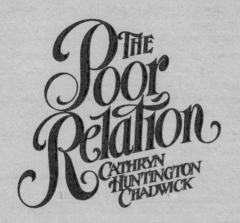

The Poor Relation

CATHRYN HUNTINGTON CHADWICK

ZEBRA BOOKS
KENSINGTON PUBLISHING CORP.

ZEBRA BOOKS

are published by

Kensington Publishing Corp.
475 Park Avenue South
New York, NY 10016

First printing: February, 1990

Printed in the United States of America

Chapter One

It was to be an evening of triumph for Lady Arabella Shallcross. Every object and inch of Shallcross House had been dusted, polished or decked with flowers. Creams and jellies, lobsters, and bottles of champagne awaited the delectation of the very pink of the ton. And Lady Arabella, if she had not feared to mar the perfection of her much-admired, gardenia-petal skin on this most important of all nights, would have pinched herself to see if she were awake and not dreaming.

If only her late, lamented and dirt-poor parents could see her now, rubbing elbows with the nobs. Arabella Winton had arrived in London twenty-three years ago on a common coach and now rode through the metropolis in a crested barouche. Not a bad come-up for a damsel who, if the truth were to be told, had been at best a mediocre actress fortunate to be blessed with quite startling beauty. Her ravishing looks served her far better than mere talent ever could have.

Miss Winton had been fortunate to captivate a titled gentleman's heir, whom she succeeded in cajoling into marriage before maturity and his horrified parents could intervene. She could have had a grand career, she reflected complacently, as an even richer nobleman's mistress. But Arabella Winton, though willing to take advantage of circumstances, had been no light skirt. Marriage had been her object when she took the metropolis by storm, not a notorious career as the paramour of a succession of peers, ending in a lonely death surrounded by mementos of her past glory and empty bottles of blue ruin.

Empire decor was all the crack now that England was at war with the French, and the viscountess, not to be outdone in the prompt embracing of any fashionable trend, had ruthlessly disposed of the comfortable furniture that had graced her husband's town house for generations and replaced it with all that was classical and elegant. It was a triumph, she observed in self-congratulation, worth every guinea of the modest fortune it had taken to transform Shallcross House into a sort of pagan shrine to Arabella's vanity.

Tonight her seventeen-year-old daughter Melanie would be introduced to the ton with all the pomp and ostentation that her mother could contrive. Lady Arabella had spent a fortune on her darling's debut as well as the refurbishing, compounding the displeasure of her long-suffering spouse. But it would be well worth it. At the height of the evening, Lord Shallcross would announce Melanie's engagement to Phillip Bentley, Lord Windom, heir to an earldom and one of the wealthiest young men in the kingdom.

The prospective bride's father had argued persuasively that Melanie should experience some freedom before shackling herself to a husband at her tender age, hinting, much to his wife's displeasure, that young persons toiling in the throes of their first romances tend to repent their choices in later life.

6

She had no doubt that he was thinking of his own marriage, and she also knew he deliberately made the remark to annoy her.

Lady Shallcross was well aware that her husband regretted marrying her, but that didn't mean she had qualms about helping her younger daughter entrap a wealthy gentleman into marriage. If nothing else, her own experience underscored the importance of a young lady's taking steps to ensure her future security while her beauty was at its most tender.

Arabella had had the devil of a time convincing her daughter that Lord Windom's wealth and social position outweighed the young gentleman's unfortunate tendency to corpulence and his rather unattractive air of self-importance.

In this endeavor she was not aided by her elder daughter, Kate, who wondered aloud in her impressionable sister's presence that she could entertain the prospect of marrying a man with such a horrid squint. Lady Shallcross accused Kate, who had not been able to produce even one respectable suitor by the end of her own shockingly expensive first season as a debutante, of being jealous.

Lady Shallcross roundly told her spouse she had no intention of permitting the catch of the season to get a look at the rest of the season's debutantes until he was publicly committed to Melanie. Lord Shallcross rather bitterly reflected that it was also fortunate the deed would be done before the young man's parents had a chance to get to know his future mother-in-law.

This was not to say that Lady Shallcross was vulgar in the way other women who had married above them often were. Although her brilliant auburn hair had faded in color, Arabella would never dream of attempting to restore its formerly startling hue. She painted her face, but discreetly. Her dress was always understated, allowing the excellence of the cut, the impeccable choice of color, and the sensuous textures of the most expensive fabrics in themselves to make the desired impression.

Lady Shallcross would never have compromised her dignity by being seen in overly theatrical gowns, for she had a horror of presenting the appearance of aping her betters. Happily, the elegant style she affected enhanced her striking, statuesque beauty in a way that frills and furbelows never would. In company she always contrived to behave with the regal assurance of one who has no social superior.

But Charles Verelst, Lord Shallcross, although he would never have demeaned himself by uttering a criticism of his spouse to any but that lady herself, often wished that the bride of his youthful infatuation were less ruthless in her ambition to see her blood intermingled with the highest in the land. She had a certain heiress in mind for Jeremy, her son, and she had the supreme confidence of the single-minded that she would be able to promote this match as soon as her first-born gave up his rather alarming penchant for rough companions and strong drink. She refused to see his dissipation as anything but boyish high spirits.

Because of their mother's scheming, Melanie's and Jeremy's futures were already assured. The only problem on Lady Shallcross's horizon was the question of what to do with her elder daughter, Kate, who steadfastly refused to fall in with her mother's stratagems to marry her off creditably.

Lady Shallcross fussed over the fragile hothouse roses which graced a pair of alabaster vases on vaguely Romanesque columns at the entrance to her dining room as she pondered the question of how to

8

thrust Kate into the arms of a suitable man without seeming too obviously to do so. The thoughtful look on her face was replaced by a frown, however, when she heard the voices of her daughter, Kate, and her husband's ward, Serena, raised in quite unbecoming laughter.

Her daughter Kate, dressed in a demure gown of blue muslin with white ribbons arranged in her glowing light chestnut hair, turned to her mother with a guilty look in her soft blue eyes. She knew she and Serena had been behaving in a manner Lady Arabella would condemn as hoydenish, and that as usual her annoyance would fall on Serena's head rather than on her own.

The girls tried in vain to hide behind them the evidence of the tarts they had pilfered from one of the refreshment tables set up in another room. Serena always seemed to be starving, and her sympathetic cousin had been helping her choose some refreshment for later in the evening when, both knew, Serena would be confined to her own room.

"Kate, my love," said Lady Shallcross, the tone of her voice belying the endearment, "we have only an hour before the musicians begin arriving, and you aren't ready."

Kate Verelst looked down at her wide-sleeved, high-necked gown and elegantly shod narrow feet with surprise.

"But, Mother," she protested, "I am ready."

"Don't be impertinent, Kate," said Lady Arabella, who would brook no nonsense from nineteen-year-old spinster daughters bent on disgracing their families by not bothering to exert even the tiniest effort to attract a husband. "You know very well I planned for you to wear the pink crepe tonight with the garnet set. I won't have you looking dowdy at your

9

sister's debut. That blue gown is at least a year old."

Kate sighed. "But, Mother, I would rather wear this one."

"Change your gown, Kate," said Arabella crossly. When Kate had left the room, she turned to her husband's niece.

"And what are you doing here, miss, when I expressly forbade you to leave the schoolroom? You know I don't want you underfoot tonight." She signaled a footman to dispose of the plate of pastries, and Serena watched its removal with great sorrow.

"Please, Aunt Arabella, might I watch from the stairway as the guests arrive?" asked Serena wistfully.

Lady Shallcross dispassionately assessed her niece's bright dark blue eyes, dusky brunette hair and glowing pink cheeks.

At fifteen, Serena didn't look in the least like a child, and her beauty was becoming too alarmingly apparent for her aunt's peace of mind. Lady Shallcross deplored the sense of duty that had prompted her husband to inflict this disturbingly lovely, orphaned young woman upon their household.

Poor relations, in Arabella's opinion, ought to be past their first youth, paralyzed with gratitude at being provided with a home, and willing to dedicate their lives to fetching and carrying for their benefactors without complaint.

Arabella had no delusions about this minx her husband had thrust upon her, and she didn't for a moment think she'd have much luck betrothing her elder daughter to a suitable gentleman with Serena standing there forcing Kate even farther into the background. She was determined to keep Serena under wraps until Kate was safely married. She had no intention of seeing her husband's niece married

10

before his own daughter, not that Kate wouldn't deserve it.

"No," said Lady Shallcross, seeing that Serena was waiting for an answer to her question. "What kind of an impression would it make on our guests if they were to see a half-grown schoolgirl staring through the banisters like a looby? You will keep to your room or incur my severest displeasure."

Serena, who had often found her aunt's severest displeasure a most uncomfortable state, meekly assented, but once upstairs, disobediently walked past the doorway of her own room, which was near the one where Kate was changing her dress. She stole into her favorite cousin's bedchamber and flopped inelegantly onto the bed.

Kate, struggling with the hooks on her new pink crepe gown, greeted her with relief. "How did you know I needed help with this?" she asked her cousin rallyingly. "I can't find my mother's serving woman."

Serena gave her a half smile and began doing the hooks. "Do you think I will ever wear a dress like this?" she asked glumly.

"I profoundly hope not," said Kate in disgust, making a face at her reflection in the mirror.

"It must be lovely to wear truly fashionable clothes and not be hidden away like a scratched table when guests arrive," said Serena.

"Well, you can have this one with my good grace," said Kate, regarding with disapproval the low-necked, high-waisted gown designed in the French classical fashion.

It had cost Lady Shallcross a modest fortune, and the workmanship was of the very finest. But it was not particularly flattering to Kate, who was short and prettily plump.

Whereas a less form-fitting, more feminine gown

11

would have made her look ethereal and dainty, this gown made her well-developed figure look, as she had so inelegantly informed Serena earlier, like a potato sack full of tennis balls. In truth, the gown didn't look *that* bad, but Kate didn't have the confidence to carry off this highly sophisticated confection of continental fashion, and she probably never would. For all of her nineteen years, Kate's face and figure were still childishly rounded, and she gave the impression of nothing so much as a youthful damsel dressing up in her mother's evening gown. She longed for ruffles and ribbons, but her mother reasoned that white satin shoulders and partially exposed bosoms were of more use in attracting the attention of gentlemen of marriageable age than sweetly insipid ribbons and bows.

"I will feel that everyone is staring down my bodice all night long," complained Kate, blushing a little, "and I am certain that is exactly what Mother had in mind when she chose it."

"I would kill for that dress," said Serena enviously.

"I agree that *you* would look delightful in it," said Kate forthrightly, eyeing her cousin's taller, slimmer figure with admiration untempered by jealousy. "You don't have as much on top as I."

"Are these the garnets your mother wants you to wear?" asked Serena, holding up a magnificent collar of large, polished stones set in gold. "How beautiful."

"How ostentatious," said Kate, after Serena reverently fastened the bauble around her neck. "They've been in the Verelst family for simply ages, and Mother insisted that I wear them so the guests can be assured of my pedigree. That great, gaudy central pendant *would* hang right between my—"

"Kate, dear," came her mother's voice from the

hallway. Lady Shallcross entered the room and observed with approval that Serena was making herself useful by helping Kate dress. Serena's occupation in acting as her cousin's maid was so in keeping with Arabella's perception of how a dependent relation ought to behave that she forbore to scold her for not going to her own room as she had been ordered. "I need you. Come with me, please. You will go to your room, Serena."

"Yes, Aunt," said Serena, her eyes alight with curiosity.

"Kate, the most unfortunate thing. Your cousin Mark is here," said Lady Shallcross when Serena was out of earshot. "I would not have had this happen for the world. Just now, when Melanie finally has seen reason—"

A lump promptly lodged itself in Kate's throat. "But, Mother—"

"You must go down to him, Kate. There probably will be a dreadful scene, and you must help me keep him away from Melanie. If she sees him—"

"Why do I have to tell him? Why don't you—"

"I can't be bothered with him now," said Lady Shallcross, displaying, for her, unusual cowardice, "and someone must tell him. He always had a certain affection for you. He will naturally think that I persuaded Melanie to accept Lord Windom—"

"Which you did," said Kate in an uncompromising tone, which made her mother's brows rise with vexation.

"Which I did for the sake of her future happiness, Kate," said Lady Shallcross firmly, "and I refuse to be made to feel like a murderess because I won't see my beautiful daughter wasted on a poor relation!"

"Mark is *not* a poor relation, Mother," said Kate angrily. "His blood goes back to—"

"I am not talking about his *blood,* Kate, I am talking about his purse," said Arabella bluntly. "You must keep him occupied. You must explain to him that he would be doing Melanie a grievous injury to force his attentions on her—"

"I?" said Kate in a choked voice. "No, Mother, I can't tell him Melanie is rejecting him to marry Phillip Bentley. You know as well as I do that they had an understanding, and that he intends to offer for her now that he's received his promotion."

"What nonsense! If you ask me, it was quite improper for him to make up to such a young girl without her father's permission," said Lady Shallcross, who felt a twinge of guilt, despite her airy assurances to her husband that the understanding that had developed between Melanie and her cousin could be put aside as mere calf-love.

She knew very well that Mark had intended to ask his uncle for Melanie's hand in marriage as soon as he could afford to support a wife. Melanie, feeling all the rapture of being in love for the first time last summer, had told everyone who would listen about their romance. After receiving her last letter from him some months ago, she had announced that he was coming home on leave to ask her father for her hand in marriage. She often read the girlish effusions she wrote to her lover for the edification of Kate, Serena and the maid who waited on her mother, before she posted them.

"If the truth be told, Mother, you know very well that Melanie probably made up to him first. And now his heart will be broken," said Kate melodramatically.

"How dare you accuse your sister of anything so improper! Of course it won't break his heart," Arabella insisted. "He will simply find someone more

14

suitable for following him and his regiment through its various disease-ridden camps. Surely even he cannot think a delicately nurtured young girl like Melanie could be happy as the wife of a common soldier."

"He is not a common soldier, Mother. He is a captain. He is on his way to being a—"

"I know, darling. I am sure it is perfectly splendid that Mark has made such a success of being in the army, but that doesn't mean he's a suitable match for my daughter," said Arabella, avoiding Kate's accusing eye.

She knew what Kate was thinking, although the girl would never be so dead to propriety as to remind her mother that generations of Wintons were tenant farmers before Arabella became an actress on the common stage and contrived to enslave the present Viscount Shallcross.

"Now, be a good girl," Arabella continued hurriedly, "and go talk to your cousin. Make him see that no good will come of agitating Melanie and ruining her come-out ball. If he won't be reasonable, you must persuade him to leave. On no account must he see your father."

"Naturally Mark will want to see his sister."

"And he may do so, of course, but only after Melanie's engagement is announced. I can't have Melanie upset now, and if Serena gets wind of the fact that her brother is here, she'll kick up enough of a commotion to rouse the household. I must go to Melanie and keep her from coming downstairs."

Lady Shallcross lifted her yellow lace over taffeta skirts and made good her escape. Kate took a deep breath and stepped into the parlor where she saw her tall, raven-haired, magnificent cousin Mark, resplendent in his regimentals, staring out of the window.

Captain Mark Charles Verelst, age twenty-five,

greeted his cousin with a smile and a penetrating look, which made Kate want to sink. He looked exactly like a nervous young man preparing himself to ask the head of his family for the hand of his cousin in marriage. Most people would have missed that fleeting look in his serious brown eyes, but from Kate, who had memorized every nuance of Mark's handsome face, no expression could be hidden.

"Ah, Cousin," he said cordially. "All ready for the ball, I see. How delightful you look."

"Thank you, Cousin," said Kate, accepting what she interpreted as a polite lie. She thought her gowns grew more and more unsuitable as her mother's desperation to get her married off intensified. Blushing slightly under his regard, she was glad she'd had the presence of mind to wrap a gauze scarf around her shoulders and bosom. "How nice to see you," she added lamely.

"I was sent on one of the transports with dispatches from my commanding officer," he said. "How providential that my assignment as courier should coincide with Melanie's ball. Where is she, by the way?"

"Getting dressed, of course. Mark—"

"Do you suppose your father could spare me a few moments?" he asked a trifle nervously. "I have to discuss something with him—"

"Mark!"

In frustration, Kate had grasped his forearms. Tears glistened on the ends of her long lashes. It was going to hurt her so much to hurt him.

He looked at her, startled.

"What is it, Kate?" he asked, automatically putting his strong hands on her shoulders in concern as he perceived her distress. "Is it bad news? Serena—"

"No, it's not Serena. It's Melanie."

16

"Is she ill? What—"

"She's not ill; she's betrothed to Lord Windom."

He stared at her, and for once her lovers' instinct was at fault. She didn't see the look of relief on his face, because she was looking straight at the top button of his uniform in confusion at the delicious feelings his touch on her shoulders aroused in her. Shakily, she released herself from his hold.

"Phillip Bentley!" he exclaimed. "That squinney-eyed—"

"Yes," she said baldly, feeling like a villainess.

"This is my aunt's doing, of course," he said. He was so indignant that a young and beautiful girl should be forced into marriage with a coxcomb like Phillip Bentley that he almost forgot why he had sought his interview with Melanie's father. "I'll not believe that Melanie—but this is monstrous." Purposefully, he stepped around Kate to get to the doorway. He found his uncle waiting there.

"Go to your mother, Kate," said Lord Shallcross quietly. Kate thankfully made her escape, knowing her father would handle the awkward scene that was to follow with far more delicacy than she could.

She wasn't to know what was said after she left the room, and she didn't want to. She knew her mother would be annoyed that Kate hadn't succeeded in keeping the men apart, but she didn't see how she could have avoided their meeting.

Her mother, seeing her in the hall, pulled her into her chamber.

"Did you tell him?" she asked anxiously.

"Yes. Father is with him now."

"Oh, blast! Nothing could be more unfortunate. He'll probably allow Mark to see her before the ball, and I won't have it. You must go back down again and tell your father—"

"No," said Kate firmly. "I won't."

Lady Shallcross looked at her eldest daughter speculatively.

"I don't like that tone of voice, young woman," she told her least favorite child, "but you're probably right. Surely your father will have the wit to impress upon Mark that his suit is hopeless. After all, Mark never did apply to your father for Melanie's hand in form."

"His suit wouldn't have been so hopeless before his father lost his fortune," Kate pointed out. Naturally she had not been overjoyed to learn that her sister expected to marry the man she, Kate, wanted, but she resented any inference that he was unworthy of marrying into his own family.

"Even so," said Lady Shallcross, "it wouldn't have been the match I wanted for her. Now, of course, it is impossible. Someday Melanie will thank me for this."

"What are you hiding from me?" asked Melanie, framed in the doorway. Despite her agitation, Lady Shallcross couldn't conceal her maternal pride in the delightful picture her youngest daughter made in her white lace-trimmed gown and her golden hair dressed in a cascade of fashionably short, gleaming ringlets. Pearls formed a fillet across her smooth forehead and encircled her long, graceful neck. "He's here, isn't he?" she added in throbbing accents.

"If you mean your cousin, yes," said Lady Shallcross, "and your father is dealing with him."

"Oh, Mother, I can't see him—"

"Now, all will be well, Melanie," said Lady Shallcross, relieved that Melanie did not want to see her rejected suitor. It would make the whole awkward business so much more manageable if she could count on Melanie not to renege on her accept-

18

ance of Phillip. Lady Shallcross started herding her favorite daughter toward her own room and watched only long enough to see that she turned into the doorway. She turned back to her elder daughter. "Kate—" she hissed.

"Yes, Mother?"

"Go downstairs and see what your cousin is doing. You don't have to *say* anything to him. No doubt your father is representing to him the folly of making a scene. If he and your father have finished talking, give him some refreshment. If he insists upon staying for the ball, you must keep him occupied and away from Melanie. If only we could count on his retiring upstairs with Serena!"

"I know you said she must stay in her room, but perhaps we should take Serena down to him," said Kate. "After all, she *is* his sister. And now that Melanie knows he's here anyway, Serena might prove a distraction. I know Serena would like to see him."

Lady Shallcross thought about it. "Very well. But be sure the little hoyden is back upstairs before the guests arrive. It wouldn't do for them to see her in that old gown."

"It's the best one she has," said Kate, not bothering to keep the note of condemnation out of her voice.

Lady Shallcross looked at her daughter with exasperation. "I suppose you are next going to say I should dress my husband's dependent in the first stare of fashion."

"No," said Kate, "but a new muslin gown or two would certainly make her look more like a gentleman's ward. The one she has on is quite shabby in addition to being *brown*."

"Oh, very well," said Arabella guiltily. Kate had not accused her in so many words, but she suspected

Kate knew her mother had given in to an unworthy impulse when she had chosen brown for most of Serena's gowns, knowing that the color did not become her. "I dare say I should have seen to it. She's grown so tall that her dress is almost indecent. Now your father will probably accuse me of neglecting the chit. Tomorrow you may take her to town and buy some lengths of muslin for new gowns. But for today she will have to be hidden from our guests."

"Very well, Mother," said Kate. "And thank you." She went to her own room, where Serena was holding one of Kate's evening gowns up to herself and smiling into a mirror. She looked guilty when Kate entered.

"I'm sorry," she said. "I couldn't resist. You have such *delicious* clothes."

"Yes. Fine wrappings with which to disguise inferior merchandise," said Kate, but she had a smile on her face. "Your brother is here, and Mother said you could go down to see him before the ball. I think I should tell you he's upset just now. My father has told him that his suit for Melanie is hopeless. As you know, her engagement is being announced tonight. My mother is afraid he'll make a scene."

"Mark never makes a scene," said Serena. "It is what one likes most about him. Perhaps Aunt Arabella would treat him and me better if he did."

"Mother did give me permission to take you to the shops to buy some muslin for new gowns tomorrow," said Kate teasingly, "but if you feel that way about her, you probably won't want to accept—"

"She did?" exclaimed Serena. "How wonderful! But why?"

"She said I could take you downstairs to see Mark before the ball, but I would have to take you upstairs before the guests see you in that old gown. I had only to point out that you have none better."

"But surely she knows the deficiencies of my wardrobe by now," said Serena bitterly.

"I think she's so busy trying to launch Melanie and me into society that she doesn't give you a thought," said Kate. "She isn't all bad, although I do think she could be a little more generous with you. I think she's afraid if any of the gentlemen see you, she'll have an even harder time getting rid of me."

"Flatterer," said Serena. "I must say I cannot understand why you seem to have trouble attracting a husband. I think you are very pretty, but you don't pay any attention to the gentlemen. When we're out walking in the park, you never flirt like Melanie does. The way you ignored poor Mr. Marlowe when he tried to start a conversation with you—"

"Poor Mr. Marlowe was so engrossed in staring at my bosom that I rather doubt he noticed my lack of conversation," said Kate dryly. "I assure you *that* kind of offer is not at all what Mother has in mind for me, my innocent. Let us go downstairs and see if your brother has offered to call poor Phillip Bentley out."

The thought of the ponderous Lord Windom dueling with someone was so humorous that Serena could not repress a giggle, but she sobered instantly when she was ushered into her brother's presence.

He was alone now, and Serena looked at him with so much sympathy in her glance that he immediately held out his hands to her. She knew as she gave him a sisterly hug that he must be very broken-hearted because he had lost the one he loved to another. She was relieved to see that he didn't look as if he might cry. The only man she had ever seen cry was her father on the occasion of her mother's death, and that had been horrid.

If Mark had been angry, Kate would have been less dismayed. Instead, he looked and behaved much as he always did.

"Serena, how you've grown up," he said by way of greeting.

"You always say that," replied Serena, who always said "you always say that" in disgust when her brother told her how much she'd grown up. Serena was anxious to be accepted as an adult, and she didn't like being reminded that she still had some growing up to do. "I'm almost sixteen."

"Yes," he said, as if much struck. "So you are. Lord, I suppose it will be up to me to find you a husband."

"You might find Kate one, too, while you're at it, brother mine," said Serena.

"Why? Do you wish to be married, Kate?" asked Mark, smiling at his cousin. "I know several good fellows, but I doubt they'll pass muster with my aunt."

He was so brave and so droll. At that moment, Kate fell even more deeply in love with him.

"Yes, Mother's standards are so high when it comes to suitors for me," she said rallyingly. "First of all, he must be able to walk into a room unaided. Then, very important, he must still be able to breathe—"

"Silly," said Serena, changing the subject to one of more immediate gratification to her. "Mark, my aunt said I am to have some new gowns."

"How kind of her," said Mark, who didn't for a minute think kindness had a thing to do with it. It pained him to see his lovely sister dressed so shabbily. He vowed that someday he would shower her with pretty clothes and jewels. "I bought something for you in Spain, love. I hope you like it. It's noth-

22

ing, really, but, well, I hope you like it. I'll fetch it directly when I find out where the servants have put my gear. My batman will be here as soon as he sees to the stabling of my horse."

"Your usual room has been readied," said Kate, who had seen to this on the way down to greet Mark when he first arrived. Privately, she thought it was absolutely churlish of her mother to insist that Mark stable his horses at Tattersalls when visiting them, and poor-spirited of her father to allow it. She knew there was plenty of room in their own stables, and her mother's dictum was nothing but an act of petty harassment designed to put Mark in his place. "I can have Serena's gift brought down if you wish."

"No," said Mark. "My aunt will not appreciate my putting the servants to any bother while they are getting ready for the ball. Jack will see to my needs. The house looks splendid. I thought for a moment I was in a pagan temple. All of these ancient Romans in gilded armor on pedestals are quite effective once one's eyes become accustomed, and all of the chairs are so uncomfortable that I am sure they must be all the crack."

"Yes," said Kate mischievously. "It is always best for a merchant to present the wares in a lavish setting."

The look of reproach on his face wounded her. Of course, she was referring to her mother's attempts to marry her off. Since her own ill-fated come-out two years before, she and Mark had often joked about the subject. But she realized her words could also be taken to mean her mother's attempt to marry Melanie off creditably. Although Lady Shallcross would make the usual maternal protestations about her innocent child being carried off straight from the schoolroom to the nuptial couch, anyone acquainted

23

with the lady knew she would be in high croak at marrying Melanie to Lord Windom. Kate could have bitten her tongue.

Fortunately, the awkward moment passed when the butler and a maid brought in modest refreshments of tea and cakes.

"Oh, famous!" exclaimed Serena. "I'm famished!"

"You are always famished, love," said Kate, smiling. "Do have one of these cakes. I don't dare for fear of getting something on my gown. Mark, what can I give you?"

"A cup of tea would be ample, Cousin. I'm not hungry."

Serena had already bitten into a white confection which left a dusting of sugar on her cherry-red lips.

"Do you mean because of Melanie?" she said, disconcertingly direct. "I'm sorry if you're vastly unhappy, Mark, but I can't help but think it's rather a good thing you won't be marrying her."

"Serena!" exclaimed Kate. "Have you *no* delicacy?"

"Well, it's not as if we were in company," Serena pointed out. "Mama always said awkward things were best gotten out in the open. Melanie is not the only woman in the world. Nor even the prettiest."

"Perhaps for your brother she is," said Kate repressively.

"How perceptive of you, Cousin," said Mark. "I am obliged to both of you, but I would rather not discuss it, if you don't mind. After all, it is not very chivalrous for me to bandy a lady's name about when she is promised to another."

"It just *shows* what a flirt she is," said the incorrigible Serena. "When I think of how she positively threw herself at your head last summer when we were in the country, I should think she would be mortified

24

to cry off now. When she told me she persuaded you to meet her in secret—"

"Serena!" Mark and Kate exclaimed together.

"She told you that?" said Mark, taken aback. He remembered the incident well. Melanie had asked him to meet her in the garden, and he, not dreaming what she had in mind, had had the devil of a time persuading her to go back inside the house. He still broke out in a cold sweat at the thought of having to explain what his then sixteen-year-old cousin was doing in his company out in the dark if anyone would have discovered them.

"Oh, I think she told everyone," said Serena ingenuously. "It was the most affecting thing. All of us were quite jealous. Or, of course, I wasn't jealous, exactly, because you're my brother. But it was just the idea of having a man fall in love with one and—"

"All of us?" he asked in dismay, wondering with lively dread exactly what the imaginative Melanie might have told them. "Just how many people did Melanie take into her confidence?"

The question was directed at Kate, not at Serena.

"Oh, not too many," said Kate uncomfortably.

"Well," said Serena helpfully, "Lydia and Jane Thrasher knew about it, and of course Aunt Arabella's maid, and she probably told Aunt, which is where the mischief started. And Melanie must have told Caroline Smythe, because she told me it was the most romantic thing and we'd probably have Melanie off to Gretna Green, and—"

"Really, Serena, that will do!" said Kate, alarmed by Mark's stony silence. "Mark, Melanie is only seventeen—"

"I know, Kate," he said. "Naturally I don't expect you to understand how it was. Melanie is so young and biddable—"

25

"Biddable? Melanie?" said Serena in some amusement. "You wouldn't think so if you could have heard her threatening my aunt that she would run away and embark on a life of shame if her parents tried to stop her from marrying you."

"Serena, I think you should be going upstairs," said Kate, desperate to change the subject.

It was bad enough for him that Melanie had thrown him over for a wealthier man, Kate thought, but it was cruel and unusual punishment for him to have to listen to his sister tell him that the object of his devotion had made free with his name to all of her acquaintances. Although Kate privately thought that Mark would have found out all too soon how much like her masterful mother his Melanie was, Kate did not think he was ready to have Melanie pushed off her pedestal so abruptly.

"I know," said Serena, mercifully taking the hint. "Let us go to Mark's room and see what he brought us. You did bring Kate a present, too, didn't you, Mark?"

"I brought presents for everyone," he said. "You shall tell me if I have chosen well."

Kate looked at him sympathetically. Of course he had brought presents for everyone. He thought he was bearing gifts to his future in-laws.

Kate knew she should be at her mother's side, making sure the musicians didn't knock over any vases, and rehearsing the servants hired for the dinner, but she hesitated to leave Mark to his sister's tender mercies. He seemed to be holding up tolerably well, however, and perhaps Serena would behave herself if distracted by whatever present he brought her, Kate thought optimistically.

Kate loved Serena almost as much as she loved Mark, although in a much different way. There had been far too few presents in Serena's life the past two years. Yet Serena remained sunny and cheerful, and not even her aunt's coldness could quell her liveliness. She was much the same child she had been before tragedy had clouded her young life. She'd survived the deaths of both her parents and the loss of her family's fortune. Even being forced to live as a dependent in her aunt and uncle's household didn't have the power to crush her buoyant spirit.

Kate hesitated, then excused herself.

"You go ahead," she said. "I'd best see to Mother."

"Yes, you'd best," said Serena with a twinkle in her eye. "You're the only one who can soothe the servants when Aunt Arabella has been agitating them. Wouldn't it be shocking if they walked out before the ball?"

Serena took her brother's arm and led him away. Kate found her mother bullying the musicians.

"Mother," she said, smiling and patting one of Arabella's auburn curls into place. "There you are. Where is Father? We must find him before the guests arrive."

She put her arm around her mother's shoulders—which wasn't easy because Arabella was much taller than Kate—and led her away from the musicians.

"Kate, dear," said her mother, "why do you have that gauze thing on? It hides your dress. And you aren't wearing any rouge!"

"No, and I'm not going to," said Kate cheerfully. "I am enough of a sight in this gown."

Lady Shallcross regarded Kate with dismay and faint sorrow. How on earth, she wondered, did she manage to give birth to this incomprehensible child? Arabella had truly thought Kate would love the pink dress. Arabella would have adored it at her daughter's age. It *was* cut rather low, but Arabella's own

27

gown was cut just as low.

Kate had a lovely bosom and shoulders, so why did she want to hide them? In the blue dress Kate preferred, she looked exactly like all the other miss-ish young damsels one was forever meeting in soci-ety.

Arabella considered it only common sense for an unmarried woman in her third season to dress in a way that set off her physical charms, and if the fashionable matrons who dictated to polite society disapproved, who cared? The only useful purpose served by a young woman's cultivating the friendship of other ladies, Arabella believed, was to get invited to the right parties where she could be introduced to eligible gentlemen.

Well, perhaps tonight would be different, Arabella thought hopefully. She let Kate lead her into a small salon, where she gave her appearance an inspection in a long mirror.

"You look lovely, Mother," said Kate, admiring her mother's still beautiful if faded auburn hair, shining green eyes and petal-perfect complexion which was only lightly touched with rouge.

"And so do you, my dear," said Lady Shallcross in an unusual burst of affection for her least under-stood child. "Do try to smile more tonight, my love. And don't freeze all the young gentlemen with a look if they approach you. And don't sit in the corner with all the dowagers tonight. I know you consider it your duty to entertain them, but you don't have to spend *all* evening fetching tea for them and moving them closer to the fire and fussing over them."

"Yes, Mother," said Kate.

"Oh, bother! I almost forgot about your cousin Mark. Darling, promise me you will keep Mark away from Melanie. I *won't* have her ball spoiled by his attentions."

"Mark won't make a scene, Mother. He's too much the gentleman for that. I'll engage to keep him occupied."

"Thank you, Kate," said Arabella, her brow serene. "I knew I could depend on you to see that all goes as it ought. That dreadful cook—"

"Don't worry about Gaspar, Mother. I'll see him while you join Father. It would be shocking for the guests to be greeted by no one but the butler."

"Yes, dear, and thank you. And Kate, love, *do* take that gauze thing off so the gentlemen can see your lovely shoulders."

"Yes, Mother," said Kate resignedly.

Three hours later, Kate saw Mark enter the ballroom and look quickly around. He's searching for Melanie, thought Kate, pitying him. But instead of following Melanie's golden progress around the room in her betrothed's arms, Mark's eyes seemed to be seeking someone else. Herself.

"There you are, Cousin," said Mark. His gaze dropped and his eyes danced, lightening the serious expression he had worn on his face when he entered the room.

Kate blushed. She knew he was amused by the low neckline of her gown. His words confirmed it.

"I must compliment my aunt once again on her exquisite taste," he said.

"You might have the civility," Kate said tartly, "to glance at my face now and again."

"With the greatest of pleasure, my dear," replied her cousin gallantly. "When is the happy announcement to be made?"

She sobered at once, and she looked across the room to where Melanie contrived to give the impression of laughing up into her fiancé's infatuated face

29

despite the fact that she was only two inches shorter than he.

"Not for some time yet," she said sympathetically. "If you'd rather not stay—"

"I could never be so churlish as to miss my cousin's come-out ball," he said frivolously. "Especially when it seems that all of her acquaintance is watching me avidly for signs of mental deterioration. How poor-spirited it would be to disappoint them. Do you think I will be expected to call young Bentley out?"

"Oh, no," said Kate in alarm. She remembered her facetious remark to Serena about the possibility of Mark's challenging Windom to a duel, but she hadn't seriously considered such a thing. She did so now.

She looked so upset that he flicked her soft cheek with a careless forefinger, making her glad she hadn't rouged her face.

"My dear, is all of this distress for me? Or do you have a *tendre* for his lordship yourself?" he teased.

"How can you even say such a thing," she snapped, her eyes sparkling brilliantly with indignation. "I think Phillip Bentley is a beastly little—"

"Hush, my sweet," he said softly. "I quite agree. But it isn't quite the thing to say so, particularly tonight."

"It must be dreadful for you," she said, hanging her head a little. The old-fashioned lavender scent she always wore wafted up to him from her long, glossy ringlets. "You won't meet him, will you?"

"No," he said, enchanted by her sympathy. Being consoled in his supposed sorrow by Kate, he thought, was a benefit to being jilted that he hadn't anticipated. He began to enjoy himself.

"I hope I am not a coward," he continued, imposing shamelessly on Kate's tender-heartedness, "but I would feel ridiculous dueling with a man who couldn't hit a wagon at five paces. And I am not enough of a hero to fire into the air. I'm not sure I could depend on him not to shoot me quite by accident."

"You must not say such things," she said vehemently.

"Then you must distract me," he said. "They're playing a waltz. Dancing the waltz with a beautiful lady always soothes me when I'm contemplating violence."

She looked at him searchingly. "Does it hurt very much, Mark?"

"No, Kate. I am becoming resigned, as your father told me I would," he said, leading her into the dance. "Never let it be said that I gratified your sister's vanity by standing at the side of the room watching her dance with my rival."

Kate kept her mind on her steps with great difficulty. His arm lightly encircled her waist, and she felt oddly breathless. Drat the effect this man had on her! She thought of how often during her come-out season he had sought her out and danced with her, she was convinced, out of kindness. She had been so grateful to him then. She tried to comfort herself with the reflection that he often sought her company, even if he didn't love her.

"Does your appearance here mean that you are actually going to stay in London for the season," he asked, "or do you mean to run away to the country like you did last year?"

"I imagine I will have to stay here until Melanie's wedding," said Kate. "Mother says it would give a very off appearance if I didn't appear at all the parties, although I don't see why. Who would miss the bride's sister?"

31

"Do I detect a note of self-pity?" he asked quizzically.

"Certainly not," said Kate with a fine show of spirit. "How could I envy a woman who is about to be married to Lord Windom?"

"How indeed," he murmured.

They were hailed at that moment by Kate's brother Jeremy, who was, she was sorry to see, the worst for drink and at only ten o'clock in the evening.

After bumping into a column crowned with a bust of a bald philosopher and solemnly begging its pardon, he guided his all too apparently erratic footsteps to Mark's side and clapped him on the shoulder.

"M'father tells me Melanie gave you the go-by," said Jeremy in a hearty voice. Several heads turned, and Kate set her jaw at the avid curiosity in the eyes around her.

"Good evening, Jeremy," said Mark in a friendly manner. "You're looking well."

"I'm not," confided Jeremy. "I'm drunk as a lord." He giggled at his own wit.

"So you are," said Mark, unperturbed.

"Don't let m'sister make you unhappy," said his sympathetic cousin. "The girl's a minx. She'll lead poor Windom a merry dance. You should be congratulating yourself on your lucky escape."

"Perhaps I shall someday," said Mark, mindful of his role.

"You'd do well to have Kate instead," said Jeremy, to Kate's horror. "You don't have to worry about a gel like Kate being faithful. It stands to reason a gel who has so much trouble finding a husband in the first place won't be enough up to snuff to find a lover!"

"Jeremy!" exclaimed Kate. She was relieved to see

her father approaching. Lord Shallcross put an arm around Jeremy's shoulder.

"Now, Son. I can see that as usual you are teasing your sister," his father reprimanded him.

Jeremy got an idiot grin on his face. In appearance he was very like his sister Melanie, only her golden beauty was translated, in his case, into the embodiment of masculine perfection. His blond, silken hair was worn in an artistically careless style known as the *coup de vent,* and the glories of evening dress suited him admirably. He had a splendid physique which Mark reflected dourly would probably run to fat if his cousin continued on his present ruinous path of hedonism. He'd heard bad things about Jeremy even in the short time since he'd returned from Spain, and wondered if he dared give his uncle a hint. After a glance at Lord Shallcross, though, Mark came to the conclusion that Jeremy's sire had a good idea of how far his son's excesses went.

"I'd like to talk with you alone for a moment, Mark, if I may," said Lord Shallcross.

"Kate, a dance with you," said Jeremy, leading his sister away and treading so clumsily on the hem of her ball gown that she had to retire to her room eventually to affect repairs.

"I am at your service, Uncle," said Mark.

"Excellent. Shall we go to my library?"

Mark followed him, wondering what awaited him in his uncle's library. He was not happy when he found out.

"I just wanted to tell you again how sorry I am that Melanie aroused expectations she was unwilling to fulfill," said Lord Shallcross, seating himself in a leather chair at his desk.

"Oh, don't give it a thought, sir," said Mark

gravely.

"The least the girl owes you is an explanation, and I've told her that she must see you. She owes you that much."

"No, sir! Really!" Mark protested.

"She will be here in a few minutes."

"You are all consideration, but—"

"What is wrong, Mark?" asked Lord Shallcross, puzzled. "Surely a man who has had his proposal of marriage spurned—"

"Sir, I have a confession to make," said Mark, shamefaced.

"What is this? *You*, I am persuaded, have behaved with propriety throughout, although I would have wished if you wanted to marry my daughter—"

"I never wanted to marry Melanie, sir," Mark said, making a clean breast of it.

"I think," said Lord Shallcross, controlling his confusion with an effort, "that you should sit down and tell me exactly what has happened between you and Melanie."

Mark seated himself on the chair, stretching long legs before him.

"I am thankful to see, sir, that we are sitting on sturdy English chairs and not on Roman couches," said Mark, his eyes gleaming with mischief. His uncle grunted in reply. It had been a battle to keep Arabella's ruthless, reforming hands from giving his library a more modish look, but he had won.

Lord Shallcross marveled at how well full-dress uniform became his once sickly nephew. The military had been the making of the boy, although at the time he had been shipped off to Spain it seemed that nothing but misfortune had come out of the necessity for Mark to make his own way in the world.

"Are you telling me that you didn't propose marriage to Melanie?" he asked.

"Yes, I am afraid I am."

"Explain, please."

"Well, last summer I went to visit the family in the country when I was on leave. I wanted to see Serena, and all of you of course," he added hastily.

"Very proper," said Lord Shallcross, his lips twitching in appreciation. He knew that Mark and his aunt loathed each other.

"That was the first time I had seen Melanie since I went into the army. She is very beautiful, sir."

"Are you saying you trifled with an innocent child with no intention of marrying her?" Lord Shallcross's voice was stern.

"No. Certainly not," said Mark, aghast. "I would never have dreamed of such a thing. She sought me out and I was flattered. She read to me, and I took both her and Serena to the fair. Kate had caught a chill and didn't go with us. I enjoyed taking the girls to all the booths and buying them sweets. They seemed to me then to be much of an age. When I went back into the army, Melanie started writing to me."

"Are you telling me my daughter proposed to *you?*"

"In a manner of speaking, sir, yes," said Mark, feeling foolish. "Apparently she misunderstood something I wrote to her, and thought I was in love with her. Her letters became more and more, well, er—"

"Romantic?"

"Yes, sir," said Mark, who didn't like the forbidding look on his uncle's face. "When I read her last letter, I discovered that she and her family expected me to make an offer for her when I attained the rank of captain. I suppose it was some foolishness I had written about being able to purchase a home and prepare it for a lady. Melanie thought I meant her. I meant my sister."

"I see," said Lord Shallcross, digesting this.

After a moment of silence, the older man gave a bark of mirthless laughter.

"What would you have done if Melanie hadn't cried off from this wholly imaginary engagement, become bracketed to her anyway?"

"No, sir," said Mark. "Much as I like Melanie and would hate to hurt her, I could never be married to a woman I didn't love. I was prepared to explain to Melanie that she is too young for marriage. And, if I may speak frankly, I placed some dependence on the fact that my aunt would not like the match."

"I see. You must have been relieved to hear she was about to become riveted to Windom."

"I was relieved to hear she no longer expected to marry me," said Mark. "But I am not at all convinced that Phillip Bentley is the man for her."

"He is, though," said Lord Shallcross. "The boy has an abominable squint, and he is filled with his own importance. But he is rich and can afford to give Melanie her choice of several handsome homes, her own carriage and all the clothes and jewels she could ever desire. They will do very well together."

"Is wealth so important?" asked Mark in some indignation.

"Yes," said Lord Shallcross simply. "Just ask her mother."

They were interrupted by the tempestuous entrance of Melanie, who posed prettily in the doorway with one hand caught to her breast in distress.

"There you are, my child," said Lord Shallcross sternly. "I will leave the two of you alone."

Melanie slowly approached Mark, her color much

heightened. Mark could see she was agitated.

"I am so sorry," she said haltingly.

"So am I," said Mark nobly. She looked so upset he thought about telling her the truth — that he had never intended his letters to convey a proposal of marriage.

"I imagine you must be thinking that I am a poor-spirited creature to submit to my father's wishes in the matter of my marriage," she continued.

Mark looked at her in amazement. She might have been reading from a script. In a flash of enlightenment tempered with no mean amount of amusement, he realized that Melanie had cast herself in the role of a tragic heroine. He knew very well that his uncle considered Melanie much too young to get married, and that in any case, he would never have constrained her to marry Lord Windom.

Mark made his decision. He didn't think the girl's ego could survive the knowledge that he had spent a sleepless night pondering the least painful way of telling her that he had no intention of marrying anyone yet, least of all a girl barely a year older than his romp of a sister. The brave, noble, rejected suitor it would have to be.

"Please don't distress yourself on my account," said Mark, taking both her hands in his. "I understand, of course, and I honor you for coming to me in person to explain."

"I could tell Lord Windom that we won't suit —" she wavered. She had almost forgotten how dashing her cousin looked in his regimentals, and she was a little stunned by him.

"No, no," protested Mark in horror.

"—but my father—"

"Of course, you must do as your father says you ought," said Mark soothingly. "The life of an officer's wife is not for a delicate young woman like you. I was mad to think of it. Forgive me for taking advantage of your youth and your innocence."

Melanie looked at him in a very speaking way and dashed tears of emotion from her eyes before they could produce runnels in her rouged cheeks.

"Mark, if you knew how highly I regard you—"

"I do, of course," he said hastily, groping for words suitable to this most uncomfortable of conversations. "I hope you will always know that I am your friend, and if I can ever be of service to you I should consider it an honor."

"Thank you," said Melanie. "You are so understanding and so kind."

She pressed his hand and turned to leave. She didn't want her betrothed to find her ensconced with another man in her father's library. "*Adieu,*" she added theatrically.

Mark's lips twitched, but only for a moment. The poor girl really thought she had wounded him, and the only gentlemanly course for him to follow would be to support the role he had cast himself in throughout the evening. He'd started out intending to leaven the tedium of one of his aunt's pretentious affairs by flirting with Kate, his favorite relative. After all, during her come-out season the only reason he exerted himself to go to parties at all was for the pleasure of her company. She amused him. And she was so good-hearted that she constantly frustrated her social-conscious mother by exchanging recipes with the dowagers in the corners and squandering her smiles and good nature on those who couldn't help her consequence in the least. Her impecunious soldier cousin, for instance.

He decided that there was no reason for him to abandon his first impulse, which was to spend the evening encouraging his pretty cousin Kate to console him in what she thought was his disappointment. He was quite looking forward to it.

It was almost time to go into supper when he returned to the ballroom. Lord Shallcross was about to make the announcement, and Mark realized that most of the guests were watching him furtively instead of the radiant couple. They plainly expected him to gnash his teeth, tear out his hair or give some other sign of thwarted passion.

He decided that he wasn't a good enough thespian to carry off the mien of a broken-hearted lover when what he wished most was to shout with joy at his escape from matrimony, so he went in search of Kate, who, strangely enough, was not in the ballroom.

He found her in the supper room, furtively arranging refreshments on a large plate under the benevolent aegis of the cook, who was packing a basket of delicacies with the air of a conspirator.

"Kate!" said Mark, surprised. "Your father is about to make the announcement."

"Oh, bother," exclaimed Kate, conscience-stricken.

"What is all of this?" asked Mark in surprise, looking at the plate she was preparing.

"This is for Serena," said Kate distractedly. "She loves lobster patties, and I know if I don't get these for her now there will be none left."

"How very kind you are to her," he said gratefully.

"Well, she's very kind to me, too," said Kate, smiling.

"Mademoiselle Serena is very partial to the veal," interjected Gaspar.

"Yes, a little of that, if you please, Gaspar," said Kate.

Mark's eyes widened at the array of victuals. "Is

my sister capable of eating all of this by herself?"

Kate giggled. "Silly. Of course not. I plan to share her supper. No one will miss me."

"I would. So much so, that I think we'd best have more of the beef. I am very partial to beef."

Kate looked surprised and pleased. "You are going to eat supper with us, Mark? How delightful. Serena will be thrilled. But you'll miss—"

"—the announcement. Quite so, Cousin," said Mark in what he hoped was a crestfallen tone.

The pleased surprise on Kate's face abated somewhat. Of course. He hadn't wanted to eat supper with her and Serena. He only wished to save himself the pain of sitting at a banquet table watching the guests toast Melanie and her brand new fiancé.

Kate could have cried for him, but with her usual common sense she determined not to let her sympathy for Mark ruin her pleasure in having his company during an evening that she had expected to dislike excessively.

While Gaspar guarded their horde, Mark and Kate returned to the ballroom for another dance, and as the guests filed into the supper room, they stole upstairs for their private supper, which was being spirited up the back steps by two footmen.

Little did Kate suspect that their absence from supper would be remarked by the gossips and that by teatime the next day the town would be buzzing with the rumor that Captain Mark Verelst was going to punish the faithless Melanie by trifling with her elder sister.

Chapter Two

Lady Arabella would have been aghast at the gay dissipation going on in her elder daughter's pristine bedchamber.

Serena, who much against Mark's better judgment had decided to enjoy her first glass of champagne in defiance of convention, sat giggling in the middle of the bed and eating raw oysters. The black lace mantilla and ornamental comb that were gifts from her loving brother were set slightly askew on her disheveled curls.

Kate, helping Mark to more beef, looked mischievous as she described to Serena some of the more flamboyant toilettes in the lower rooms. To Kate and Serena's amusement, Lady Buxted, one of Lady Shallcross's least favorite acquaintances, had brought her three daughters to the ball, even though she and Lady Shallcross were barely speaking after Arabella had said something quite malicious about the daughters' plain looks not quite out of their fond mother's earshot some time ago.

Although Lady Buxted could become quite fierce in defense of any one of her rather unsatisfactory children, she would not have dreamed of forgoing the masochistic pleasure of watching that shameless

41

woman launch her simpering daughter into the laps of the ton. Unfortunately for the Buxted girls, each of them was afflicted with singularly deplorable taste, and Kate, who knew Serena disliked them excessively, was entertaining Serena by telling her how hideous they looked in their billowing, over-embellished dresses as they simpered at all of the bachelors.

Mark had removed his dashing red coat and undone his stock so that his muscular neck was partially visible. He laughed so much at his sister's coy sallies that Kate was lost in admiration of his brave attempt at putting his disappointment behind him.

He was, in fact, finding it difficult to maintain his pretense of being crushed by Melanie's rejection of his wholly imaginary proposal of marriage.

He had been traveling hard for several weeks, and prior to that time he had been sleeping in a tent with nothing but his cloak to protect him from the cold. Well-being surrounded him like warm blanket.

His mother had died when he was a mere youth, so he was very much enjoying the novelty of surrendering to Kate and Serena's feminine ministrations to his comfort.

After settling him in a comfortable chair by the fire, Serena had brought over a small table and spread it with a cloth as Kate put the most tempting morsels from their pilfered horde on his plate. She would, in fact, have given him the lion's share of the lobster patties if Serena had not strenuously objected. Serena loved her brother more than anyone on earth, but there were limits, after all, to her altruism.

Mark felt warm, secure and happy for the first time in many weary months of traveling with Wellington's army. He had actually dozed off for a few minutes, lulled by the sweet voices of his cousin and his sister. He opened his eyes to find Kate regarding him with a tender light in her eyes.

With very little encouragement he was sure his accommodating cousin could be persuaded to feed him nutmeats by hand, a hedonistic pleasure he had read about but had never actually experienced. He was just trying to figure out how to bring about this most desirable state of affairs when his sister broke in on his pleasant reverie.

"I love you both," said Serena soulfully. "You are the only ones in the world who care about me."

"That's not true, love," said Kate, hoping this sentiment did not herald the arrival of the maudlin stage in Serena's progress toward inebriation. Kate strongly suspected that her scapegrace of a brother was responsible for Serena's condition. In Mark and Kate's presence, Serena had drunk only a half-glass of the wine. It would be just like Jeremy, Kate thought shrewdly, to initiate his young cousin into the pleasures of champagne on the sly for the sheer deviltry of it. Apparently Kate wasn't the only one who knew how her brother's mind worked.

"When I see Jeremy," said Mark pleasantly, "I am going to wring his neck."

"Jeremy is my friend. He doesn't grudge me a little fun," said Serena, confirming her elders' suspicions. Her sentence ended on a hiccup.

"Yes, Jeremy's a fine fellow," said Mark grimly. "And it's time for you to be in bed, sister of mine." He shook his head at her protest. "You may as well go to bed, Serena. You've already eaten all of the lobster patties, so there doesn't seem to be much else to stay up for."

"Very true," said Serena docilely. "Wasn't it the most splendid supper?"

"It was indeed, pet," he said, dropping a kiss on her forehead. "I'll escort you to your room."

Smiling, Kate watched them leave and pulled the bell rope. Her mother's maid answered and seemed surprised to see Kate surrounded by the broken meats of her cousins' revelry.

"Please send someone to tidy up in here," said Kate.

The woman clucked—that's the only description Kate could think of for the sound—and picked up one of the plates with a surly look. Fate had been most unkind to send Higgins in answer to the bell. Any of the other servants, almost all of whom regarded their master's ward as a sort of pet, would have been glad to see Miss Serena have a bit of a frolic; but she knew Higgins would tell her mother, and Lady Shallcross would, Kate knew, make Serena pay for her enjoyment when neither Kate nor her father was near. It was useless to hope that Higgins' sharp eyes would miss the significance of the three food-soiled plates and crystal glasses on the small tables.

"Fine doings, Miss Kate," the woman grumbled. Kate lifted her eyebrows, startling the woman with an almost uncanny imitation of Arabella in one of her haughty attitudes, and the woman stiffened. Kate went down to join the rest of the guests and ran headlong into Lady Buxted, the magnificently dressed but elephantine creature who was Arabella's sworn enemy.

Lady Buxted licked her lips in anticipation.

"Let me commend you on your common sense, my dear Miss Verelst," she said in a patronizing tone.

"Why, thank you, ma'am," said Kate, smiling pleasantly. "Upon what am I to be commended? Have I done something clever?"

"Don't be coy with me, miss," she said insinuatingly. "I saw you sneak away with your cousin. What a handsome man! What an air! What address! How clever of you to use this opportunity to attract his attention to yourself."

"I beg your pardon, ma'am?" asked Kate with cold dignity.

"Now, don't get poker-faced with me," said Lady Buxted, taking Kate's arm in a surprisingly strong grip. "Of course, I would not be gratified by the sight of any of *my* daughters so plainly pursuing a gentleman, but then they're so much younger than you that they have plenty of time to captivate the attention of suitable persons, while you must make good use of the little time you have left."

Kate's eyes narrowed. "I am glad to see that my sister's ball is affording you so much entertainment," she said ambiguously.

"Indeed," her tormentor continued, "censorious tongues will wag, but I am sure neither you nor your mother will care for that once you are creditably established. Some may say it is in questionable taste for you to so eagerly take advantage of a young man's vulnerable state after your sister's rejection of him, but such evil musings would never cross my lips."

"You relieve my mind, ma'am," said Kate with a forced smile. Kate recognized Lady Buxted's words for the clumsy shafts they were, and with magnificently heightened color, she swept into the ballroom in time to dance with a sprightly old gentlemen who had, he declared rather too loudly, dandled her on his knees during her infancy. These appendages were so thin and so bony that Kate could not believe this had been anything but a most uncomfortable experience for her, but she accepted the remark in the spirit in which it was meant and consented with good grace to, as he so jocularly put it, do a turn around the room with him.

After towing her about so energetically that she was almost dizzy by the end of the dance, he escorted her to her mother's side before Kate realized what he was about.

"My love," said her mother in a tone of much-tried patience when the gentleman retreated in search of fresh prey, "where have you been? And why are you wasting your time on old dotards who would be better off playing cards in one of the salons?"

"He asked me to dance, Mother; I didn't ask him," said Kate, smiling. "The ball is a huge success, as I knew it would be. You must be very pleased."

"Letitia Buxted is green with envy," said Arabella gleefully, allowing herself to be distracted from her criticism of Kate's choice of dancing partners.

Kate lifted her brows quizzically.

"I can't help it, Kate," said Arabella, interpreting Kate's look correctly. "I *had* to invite her. It would have occasioned remark if I had not. But never did I think the woman would have so little breeding as to accept an invitation that even a person with a skull as thick as hers must have known was not extended with any expectation of being accepted."

"It was most inconsiderate of her," agreed Kate, her eyes sparkling.

"Do dance with someone young, love," her mother coaxed.

"I will try, Mother," said Kate docilely. She glanced across the room, caught Mark's eye and, mindful of Letitia Buxted's poisoned words, quickly looked away. He walked straight to her.

"Delightful party, Aunt," he said by way of greeting to Arabella. "My dance, Kate?"

"You have danced with your cousin twice already, Mark," said Arabella, who saw no reason to waste words of ceremony on Mark. "To do so again would cause talk that I am sure Kate would dislike."

"Oh, surely not, ma'am," said Mark humorously. "I quite consider myself one of the family. And, anyway, I don't count the dance that Jeremy interrupted. Surely you must see that Kate owes me compensation."

Arabella, naturally enough, had no answer for this speech, and Mark took advantage of this happy and most unusual state of affairs by taking Kate's hand and leading her away. He looked down in surprise at her initial resistance.

"Tired, Kate?" he asked sympathetically.

"A little," she lied, joining the dance with him. She began to examine her conscience. *Had* she been throwing out lures to her cousin? She hadn't thought so, but perhaps she *was* taking advantage of Mark's vulnerability. He didn't look distracted with grief. Far from it. But perhaps he was just being brave.

"My mother is probably right," she said carefully. "Being so particular in your attentions might cause a little talk. Of course, *we* know there's nothing in it but friendship, but—"

"It seems I am going to be an object of some talk anyway, from the way people have been staring at me," he said, thinking her missish attitude rather odd. "Does it matter? Surely dancing with your own cousin couldn't damage *your* reputation, especially when everyone knows my sister is your father's ward."

"I suppose not," she said uncomfortably.

"What is it? Has Aunt Arabella been pinching at you again?"

"Certainly not. She would never do so in public,"

said Kate, feeling sure she could not share Letitia Buxted's hateful words with him.

"Is Jeremy's behavior bothering you? I wouldn't mind dusting that young man's breeches for him, but there isn't any real evil in the boy," said Mark, who still thought of Jeremy as an immature youth even though he was only five years younger than himself. "And Serena has taken no harm. She was still incoherent with joy when I left her, poor child. She will have a devil of a head in the morning."

"She will be fortunate to get off so lightly," said Kate in some amusement, "after the huge dinner she consumed. I wouldn't blame you for having the impression that we are starving Serena, but I assure you she made an excellent supper several hours before the ball."

"I don't dispute that," he said.

Kate looked embarrassed. "Mark, you're crushing my dress," she said breathlessly.

He was holding her rather closely, possibly so they could converse without shouting over the noise, and she had seen several dowagers glance their way with malice glittering in their eyes. At that moment Kate hated every one of the harpies, the more so because she probably would have devoted her evening to making them comfortable if she hadn't been so occupied with Mark and Serena.

"Is that possible?" he asked with raised eyebrows. "It clings to you so delightfully that I would have thought it would be difficult to damage it by close contact."

He couldn't have said anything worse to a damsel who was still smarting from being styled as a manchaser by Letitia Buxted, but he wasn't to know that. Meeting her eyes, he saw she was looking rather conscious, and he capitulated, holding her at a more decorous distance.

"Very well," he said quizzically. "I will behave myself, although I ask you, are you being entirely kind to a man who has been risking his life for his country these many months?"

Kate was spared the necessity of answering because Mark was distracted by the sight of her brother lurching rather awkwardly for an exit from a ballroom which was becoming stuffy and unpleasantly redolent of the sickly sweetness of far too many wilting hothouse roses.

"Oh, lord, there goes Jeremy," Mark said, regretfully releasing Kate. "He looks a bit green, my dear, so I'd better go along to see that he doesn't desecrate my aunt's garden. The ladies wouldn't like it."

"How do I know you won't make good your threat to wring his neck?" asked Kate, only half jokingly.

"You'll have to trust me, my sweet, which you know you can always do." He kissed her hand gallantly and followed Jeremy out one of the long French windows at one end of the ballroom. Flushing, Kate turned to meet the avid birdlike gaze of Millicent Buxted, one of Lady Letitia Buxted's angular daughters.

Kate turned from the girl and walked into one of the little salons, seeking privacy. There had recently been a card game there by the looks of the littered tables. Several teacups and tiny plates were discarded at the side, and Kate, who couldn't abide such clutter, absent-mindedly picked up some of the cups and prepared to hand them over to a servant. She was crossing the room when she heard a pair of elderly voices coming from a hidden alcove at one corner. She prepared to withdraw with an apology for the intrusion when she realized that the speakers, because of an overly ornamented and vaguely oriental screen, were unaware of her presence.

"I, for one, hope she gets him," said one disastrously clear voice.

"I quite agree," said the other, "if only because Arabella Winton will hate it so. As if that vulgar upstart had any right to be so nice in her taste of suitors for her girls. I'll grant you that Melanie is a little beauty—although if she has two brains to rub together in her head, I'll declare myself much surprised—but one would think even so gauche a young lady as Kate would be less obvious in her haste to entrap her good-looking cousin."

"I disagree," said Kate's unsolicited champion. "She is far from gauche, although it's a miracle with that mother. I think she's a very pretty-behaved gel."

"Pretty-behaved? Well, if it is pretty-behaved to wear a bodice cut so low as to pass for a sash, and practically throw herself at a man so recently disappointed in love, then I suppose Kate Verelst can be deemed a pretty-behaved female. I wonder what dear Arabella can be thinking of to allow her plump little partridge to parade her rather too well-endowed charms before the fascinated gazes of our bachelors and husbands."

Kate, her cheeks on fire, backed out of the room soundlessly; so it was perhaps unfortunate she didn't hear what her champion had to say in her defense.

"As to that," said Kate's benefactress, who cast caution to the winds and managed to alienate a woman who until that moment had counted her as one of her dearest friends, "your youngest granddaughter's bodice is quite as low as Kate's. Don't blame Miss Verelst because nature gave her a lovely shape and your Maria inherited your own figure, which even at full bloom was about as voluptuous as a broomstick. Your real complaint is that Kate seems in a fair way of snagging the captain, and you have your eyes on him for your own granddaughter."

Kate, meanwhile, sought out her father, intending to make her excuses to him of a headache and escape to her room. The fact that the ladies attending the ball considered her dress immodest enough to remark upon made her want to hide in her humiliation. This, when she had almost convinced herself that its décolleté was nothing out of the ordinary, which indeed, in the eyes of most of society, it was. She didn't know how she could ever again hold her head up in public. Her evening was quite spoilt.

"A headache, Kate? I'm so sorry, my dear," said her father, interrupted by his daughter at cards with some of his friends. "Very well, I'll tell your mother for you when I see her."

"Thank you, Father," she said, grateful not to have to make her excuses before her mother's penetrating gaze.

She was about to ascend the staircase when Mark met her at the foot with his arm around a melancholy Jeremy. Jeremy had been quite abruptly catapulted into sobriety and was finding this state as unpleasant as it was unfamiliar.

"Kate," Jeremy asked remorsefully, "have I disgraced myself?"

"No. Of course not," she said.

"Fortunately you got sick before you attracted too much attention, Jeremy," said Mark in an unsympathetic tone. "And if you ever again give spirits to my sister, I'll—"

"I know," Jeremy said, chastened. "I couldn't help it. I wasn't quite sober at the time. I went upstairs to get my flask, and there she was, peering through the banisters. I knew m'mother told her to keep out of sight. She looked so sad that I wanted to cheer her

51

up, so I took her some champagne."

"Well, you cheered her up," said Mark grimly.

"I'm glad," said Jeremy defiantly. "This is the devil of a house to live in, thanks to the atmosphere my parents' arguments leave about the place. If I've made it any more pleasant for Serena tonight, then I'm happy."

On this altruistic note he slid into an untidy heap at Mark's feet.

"Sobriety was just too much for him, I imagine. If he weren't your brother," said Mark, grimly shouldering his burden, "I'd have left him outside retching his guts up."

"Oh, Mark," said Kate, appalled. "Surely he wasn't —"

"Wasn't he just, my pretty innocent?" he said with wry humor. "I hope your mother's guests watch their step when they go out to the garden for air."

"You're horrid," said Kate, looking at her brother with some concern.

"He's all right, Kate," said Mark. "And he'll be the better for some sleep. Where were you going?"

"I'm going to retire," she said. "I have a headache."

He gave her a penetrating look. "Something *is* wrong. What is it? The truth, now."

"You'll drop Jeremy," said Kate in alarm as Jeremy began stirring.

"It would serve him right," said Mark callously. She pursed her lips in disapproval, and he capitulated. "I'm sorry. Let's get him upstairs and hand him over to his valet. Then we can talk."

"There's really nothing to talk about," said Kate politely but firmly. "I enjoyed our feast. Thank you."

"Thank *you*, Kate," he said, looking after her with some puzzlement on his handsome brow as she walked rather too briskly for an ailing female up the winding stairway.

He remembered the glow of pleasure in her fine blue eyes when he gave her the elaborate silver filigree earrings he had brought her from Spain. He felt warm just thinking about the way she had looked at him then. What could have happened to make her stiffen in his arms, then unceremoniously announce she had a headache and go to bed when none of the other guests would dream of abandoning the festivities until dawn, at least? He didn't believe her excuse of a headache for a moment. Kate never had headaches. She was the most tireless woman of his acquaintance, next to his sister.

"Kate," mumbled Jeremy.

"She's gone, you young lout," said Mark impatiently.

"Need to talk to her," Jeremy said urgently.

"So do I," Mark muttered, helping Jeremy none too gently up the stairs.

Morning broke excruciatingly early and far too brightly for Serena, rudely interrupted from her slumber by a shaft of sunlight falling over her eyes. Her tongue felt dry in her mouth, and her head pounded. She opened one afflicted eye and stared reproachfully at Kate, who looked tidy and efficient in a neat blue-and-white-striped spencer over a muslin gown. She was wearing a chip hat with cherry-red ribbons and was just drawing on her spotless white gloves.

It was only because Arabella had not seen fit to provide her niece with a vase or porcelain ornament to soften the austerity of her spartan bedchamber that Kate was spared having a small, heavy, possibly lethal object hurled at her pretty head.

"*Must* you do that?" snapped Serena when Kate pulled the curtains a little farther apart, flooding the room with unwelcome sunlight.

"Time for you to get up, love," said Kate. "Everyone else is still abed, and if I know my mother it would be wise to go to the shops before she can repent of her promise or inflict Higgins' dour company upon us."

These magic words had a reviving effect on the sufferer. She sat bolt upright in bed.

"Oh, Kate. If only I didn't feel so *wretched.*"

"Was it worth it?"

"No. It didn't even taste good, although it certainly makes one feel jolly at the time," said Serena, gingerly extracting herself from the bed and groping in her wardrobe as if hoping a garment that was not made of the hated brown would materialize. "I don't want to be greedy, but do you think my aunt's generosity would extend to a new hat?"

Kate frowned at the outmoded object that Serena withdrew from a shelf.

"I think it can be made to do so," she said thoughtfully. "And a new pelisse, too, if Mother scolds me until my dying day."

"Oh, thank you, Kate! Let us go quickly or we'll have to take Higgins."

A few minutes later the two girls were bowling toward the Pantheon Bazaar in Arabella's carriage with one of the kitchen maids to lend them consequence. She was a strapping damsel fresh from the country. Kate chose her carefully. She wanted someone who would be so grateful for the chance of an outing that she would be willing to carry the shoppers' parcels without complaining for as long as it would take to turn Serena out in respectable style.

Elbow-to-elbow with other shoppers intent upon giving their wardrobes a fashionable touch at dirt-cheap prices, Serena aggressively clawed her way to a shelf containing bolts of fabric and, with unerring if hitherto untried taste, selected a sapphire blue wool, an apricot sprigged muslin and a rose-pink satin. Kate regretfully vetoed the satin because she knew Arabella would never allow her niece to appear in public in so dashing a color or so rich a fabric at her tender age, but she had no fault to find with Serena's other selections. They added a green striped muslin and were surprised by Lady Buxted and her daughters, during their inspection of a selection of ivory buttons. All six ladies rather self-consciously attempted to persuade the others that in the common way, of course, they would never dream of shopping for anything really important in the Pantheon Bazaar. But it was so diverting, really, to see what was available in such a fascinating place. One often found some quite good bargains of a trifling nature.

With many similar protestations, all of the ladies somehow found themselves with arms full of merchandise. Sally, the kitchen maid from Shallcross House, stoically carried all of the Verelst ladies' bundles to the carriage and awaited Kate and Serena, who were intent upon looking for a hat that would not disgrace Serena's guardians. In the end, they settled on a straw chip hat trimmed with silk roses. Kate knew her mother would think the hat too fine for a poor relation, but Kate couldn't resist Serena's blandishments, particularly since the child had been so good about the satin.

They were about to return to the carriage and home when Serena, hoping to prolong the treat of being out of the range of Arabella's caustic tongue, begged Kate to accompany her to Hookham's Library.

"It would be so pleasant to have some diverting novels to read," she said wistfully, "when I'm home alone and you and Aunt Arabella and Melanie are at balls and parties."

Kate felt guilty enough about Serena's confinement to the schoolroom while her elders enjoyed themselves that she allowed herself to be persuaded. Besides, Kate herself was very fond of a good book on a cold winter evening. The Shallcross House ladies did not go to parties every night, after all.

They had greeted the librarian and were absorbed in examining some volumes on a high shelf when they heard familiar and most unwelcome voices raised in conversation on the other side of the bookcase.

"Did you see that ugly brown dress and that quiz of a hat?" asked Felicity Buxted of her sisters. Felicity's impeccable taste on this particular morning ran to an extraordinarily virulent hue of green that made her rather spotty complexion appear even more sallow than it was by nature. "Who would believe she has such a handsome brother?"

"Not that it will do you any good now that Kate Verelst has her hooks in him," said the unsympathetic Millicent Buxted, dubbed "The Nose" by those who did not admire the way the young lady's most distinctive feature dominated her rather shallow profile.

"I wish he had turned to *me* for consolation," said Mary Buxted, giggling. In addition to the irritating giggle, Mary had a lisp and large white teeth that made her rather narrow face resemble that of a horse. "But naturally she has stolen a march on us, now that she is fortunate enough to be living in the same house with his sister."

"For my part," said Felicity virtuously, "I would be ashamed to attempt to marry a man who was in love with one of my sisters. I think she's taking advantage of his vulnerable state, and I think it's disgusting."

"You know, I thought so, too," said Millicent, "but I wonder if it isn't the captain who is taking advantage of Kate rather than the other way around."

"What can you mean?" asked Mary.

"Can you think of a better revenge for his being jilted than to make Melanie's sister fall in love with him? His attentions to Kate were *most* particular last night. Melanie *must* be a little in love with him still. One does not transfer one's affections totally overnight, particularly to such a pudding-face as Phillip Bentley. What could be more painful for Melanie than to see Captain Verelst making up to her sister Kate?"

"I must say," returned Felicity in a dry tone, "Kate seems a willing enough victim. She's either not wise enough to see what he's about, or doesn't care."

"I suppose when you're as old as Kate Verelst you can't afford pride," tittered Millicent with all the complacency of her seventeen years. "She's in her *third* season, you know."

Kate whispered urgently to Serena that they should be leaving for home or they would be missed.

"In a moment," hissed Serena with fire in her eye.

Unfortunately for Kate's unkind critics, Serena was still feeling cranky and out of sorts for her excesses of the prior evening. Otherwise, she later assured Kate virtuously, she would never have resorted to violence. She dragged a small stool to the shelf and gave a mighty heave to several large volumes that were precariously balanced on the top. She smiled with grim satisfaction as she heard the squeals of the Buxted girls as they dodged the heavy books that with no warning came raining down upon them.

"Such a pity," said Serena, briskly wiping her hands together to brush the dust from them, "that someone put the heavy books on top. It takes only the slightest movement sometimes to dislodge them."

Serena stalked past Kate, who followed with reddened cheeks. It seemed that everyone in town thought she was pursuing Mark. It was bad enough to be styled a cold-hearted hussy out to take advantage of a heart-wounded man. It was worse for people to think he was trifling with her in order to be revenged on her sister and that she was naive enough to welcome his attentions.

Could it be true? Mark had been especially attentive during the ball, but Kate had assumed his behavior was merely an extension of the friendship he had always shown his younger cousin. Kate couldn't bear the thought that he would deliberately use her in order to punish Melanie for rejecting him.

She resolved to keep Mark at arm's length, no matter how painful that would be, but after they returned to Shallcross House, Kate was dismayed to learn she wouldn't need to exert her determination to avoid her cousin's company for much longer.

"I must leave tomorrow," he told Kate without ceremony when they left Serena with an unprecedented desire for a nap in the afternoon. It had taken some ingenuity to manipulate Kate into the position of riding with him in the park, and he was puzzled by her reluctance. Sensing it, he stooped on the stratagem of pretending that Melanie and Jeremy were to join them, and informing her only when she had changed into riding dress to accompany them that her siblings both had declined his suggestion of exercise.

To Kate's dismay, they attracted speculative stares from all of Melanie's particular friends, whom Melanie already had managed to regale with her version of her parting scene with her crestfallen cavalier. Suddenly, however, their titters didn't matter.

"Leaving?" she faltered. "For Spain again?"

"Yes," he said. "After all, I was only sent to London in order to deliver the dispatches. This wasn't a real leave. Dare I hope you will miss me?"

When she didn't answer, he continued on a lighter note.

"In fact, if everything goes well I should have leave in the spring," he said, "and perhaps it will coincide with Melanie's wedding. Serena will be a bridesmaid, and I've promised her that if I can get leave, I will be here. At that time, I will have an opportunity to look around for a better situation for Serena. Your parents have been kind to shelter her, but now that I can afford to do so, I intend to establish a modest household for her. She won't be housed as richly as she had been under your father's roof, but she won't complain, I'm sure. It's time she had a home of her own."

"Won't the wedding be awfully painful for you?" asked Kate, fastening on what she considered the most puzzling part of his conversation. She would have thought Mark would avoid Melanie's wedding at all costs.

"Painful?" He looked puzzled for a moment. "Oh, yes. Very painful." He avoided her eye, which reinforced Kate's conviction that he was still suffering because of Melanie's defection.

"One must face these things," added Mark, recollecting his supposed bereavement. Her eyes went soft and dewy, and she looked so sympathetic that his

59

evil genius prompted him to add, "Only by seeing the deed done will I be able to accept it."

"I see," said Kate miserably.

He reached out and covered her hand with his. "Kate?"

"Yes?" she asked cautiously.

"Have I done something to offend you?"

"Why do you ask?"

"I detect some reserve on your part that wasn't there when we had dinner with Serena last night."

"I don't know what you mean."

"I think you know exactly what I mean," he said, frustrated, "but let it rest for now. Just remember that I am your friend, and if something is troubling you I will do my best to help you."

Kind words. Kate might have been reassured by them if she hadn't heard Melanie tell an impressed Higgins about her last poignant interview with her rejected suitor in her father's library. Kate had gone upstairs to change into her black velvet riding dress and remembered that Melanie had borrowed her favorite black hat. When Kate paused at the doorway of Melanie's room to ask her sister if she still had the hat, she overheard Melanie telling Higgins about Mark's nobility in their touching scene of farewell.

She had knocked politely on the door to announce her presence to Melanie and Higgins, but not before the damage was done.

According to what Kate overheard, Mark had expressed much the same gallant sentiments to Melanie in her father's library as he had just expressed to Kate herself in the park.

Noble words.

She wondered if he meant them either time.

Chapter Three

It was a beautiful day for a wedding. Naturally Melanie was being married from Shallcross House, and Arabella was giving full rein to her ecstasy at marrying one of her daughters to a really worthy suitor.

She had high hopes for the day, quite apart from the maternal satisfaction of seeing her darling, most favorite child outshine all of the season's debutantes with this brilliant marriage. Melanie was in high beauty, and unquestionably she would be the star of the day. But she was no longer the centerpiece of her mother's vaunting ambition.

Kate would be Melanie's maid of honor, and Arabella thought with satisfaction that those who once considered Kate too plump for real beauty, in an age when the reigning toasts looked positively emaciated when compared to the more generous standards of an earlier day, would be surprised by the change in her.

Somehow over the winter and early spring Kate's puppy fat had melted away.

Her limbs had retained their formerly graceful curves, but now could be described as classically molded rather than charmingly dimpled. Her expression celestial blue eyes were almost too large in a fine-boned face above a swanlike neck. Her formerly sunny smile now betrayed a hint of oddly taking gravity, suggesting a mysterious sadness. And her figure, while retaining its generous curves, had been much improved by daily horseback rides with Serena and long, unfashionably early walks with whatever maid had the stamina to keep up with her energetic strides.

Kate herself seemed oddly unaware of the change in her appearance, which only added to her appeal. Kate was not vain, nor did she make any attempt to attract attention to herself in company. The self-conscious, over-awed damsel who had made her precarious debut at Shallcross House three years ago was gone, and a mature, dignified young lady had taken her place. Arabella was delighted with her elder daughter's new assurance.

Arabella could have wished her daughter were not so willing to let the other girls shine her down at parties, but she was generally hopeful that Kate would soon follow her younger sister to the altar.

One person who did not share his wife's raptures over Kate's metamorphosis from a plump little cocoon into a butterfly was Lord Shallcross. Her restlessness disturbed him. On the few occasions when he wasn't dining from home in order to avoid his wife's far from soothing company, he watched Kate closely, one day going so far as to send for her as he worked on his accounts in his library.

She entered with a tremulous smile, as if she were a stranger unsure of her welcome.

"Good afternoon, Father," she said. "You wanted to see me?"

It occurred to him that Kate never called him Papa these days and hadn't since she was younger than

Serena. Over the years he had expended little thought on her. She was one of those nice children who never perpetrated pranks or made demands, and although he had always been very fond of her, he had never taken much trouble to know her well.

When the family group was together, it was Melanie who was his pet. Her dulcet prattle soothed him after listening to the strident tones of her mother. Jeremy, before he became involved with low company, amused him with his exploits. But Kate had always been the quiet one. He had always taken her sunny disposition at face value, assuming that because she indulged in no tantrums or made no demands she was content in the life her parents provided for her. Now he wasn't so sure.

He signed for her to be seated.

"There seems to be no escape from this grand wedding, my dear," he said jovially. "I find it hard to believe that any of the royal princesses could have been married with such pomp. If so, I think I know why the poor mad king lost his reason. I suppose next it will be your turn to be married, eh?"

Like all gentlemen of his age, he automatically assumed young ladies thought of nothing but beaux and bridals, but he had made the remark for a reason. Kate gave him a tight, noncommittal smile which was not lost on her father, who was watching her closely for her reaction.

"Are you entirely happy, Kate? Does it bother you so much that your younger sister is being married before you?"

"Gracious, Father! Indeed not!" exclaimed Kate. "I would never say so to Mother because she would accuse me of being jealous of my sister's good fortune, but I would not have Lord Windom as a gift. I have no wish to marry a gentleman whom I could not love, and I am sure I could never love someone like him."

"Yet marrying for love is not always wise, my child," he said bitterly. "Your mother is very anxious to see you contract a suitable alliance. In fact, I have heard so much of her schemes that I am well nigh sick of them."

"It is hard sometimes," Kate admitted, hastily adding, "I know she has my good at heart, or thinks she does. But I have no wish to be married just yet."

"And you think your mother means to push you into it."

"I know she does," said Kate. "If a gentleman so much as looks at me, Mother embarks upon a most embarrassing quest to find out the extent of his family and of his fortune. She does this by questioning all of her friends."

"Do you have a partiality for any particular gentleman?"

She smiled faintly. "Save yourself, sir?"

"Stalling, Kate?"

"Yes, sir. There is a gentleman whom—but that does not bear thinking of. My mother would never approve, even if it would come about."

"Is he so ineligible? I hope you have not formed an attachment to your dancing master," he said with a smile, secure in the knowledge that this entirely satisfactory daughter would never be so dead to convention.

"Certainly not," she said, laughing. "It is only that the gentleman's affections have been engaged by another."

"I see. Then you will do very well without him. Do you fear you will be forced into marriage by your mother? Is that why you are so sad?"

"You know my mother, sir," said Kate. "It took

her no time at all to convince my sister that she would be wiser to accept Lord Windom than to honor her previous understanding with my cousin."

Her father pursed his lips. He hesitated on the point of telling his daughter that Melanie's understanding with Mark was entirely in Melanie's head, but he decided that he could not expose his daughter's foolishness, even to her own sister, when his nephew had been at such pains not to do so. He considered that Mark had behaved in a truly noble manner. Lord Shallcross privately held the conviction that his wife's taste in men left much to be desired. He voiced this last part of his musings to Kate.

"I should not say that, Father," she said, laughing in almost, but not quite, her old manner. "I think she exercised uncharacteristically good taste when she chose to marry you, although I hope you will not consider me an unnatural daughter if I confide that it was probably the last time she showed such discrimination."

Her father rolled his eyes humorously.

"I should hope that when you marry, my dear, you will not inflict low tables on crocodile legs upon your spouse for him to fall over," he said, "or that nightmare of red and gold medallion upholstery, of all abominations."

"They are all the crack," said Kate, laughing. "My comfort is that while she is exerting her genius to new heights in turning your home into a Greek or Roman temple—I don't think she has quite decided which it is to be, although the Greeks are gaining and those crocodiles are most decidedly Egyptian—she is not choosing suitors for me."

"Rest assured, Kate, that she will not force you into marriage against your will while I am alive," he said. "I only honored your mother's wishes in Windom's case because I could see that Melanie herself is enough like her mother to guarantee that the match will do very well for her, God help them both."

"But my cousin—"

"She would have grown weary of his lack of standing in the world, and she would have made him miserable," said Lord Shallcross. "I don't think your cousin will be the kind of complaisant husband Melanie requires, nor would she for long be content with living on what he can provide. Mark will do very well in the world. I am confident he will be able to amass a fortune of his own because of the splendid connections he is making. But no man by his own exertions could amass a large enough fortune to satisfy women like your mother or Melanie unless they turn to trade. She would have beggared him within a few years of their marriage."

"Oh, surely not, sir," protested Kate, unwilling to believe that any woman could use Mark so.

"But enough of Melanie," said Lord Shallcross. "She is provided for, and need not concern us. I am worried about *you,* Kate. Although I accepted Windom for Melanie, I want you to know that no matter how miserable your mother makes me, I would never consent to your marriage with someone you dislike."

"I thank you, sir," said Kate with heartfelt gratitude. She sensed the end of the interview and rose, extending a hand to her father. "I have always thought you had my best interests at heart." She smiled faintly. "I think Mother does, too, but sometimes I am quite shocked by what she considers one's best interests to be."

Lord Shallcross laughed. "I do believe, my dear, that you are the best of my children, although that is not saying very much, after all. Are you very sure you are not interested in contracting an alliance at this time? This must be a secret between us, but I am about to take steps to assure that if I should die suddenly, your mother would not be able to force you into a marriage you do not like."

"Father!"

"You will say nothing to anyone. Least of all your mother. After all, she may yet predecease me," he said bitterly, "and I may have a few years of peace before my own demise, God willing. I am seeing my man of business to make some arrangements. I know how high-handed your mother is, but you have nothing to fear from her, I promise you."

"I do not like this talk of your death," said Kate.

"One must face these things," he said, smiling maliciously. "Your mother has a few surprises in store for her, and the cream of the jest will be her frustration that I will not be available for her to vent her anger upon. A pity I won't be able to see it."

"Father, what are you going to do?" asked Kate, seriously alarmed.

"Don't concern yourself. I will do nothing rash, I assure you. I just want you to know that if I die before your mother, there will be some who will say that I have left things very carelessly. I want you to know that what I am doing, I will be doing for your own good."

"Father, you are frightening me! What is this talk of dying? You are in perfect health."

"Of course I am," he said with a smile that was not entirely convincing. "It is a man's responsibility to leave his affairs in order."

He was not being quite honest with her. Many a night over the past few months his rest had been disturbed by premonitions of disaster. They had been vague but disturbing. He was not worried about Jeremy. He was a man and could take care of himself. Nor did he worry about Melanie. She would soon have a husband to protect her. But Kate and, to a lesser extent, his niece Serena, worried him. He would not have spoken about these plans he was about to instruct his man of business to put into execution, but Kate looked so sad he felt he had to do something to reassure her. That his mission had failed was obvious. His attempt to assure her that she would be safe from her mother's machinations after his death was clumsy. But he could not say more.

"Don't worry, my dear," he told her kindly. "I didn't tell you this so I could make you look even more worried than you did when you came in. After all, I may live a good many years yet. I only wanted you to know that you are not now, nor will you ever be, at your mother's mercy in the matter of your marriage. She is not a bad woman, your mother. Only not a very wise one, sometimes."

This was quite the most charitable thing Kate had ever heard her father say about her mother, and it restored her spirits almost magically. She knew that both of her parents had been vastly disappointed in their marriage. She hoped her father's remark was evidence that they might someday deal more comfortably together.

"Of course, Kate, I cannot work miracles," he said, grinning. "I may be able to prevent her from marrying you off to the next man of fortune who shows his face to her, but I cannot prevent her from *trying* to do so. Rumor has it that you are to be almost as splendid as the bride on the grand day."

"Indeed. And it truly embarrasses me," she said, "although I must say my new gown is sumptuous, and I shall enjoy wearing it."

She didn't say so, but she was particularly relieved that even Arabella was not so dead to convention as to parade her daughter in a low-necked gown in broad daylight at her sister's wedding, although, unfortunately, she still had no qualms about doing so for evening entertainments. Propriety dictated that Kate's costume be modest so as not to interfere with her sister's magnificence, as if, Arabella reflected justly, this were even remotely possible.

Melanie, romantically inspired by a portrait of a Verelst ancestress in hoops, had insisted upon a wedding gown styled with voluminous skirts, contrary to the prevailing mode. She would be an ice maiden in pearls, crystal and a train and veil of handmade French lace, probably smuggled illegally into the country by what method Arabella refused to discuss. Arabella hoped (she said) she was a loyal citizen of England, but she didn't know what that had to do with dressing a daughter for her wedding. Kate's gown, although of domestic origin, didn't rival her sister's, but it was truly magnificent and was probably the most becoming garment Kate had ever owned.

In fact, Arabella had spent almost as much thought on her elder daughter's gown as on the bride's. Kate would be wearing a sea green gauze creation trimmed simply—and most expensively—with silver lace and pink rosebuds. Her glowing chestnut curls would be crowned with a wreath of matching flowers. The gown was rather sweetly old fashioned, with a low waistline ending in a point and a full skirt which admirably became Kate's delightfully ripened figure and graceful arms.

The fact that she also had to provide a similar dress for Serena did not bother Arabella for long.

She pled the excuse that the style of Kate's gown was too sophisticated for a chit of Serena's tender years and attired her niece in a becoming and suitably demure dress in the same expensive fabric trimmed with tiny pink roses and white lace instead of the more magnificent silver.

If she had thought the added advantage of silver lace would be enough to allow Kate to outshine her lovely cousin, she was mistaken. Kate wasn't the only one whose looks had improved over the winter. But Arabella was so pleased with the way Kate looked in her gown that she allowed her natural optimism to persuade her that no one could seriously be interested in a sixteen-year-old bridesmaid next to her more worthy and infinitely more richly dowered cousin.

It had been a hideous few months for Kate as the household anticipated that early spring wedding in 1814. Nothing could be more trying than Arabella when she was in high croak. She changed her mind about the wedding plans from hour to hour, often clashing with Melanie over them in confrontations that ended in bitter tears on both sides.

Hostilities between England and Bonaparte's forces had escalated since Mark had left Shallcross House to return to his regiment. Kate knew from reading the newspapers that Wellington's weary army had spent most of the fall crossing the Pyrenees and forcing the French out of Spain. Several times she and Serena had read about Mark's regiment being engaged in action, and twice Captain Mark Verelst had been mentioned in the dispatches. Except for that, there was no news of Mark.

In Kate's mind, Melanie and her mother were the most callous beasts in nature to be planning a wedding while Mark's fate was still unknown.

On March 30, Paris fell. But still no word had been received from him. She and Serena searched the casualty lists with frightened eyes and let out long gasps of giddy relief when they failed to find his name.

It had been months since the night when she danced in his arms and attracted the malicious whispers of the ton. When she closed her eyes at night she still saw his face and felt the touch of his lips on her hand. She heard his voice and saw him smile tenderly at something pert his sister said.

If she could just receive word that he was alive, she told herself, she would be content never to see him again. Every day she feared the official communication that would inform her father as the head of his family that Mark had fallen in battle.

Since he had left them those long months ago, no one had received a letter from him. He had promised to return for Melanie's wedding if he could get leave. In fact, Serena maintained stoutly that she expected to see him any day. But Kate couldn't avoid noticing the pinched look Serena got whenever a stranger approached the house.

Kate's state of mind would have been bad enough without her mother's acrimony. In addition to the chaos of her mother's ever-changing wedding arrangements, the bride's temperamental tears, Serena's panic over her brother, and Jeremy's outlandish escapades that compelled his tight-lipped father to spring him from various sponging houses over the winter, Kate had to endure her mother's bitter recriminations against Mark.

Before Mark departed to join his regiment, he left a considerable sum with his uncle to expend on his sister's behalf. One would think this would appease Arabella, who had always resented, if vicariously, the expense of supporting a dependent relation, particularly one, she pointed out waspishly, with as large an appetite as Serena's. But anyone who made this quite reasonable assumption would have reckoned without Arabella's rather elastic sense of justice.

"Shabby genteel, I call it," she told Kate furiously, "and exactly what one would expect of him. Now that he's come up in the world he thinks to impress us with a few paltry guineas. As if that were enough to compensate us for the inconvenience of housing a poor relation who has no sense of gratitude for our generosity, and who, besides, cannot do any sewing that would not disgrace a servant and is quite useless in the stillroom."

"I wish I might hear you," said Kate in some amusement, "if anyone, Serena included, would dare put herself forward in Mrs. Bennett's stillroom."

Mrs. Bennett was the Verelsts' housekeeper at Crossley, Lord Shallcross's country estate, a noble and remote Yorkshire residence which Arabella occupied with only the most extreme reluctance. Whenever Arabella started expressing an interest in housewifely virtues, Kate always had to suppress an inclination to laugh.

Irrelevantly, Kate broke into her mother's tirade to ask her just when was the last time *she* was in the stillroom.

Arabella pursed her lips in vexation. "You don't have to take me up so literally," she snapped.

"As for sewing," said Kate, "you admitted you were pleased with the handkerchiefs Serena embroidered for you at Christmas and the slippers she worked for Father."

"It would help if she had been taught something more useful than playing the pianoforte and embroidering," said Arabella.

"And if she had," retorted Kate, "you would have been appalled that a girl of her breeding had not been taught the refinements. She will make you proud of her at the wedding."

Arabella sniffed. "If her brother is so well heeled, why hasn't he taken steps to remove her from under our roof?" she asked maliciously.

"The girl cannot live alone," Kate said calmly, knowing very well that Arabella couldn't help but like Serena a little. No one could. "She is no more able to hold household than a babe, bless her. The servants would rob her blind, and think of the scandal if she were without the company of a respectable female in her brother's bachelor household. Besides, I know Mark intends to make some arrangement for her. He told me as much before he went to rejoin his regiment."

"And I suppose he will make a botch of it, if he returns alive from the war, which is by no means certain," said Arabella, who was so wrapped up in her own grievance that she missed Kate's painful wince. "It would be just like the man to get himself killed so his sister would be on our hands forever. And what does a military man know about setting up household, let alone taking care of a handful like Serena?"

"If he can handle the French, he can handle a sixteen-year-old girl, Mother," Kate retorted. "Serena is not a handful, and you know it. She is the most gentle creature, and she has the happiest nature. She has, perhaps, more levity than you would like, but how else could she have retained her sweet disposition in the face of all of her family's tragedy?"

Since there was plainly no answer for this, Arabella embarked upon a fresh grievance against her husband's nephew.

"I don't know why you're so quick to defend him. He hasn't even deigned to send word that he is still alive, if, indeed, he *is* still alive. He'll probably come dragging in, in all of his dirt, with that bag of moldy bones he calls a batman, if you please, toiling behind him. Very pretty, the way the man uses this house as his own. Where I am to find room for all the guests, I have no idea, without Mark coming in whenever he wishes without so much as a by-your-leave and installing himself in the biggest room next to your father's and mine."

The injustice of this remark finally succeeded in upsetting Kate's composure, because in her worst nightmares, she had been picturing Mark dead these many months.

"Mother! How could you say such a thing when it was your idea for him to have that room simply because it is the most uncomfortable bedchamber in the house," she exclaimed indignantly. "You know very well how drafty it is, and that the hangings are so faded it is almost embarrassing to have anyone see it, and that the wainscoting has been so nibbled by mice that—"

"That will do, Kate," said Arabella imperiously. "I think you should be a little concerned about what is due your own family instead of bothering yourself with imagined slights toward cousins who have no right to feel anything but the most abject gratitude to your father and me."

"Speaking of our cousins, I assume you intend to sponsor Serena into society when the time comes," said Kate.

"And why should I?" asked Arabella defiantly.

"Because you'll draw the criticism of every catty tongue in London on my father's head for being

74

such a nip-cheese to grudge the expense of one London season to his brother's child," said Kate roundly.

"Yes, I suppose that will be my duty, too," said Arabella, in the tone of one much put upon, even though Kate knew very well that none of the actual work involved in Serena's debut would fall to her mother.

Arabella had a way of accepting compliments in a voice of cheerful weariness that would lead anyone except those intimately acquainted with her to assume she had been working tirelessly on the arrangements for her parties when, in fact, most of the actual drudgery came under the province of the housekeeper and, occasionally, Kate herself.

The intricate arrangements for Melanie's wedding only owed their conception in the vaguest possible way to Arabella's imagination until they were actually being executed, at which time Arabella would begin issuing contradictory orders and throwing all into chaos. All of the actual work was done by the staff, and Kate was the one who exerted herself to deal with the various purveyors to make certain, for example, that the oysters her mother insisted upon would be available and that the violets that had to be a part of the bride's bouquet because Arabella had carried them in her own wedding bouquet would be delivered to Shallcross House no later than three hours before the ceremony.

It also fell to Kate to soothe the ruffled feathers of the servants whom Arabella had badgered relentlessly during the planning stages of the wedding. At several points during the late winter and early spring, Kate would not have been surprised to return from an outing to find that every servant at Shallcross House had departed.

Arabella insisted that both Kate and Jeremy should figure prominently in the ceremony. She invited the heiress she had chosen for Jeremy and intended to put into motion her plan to promote their match. What but a wedding, Arabella reasoned, could so effectively put a young couple in the way of thinking of marriage?

Arabella's choice of a bride for her husband's heir was a shy young woman, newly emerged from the schoolroom when Lady Shallcross met her several years ago at a provincial assembly in Yorkshire. Arabella hadn't seen the girl since, but she was convinced that this damsel would be the perfect bride for Jeremy.

True, she was a trifle dowdy when Arabella met her as a sixteen-year-old, but her prospective mother-in-law was confident the girl would improve under her own expert guidance. Arabella had only to take her to her own modiste and introduce her to the magical qualities of crushed strawberries for a slightly freckled complexion marred by unhealthy doses of country air and sunshine.

The Honorable Margaret Willoughby's situation was so desirable that Arabella, though not by nature a fanciful person, believed that fate had directly intervened to bring the girl to her notice.

What could be better for Jeremy than a young, rather pretty girl endowed with a magnificent fortune in her own right? Providentially, in Arabella's opinion, Margaret had been left an orphan at an early age, and her fortune would naturally fall to the complete guidance of her husband's family. Her trustees, though they had taken great care of the young lady's assets, had no role in her future once the girl had married. Her father's will had been most specific about that. She—and through her, her husband—would have sole control.

And, as if that weren't enough, the girl owned property adjoining the Verelsts' country seat. Nor did Arabella have anything left to desire in the girl's breeding. Although Miss Willoughby didn't have a title, she was related to most of the prominent names in England by blood, and her uncle was an influential peer.

It was time, Arabella decided complacently, for Jeremy to be married. At one-and-twenty, he had spent enough time on the town as a bachelor. He had, in fact, insisted upon taking his own lodgings instead of living with the family at Grosvenor Square for the season. Arabella thought it evidence of his maturity, although her more perceptive spouse thought it more an inclination on Jeremy's part to participate in even wilder revels than he could have pursued if his comings and goings were being monitored by his disapproving parents.

Jeremy thought a wedding was poor sport, and he told his mother so when she waxed lyrical upon the part he was to play in the day's festivities. Arabella was optimistic that once Jeremy was at the wedding he would play his role creditably. In her fondest daydreams she saw him take little Margaret Willoughby's hand and kiss it tenderly at the end of a tête-à-tête in the lovely rose gardens at Shallcross House which would be at their best on this most beautiful of all April days.

When the wedding day dawned, however, she was not optimistic enough to assume that Jeremy would present himself on his parents' doorstep at the proper time without being reminded, especially if by some ill chance some of his cronies managed to persuade him that better sport awaited him at a boxing match, a cock fight or a bearbaiting in a nearby town.

She had just left the room to dispatch a servant to Jeremy's lodging to make sure he was getting ready for the wedding when Kate was surprised at her task of cutting roses for the drawing room by Mark, who had arrived at the front door and been ushered to Kate because she was the only one whose whereabouts were known to the elderly butler.

She didn't see him at first, and he almost regretted calling attention to himself. She was far lovelier than he had remembered in her simple white muslim dress with her arms full of pink roses and the sun glimmering in the bronze lights of her glowing chestnut hair.

One minute she was alone with her tumultuous thoughts; the next she looked up to see Mark solemnly regarding her. The weary look in his eyes wrung her heart.

His coat was dusty from his journey. His face had grown thinner and would have been positively haggard in a less handsome man. She was so startled to see him that she dropped her basket and covered her confusion by bending over quickly to pick up the roses. They bumped heads, since he had given in to the same impulse.

"I beg your pardon—" she began.

"Kate, forgive me for intruding—"

They both laughed.

"Mark, you startled me! I am so happy to see you," she said, tears of relief starting in her eyes.

"Do I look that bad?" he asked with a humorous light in his brown eyes as he wiped away a tear from her cheek with one calloused finger. She was obviously relieved to see him safe from the wars, and he was encouraged to think she cared for him more than she had been willing to admit at their last meeting.

"You know that's not what I meant. You must have had a long journey. I am sure you will be glad for a rest. Your room is ready," she said briskly, her words sounding foolish in her own ears. She couldn't stop herself. Kate always would take refuge from strong emotion in housewifely bustle.

"Thank you, Cousin. We rode all night, but we made it. I couldn't send a message—"

"I know. It's all right. The most important thing is that you're here, and safe," she said, leading the way into the house with her basket of roses. She gave the roses to a footman with orders to see that one of the servants put them into water until she was free to arrange them.

"Kate, may I see Serena?"

"Of course, you may. I'll call her as soon as—"

"Mark!" screeched Serena, throwing herself into her brother's arms. "I knew you'd come. I knew it! I knew it!"

"That's no reason to strangle me, love," he said fondly, holding her slightly away from him as if she were an adorable but badly trained puppy.

"I beg your pardon, Mark," she said. "Oh, I am so happy to see you safe." She hugged him convulsively. "You must come and see the gown Aunt Arabella had made for me. It has short sleeves and pink roses—"

"All in good time, Serena," said Kate, putting a restraining arm around her young cousin and giving Mark an apologetic smile. "Your brother must rest and make himself tidy if he is to be in any condition to attend the ceremony." She broke off confusedly. "Unless you'd rather not, Mark? I am sure my father and mother would understand if you're too tired—"

"What? Come all this way and miss it? I am not

such a paltry creature," he said gravely.

"Come on then, Mark," said Serena, dragging him relentlessly toward the stairway. Kate watched them absently, conscious that the servant who had been sent to Jeremy's lodgings had returned and was having a low-voiced conversation with Arabella, who looked extremely agitated.

"That ungrateful boy! How *could* he?" Arabella demanded and, to Kate's horror, burst into tears.

"Mother! Whatever has happened?" asked Kate in concern.

"Aunt Arabella?" asked Mark tentatively.

"There you are, Mark," said Arabella, looking up to see him on the stairway. "So the French haven't managed to murder you. I do not intend to stand on ceremony with you after all these years. Go upstairs with your sister and remove all that mud from your person before anyone else sees you."

This was so much the way she had addressed him on similar occasions when he was ten years old that he grinned and winked at Kate, whose mouth had dropped open in indignation.

Being so masterfully dismissed, Mark had no choice but to follow his sister upstairs.

Arabella turned to Kate, tears of frustration glistening in her eyes. "Kate, the most horrid thing! Your brother is not at his lodgings!"

"Mother, surely he wouldn't forget his own sister's wedding," she said soothingly. "Perhaps he is on his way here."

"No. His man told Hodge that he left with some of his friends hours ago, and he wasn't dressed for a wedding."

"Perhaps he intends to return," Kate suggested desperately, saying the first thing that entered her head in order to appease her mother, who looked to be in danger of having a fit of strong hysterics.

"What is the meaning of this ridiculous scene?" demanded Lord Shallcross from the archway into the hall. "I heard your wails all the way to the library. Mark, my boy! Delighted to see you," he said, assuming the furor had been over his nephew's arrival. Mark had just been about to step out of sight at the top of the stairway and hesitated on the point of coming back down to greet his uncle, but Arabella's face looked so alarming that he decided it would be more tactful to withdraw with a smile and the suggestion of a bow toward Lord Shallcross.

"There you are, Charles," said Arabella, pouncing on her husband, "and now you see what has been the result of your lack of control over your son!"

Lord Shallcross, after years of practice in deciphering Arabella's most cryptic statements, immediately grasped the fact that Jeremy had done something dreadful once again. He accepted the culpability his wife so cavalierly assigned to him without a blink, even though he could have justifiably pointed out that it had always been Arabella, not himself, who had indulged their son and insisted that all of his outrageous exploits were merely a natural outlet for such a high-spirited boy.

"What's he done now?" Lord Shallcross asked in a tone of resignation. "If he's gotten himself clapped up again, I'll be blasted if I'm such a fool as to spring him this time. That would be the second time this month, and I won't stand for it."

"You are an unnatural father," said Arabella scornfully. "Naturally no one would expect you to exert yourself on behalf of your family to keep your son from becoming a laughingstock."

He raised an intelligent eyebrow. "Perhaps you should tell me what Jeremy's been doing to distress your mother, Kate. And please spare me the Cheltenham tragedy, if you would be so kind."

"Jeremy has disappeared, Father," said Kate. "His man says he left with some of his friends, and that he was not dressed for a wedding."

"So he's decided to escape from his sister's wedding, has he? Mighty pretty behavior on the part of your son, madam," he said, turning to his wife with a face like a thundercloud.

"It will be so humiliating if he doesn't attend," said Arabella, wringing her hands wretchedly. "How can he disgrace his family like this? What about poor Melanie?"

Her husband gave a bark of cruel laughter. "I do not think this excess of sensibility is for your daughter, madam. I think the only one who will be humiliated by this day's work is yourself. So much for your pretty scheme of inviting Margaret Willoughby for the express purpose of promoting a match between her and our son."

"You must find him and bring him back!" Arabella demanded.

"Not I," said her spouse sardonically. "I have no wish to watch you throw our only son into the path of a provincial heiress like some country auctioneer disposing of a prize stud. I profoundly hope this will teach you to restrain yourself from meddling in what is best left to nature, but I doubt that it will. In any case, you have made your bed, madam, by inviting the girl here and having no prospective bridegroom to present to her and her guardians. Now you may lie in it."

He left with a long look of distaste at his wife's seething face.

At this moment Melanie came into the room with the maid she had been scolding relentlessly throughout the morning and saw her mother's agitation.

"Why, Mother! Whatever is wrong?" she asked. She gave a start of horror. "Oh, Mother! Not the oysters!"

"Worse," said her mother tragically.

"The violets!" shrieked the distraught bride.

"No. Your brother!" exclaimed Arabella, her rich, contralto voice rising to a tragic crescendo. Here, at last, she thought, is someone who can appreciate the gravity of the situation without mouthing soothing commonplaces or making cutting remarks.

"Jeremy?" asked Melanie with a blink. "What has Jeremy to say to anything? What is wrong with him? is he ill?"

"No, he's missing!"

"Missing? How can he be missing? He lives a bare five hundred yards from here."

Kate resignedly told her sister about her brother's defection. If Arabella was disappointed in the effect this revelation had on Kate and on her husband, Melanie's reception of the catastrophe was everything her fond mother could have desired.

"Something dreadful must have happened to him," she cried in a voice so penetrating that it brought both Serena and Mark running down the steps. Mark, obviously surprised by her cries while in the act of obeying his aunt's commands to remedy the deficiencies of his appearance, looked as if he had hastily donned his shirt, because some of the buttons were undone. Kate averted her eyes from his partially exposed chest.

He arrived at the bottom of the steps in time to catch Melanie, who looked up at him and sank into a graceful swoon, although whether it was precipitated by Mark's return from near death or her brother's villainy, no one was quite sure. Much impeded by Arabella's flutterings and recriminations, he deposited his fair burden on the sofa. Melanie opened her eyes and clutched his hands convulsively.

"Oh, Mark! You must find him," she said. Selfish to the bottom of her mercenary little soul, Melanie thought nothing of dispatching a man who had ridden through the night to do her bidding.

"Who?" he asked, taken aback.

"Jeremy, of course," she said in a thread of a voice. "You must bring him back for my wedding," or it will be quite spoilt. What will people say if my own brother isn't here?"

"That he had found something more amusing to do?" guessed Serena, who had a disconcerting habit of answering rhetorical questions at the most awkward times. Kate caught Serena's eye and shook her head emphatically. Mark noticed the gesture and glanced down quickly to hide an involuntary smile.

"Mark," said Melanie, retaining her grasp on his hand, despite his attempts to withdraw it, and favoring him with a melting look from her sadly reddened eyes. "You said if ever you could be of service to me—"

"I did, didn't I," he said with resignation in his voice. He turned quickly to see if Kate was following this exchange. She was. He blushed under his tan, embarrassed for Kate to hear Melanie repeat those foolish words he so regretted. He had no idea that Kate had had the whole romantic scene poured into her unwilling ears by a nostalgic Melanie several times, as had, indeed, the entire household and most of the Verelsts' acquaintances in London.

He was no match for the four expectant pairs of eyes that regarded him so hopefully. He had little trouble reading their expressions.

Arabella thought only a paltry creature would

object to tramping all over the countryside in search of a reluctant wedding guest after spending several days in the saddle.

Melanie, whose face took on a sulky expression that he had never noticed before, was determined that her erstwhile suitor should be made to do her bidding so that every member of her family, with no exceptions, should be compelled to pay homage to her on this most important of all days.

Serena was reluctant to see any cloud mar her cousin's wedding for other reasons—today marked the first time she would be treated like a member of the family instead of like an unwanted dependent. She was, after all, very young. Was it so wrong for a beautiful child to take so much pleasure in being able to show off in her first grown-up dress? Serena had always taken it for granted that her brother was a superhuman creature with limitless strength. Having an excess of energy herself, she often overestimated the endurance of others.

And Kate. Poor Kate. Her eyes looked so vulnerable. He interpreted their expression as concern for her brother and sister when, in reality, she was actually more concerned for Mark, who was being forced to pander to Melanie's outrageous demands after his long, hard journey. The fact that he would even consider searching for Jeremy all over London when his neglected body had to be crying out for sleep only confirmed Kate's mistaken conviction that Mark was still hopelessly in love with Melanie.

Privately, much as she would have loved to get her hands on her brother at that moment, Kate rather envied him the opportunity to escape the Grand Exhibition, as she was beginning to think of it in her own mind. She wished she could escape, too. Instead, she would be forced to witness Mark's distress as he watched Lord Windom claim Melanie as his bride.

Kate's distraught look decided Mark. After all, during the past few months he had endured many long marches without sleep or food or rest. He would simply tell his weary body to consider this the end of another one.

"Just let me get my coat," he said, trying not to sound as reluctant as he felt. He had been looking forward to a hot bath and some sleep before the ceremony, which was to take place at four o'clock in St. James Church, Piccadilly. He would get no rest now, although he still was hopeful that he could find Jeremy in time to have a wash.

He gave Melanie's clutching fingers a reassuring squeeze and tried to avoid the avid look she cast up at him. Her mouth had lost its sulky look, and she was all beatific smiles now that she had gotten her own way. Even Arabella cooed a little at his capitulation.

"Oh, thank you, Mark," said Melanie in throbbing accents. "I know I have no right to ask it, but I thank you from the bottom of my heart—"

"Happy to be of service," he said with a reluctant grimace that Melanie and Kate interpreted as a bittersweet smile for what might have been and Serena interpreted, rather more accurately, although she mercifully for once did not say so, as genuine annoyance at being forced to bear-lead a grown man when he had thought his long journey at an end.

As he got back into his still perspiration-soaked clothing, Mark reflected that it was just as well young Lord Windom was unconscious of the fate that awaited him at St. James Church or he, too, might disappear.

Chapter Four

Running the Honorable Mr. Jeremy Verelst to ground wasn't as difficult as Mark had feared it would be. He found Jeremy and some of the wilder bloods in town on the outskirts of London, engaging in an activity some considered "sport." Mark was not of their number.

It had not been difficult to extract information about his whereabouts from his valet, who had known where his loyalties lay. Arabella had hired him to wait on Jeremy when he was down from school. Martin knew his work well. But if he hadn't possessed the secret to giving Jeremy's Hessians a gleam that was the envy of all of his friends, Jeremy possibly would have discharged him years ago if, indeed, Jeremy hadn't been so lazy.

Martin, despite his many excellent qualities as a valet, had one trait that Mark would never tolerate in any subordinate, be he menial or soldier. Martin spied on Jeremy for Arabella and, recognizing the captain with some fellow-feeling as her instrument on this occasion, cooperated with far more alacrity than Mark considered becoming.

Mark eyed the self-effacing valet with ill-disguised contempt as Martin told him which men had accompanied Jeremy on his outing and disclosed the spot where these young blades usually perpetrated their ghoulish pleasures. Martin had never been invited by Jeremy to this place, but he had once or twice secretly followed him there so that he could apprise Arabella of his activities.

Several young men, Jeremy included, circled a tree from which one laughing young lout was suspending a goose from its feet. Mark's insides churned. For the first time that day he was glad that no one at Shallcross House had thought to offer him anything to eat. He had heard of such amusements but, not finding them to his taste, had never watched them. He didn't want to watch now, but it looked like he would have to, because Jeremy was the first rider.

With a war whoop and encouraging, drunken cheers ringing in his ears, Jeremy rode fast toward the tree. He rode so fast, in fact, that Mark feared he might collide with it. Mark winced as Jeremy, with a nice precision that in his cousin's opinion could have been put to infinitely better use in a cavalry regiment, grasped the neck of the goose and pulled it off. Its cries during this execution were piteous, and at the last moment Mark shut his eyes. When he opened them, Jeremy was receiving the congratulations of his friends. His hands were red with blood, and he triumphantly held aloft the poor creature's neck and pathetic beak. Its entrails were still spilling slowly to the ground from its mutilated body, which continued to twitch convulsively. It put Mark forcibly in mind of worse carnage he had witnessed within recent months on the field of battle, and he reflected that if any of these young men could have been with him, they would have little relish for their so-called sport.

Mark took a deep breath and rode his horse toward his cousin.

"Mark!" exclaimed Jeremy, who Mark now saw was drunk as a lord despite the competence of his feat. "Well met! You're just in time for the fun. Did you see me twist the old honker's neck off first try?"

"Good morning, Jeremy," said Mark pleasantly. "I must applaud you on your strong stomach. I don't think I could make myself indulge in these amusements so early in the day without, er, shooting the cat."

Jeremy was amused by Mark's use of the cant expression. Usually Mark was so proper despite being, Jeremy was convinced, a right one.

"What brings you here, Cousin?" asked Jeremy cordially. "Would you care to take a turn? We have another goose—"

"No, I would not," said Mark hastily. "I came to remind you that this is your sister's wedding day, and if you do not come back with me directly, you will miss the ceremony. And so will I, if it comes to that."

"Tell you what," said Jeremy, slurring his speech. "Better not go. M'mother invited some provincial chit or other, rich as Golden Ball; she's set on having me marry. Hate weddings. Nothing to drink but wine and lemonade."

"Nevertheless, Cousin, I think it would be wise for you to accompany me," said Mark firmly. He took hold of Jeremy's bridle and led his horse apart from his cousin's companions, intending to have private speech with him.

"Who told you I was here?" Jeremy asked belligerently. "And who asked you to spoil sport, Cousin?"

"Jeremy, if we could talk—"

"I don't want to talk," he said loudly. "Either stay with us and join the fun or go home. I know who

89

told you about this place. That lying, spying, worthless Martin. I've always known he was one of my mother's tools, but I never thought *you'd* do her bidding."

"I'm not doing this for your mother, Jeremy; I'm doing this for your sister."

"Melanie," he said contemptuously. "Much she cares whether I come to her wedding."

"Nevertheless," said Mark, not bothering to disclose that it was for Kate's sake, not Melanie's, that he was chasing Jeremy instead of soaking in a hot tub, "I have promised to take you there."

By this time both men had dismounted, and Jeremy's friends, with the instinct born of all persons with low tastes, were nearly salivating at the prospect of seeing Jeremy and his impressive cousin exchange blows.

"A mill! A mill!" they shouted.

Mark saw what was happening and made yet another attempt to reach the part of Jeremy's brain that wasn't muddled with drink.

"Jeremy, listen to me," he said.

He saw a fist come down on him, and weariness had made him so clumsy that he couldn't dodge it. After that he was hard pressed to defend himself. He was at a distinct disadvantage. Not only was he too tired after several nights in the saddle to do himself justice in a fight with his cousin, but he knew instinctively that the Verelst ladies would not thank him for bringing Jeremy home with a black eye or a bloodied nose.

But fortunately Jeremy soon tired, and Mark reluctantly knocked him unconscious with a blow to the temple. He hated to do it—he was so annoyed with the young ruffian by now he would have enjoyed planting him a facer—but he knew he couldn't bruise Jeremy's jaw if he was to make a good showing at the wedding ceremony.

With what little strength he had left, Mark bent and lifted Jeremy onto his shoulder and faced Jeremy's friends, who were scattering. Now that the altercation was over, they seemed to realize the impropriety of what had happened. Mark was a captain in His Majesty's army, and they had offered him violence, or had at least encouraged Jeremy to do so. If he wanted to make things difficult for them, he could do so with little trouble.

Instead, he vented some of his frustration by shaking Jeremy roughly until he regained consciousness and ordering him to take his horse and follow him back to Shallcross House. If nothing happened to delay them, Mark estimated, they would arrive two hours before the ceremony, giving both him and Jeremy time to make themselves respectable.

He gave Jeremy a poke in the ribs to send him on his way and winced as he remembered his scraped knuckles. His ribs were sore, and his arm ached where Jeremy had produced a small knife and made a gash, a thing that never would have been tolerated in a fair fight. Indeed, Mark did Jeremy the justice to believe that he would never have drawn steel on an unarmed man if he had been sober. It was not honorable. He would have a long talk with Jeremy later, when the ceremony was over. Meanwhile, he was thankful to see the wound was superficial, although it was bleeding rather a lot. Mark got a grip on himself. It would be a grave strategic error to faint from loss of blood before he returned the truant to Shallcross House.

Jeremy was looking pale, and Mark couldn't guarantee that Jeremy would have the wit to deliver his unconscious cousin home if Mark swooned. Finding his jailer out of commission, Jeremy was more likely to go back to his friends and murder some more helpless animals. Besides, it would be too ridiculous to get through the war unscathed only to be brought low over a mere pin-prick from a civilian's knife.

Mark managed to stay on his feet long enough to deliver Jeremy to Martin's tender ministrations. The valet, who had repaired to Shallcross House with Jeremy's garments for the wedding upon seeing Mark on his way to find Jeremy, greeted the captain with an ingratiating smile. Mark glared at him, and Martin winced a little at the fierceness of the captain's scowl.

"Oh, Mark!"

He turned to see Melanie, wrapped in a white dressing gown, come toward him.

"Melanie. You see I've brought him to you," he said. "He's a bit worse for wear, but he'll do, I think."

"I knew you could not fail me," she said in throbbing accents. "How can I ever repay—"

"It was nothing," said Mark, thinking of the hot bath his body was crying out for and the undressed knife wound that was dripping his life's blood on the inside of his sleeve. He thanked fate that he wasn't wearing his best uniform.

The tiresome chit didn't seem to have any idea how desperately he wanted to escape from her, he realized with some resentment. He knew his aunt's household. It might be a long time before he could persuade one of the servants to bring him water to wash in, and he knew his batman was now domiciled at the Bird In Hand, a hostelry that Mark thought dubious, but that the man assured him would do very well for him while his master was visiting his relatives. Arabella disliked putting up Mark's servant, so Mark had decided to send him to an inn to avoid a confrontation with her at a time when he knew the house would be crowded with strangers. Such was his reward, he thought with uncharacteristic self-pity, for being considerate of his hostess's feelings.

Melanie showed no sign of releasing him.

"Mark, I hope you won't grieve for me forever," she said soulfully.

He looked at her in genuine astonishment. For a moment he was so weary that he couldn't imagine what she was talking about.

He sighed.

"We mustn't speak of it," he told her kindly. "I will become accustomed, my dear."

He took her hand, and since she plainly expected it, he kissed it fleetingly. At that moment Kate came sailing down the hall in her sea green gown, with her chestnut hair dressed in cascading ringlets crowned with roses. She looked so beautiful that it almost took his breath away. Unfortunately, she appeared just in time to see him kiss Melanie's hand and witness the long, languishing look the bride gave him before retiring to her room, scattering pins from her elaborate coiffure in a little trail behind her. Mark only hoped Kate hadn't heard his silly little speech.

"Kate, you look charming," he said, smiling.

"And you," she said roundly, "most certainly do not."

To his delight she took him by the hand and led him directly to his bedchamber, where she ordered him curtly to sit on a stool while she examined his hurts.

She rang the bell rope and stamped her foot impatiently when it was not answered.

"Excuse me, Cousin," she said, going out to the

hall. "Where can all of the servants be?"

"They're probably busy, Kate. I can see to myself—"

"Nonsense," she said tartly. "With all the servants eating their heads off in this house, one would think that at least one of them could be spared to wait on you."

Her tone was such a skillful parody of her mother's that he laughed in spite of himself, earning a sharp look from his benefactress.

"Little shrew," he said, his discomfort almost forgotten in his amusement. "There's nothing wrong with me. But if you could persuade someone to bring me water to wash in, I'll be your debtor forever."

"You shall have it, I promise you," she said with steel in her voice. "You! Hodge! Come here at once. Did you not hear Captain Verelst's bell?"

Hodge looked most embarrassed when ushered unceremoniously into the captain's presence by a magnificently angry young lady.

He looked from her indignant face to the captain's rueful one. He was not about to blurt out that his mistress had told him to ignore any summons that came from her husband's upstart nephew, who could precious well wait upon himself. Indeed, during his tenure in the house, Mark had never once pulled the bell rope. He usually had his batman in the house to wait on him.

"Hot water, cloths and bandages at once, Hodge," Kate demanded, dismissing him abruptly and returning to her cousin. "And now take off that coat, if you please."

"Kate, I had better wait until I'm alone. My arm is bleeding, and you may turn dizzy—"

"Such nonsense," she said contemptuously. "I am

94

not so paltry a creature, Cousin, I promise you. I am well aware your arm is bleeding, for the sleeve is soaked through. What that ninnyhammer of a sister of mine meant by detaining you in the hall when you look about to drop of fatigue, I'll never know."

She caught herself up guiltily and looked at Mark, who seemed to be taking this criticism of his lost love with tolerable composure. His face was almost gray with weariness, but his eyes had such a warm look in them that she felt her pulse quicken. Martin had returned with the hot water, bandages and towels, and took himself off as fast as his legs would carry him when Kate nodded an abrupt dismissal.

Kate dipped a towel in the water and began sponging Mark's bruised knuckles.

"Kate, you'll spoil your pretty dress," he objected when he saw she meant to treat his wounds herself. She gave him such a sharp look that he meekly held out both hands without further complaint.

"There," she said into the tense silence between them. "Now if you'll remove your coat, Cousin."

He did so, and although she paled a little, Kate did not swoon. She cleaned the wound carefully and bandaged it neatly.

"There, Cousin. You'll do," she said softly, looking into brown eyes that seemed to draw her into them.

He smiled and touched her soft cheek with his index finger. "Have you stopped scolding now, little shrew?" he asked, caressing one of the loose curls clinging to the curve of her jaw. Then, intoxicated in his weakness by the old-fashioned lavender scent he always associated with her, he bent his head and kissed her.

She drew back after a moment, her eyes huge in her face. She looked, not outraged, but unhappy.

For an instant she had responded. He was sure of it.

"Don't look at me like that, Kate," he said. "I meant no insult."

"Of course not," she said, swallowing hard. "We'll pretend it never happened."

He smiled.

"It didn't just *happen*, and I assure you I enjoyed it excessively," he said. "I'm fond of you, my dear. I hadn't intended to ask you now, when I look more like a scarecrow than a gentleman, but if you think you can bear the thought of marrying an elderly cousin with moderate prospects and taking on a sixteen-year-old hoyden into the bargain—"

"Please say no more, I beg of you," said Kate with a catch in her voice.

"But, Kate, I am asking you to marry me," he said. "Is it so impossible?"

"Yes," she said, "but I do not blame you. If I were in love with someone who spurned me for another, I think I might want to marry the first eligible person who presented himself, too."

"If you did, you would be a complete fool," he said in some indignation. "You are mistaken if you think I—"

"Please, Cousin," she said, throwing up a hand, "let me finish. I know you think you will never recover from your disappointment over losing Melanie—"

"I *have* recovered," he said, gritting his teeth in frustration.

Kate was addressing him in the kind tone she might use to a child who wanted something that she, in her adult wisdom, knew would not be good for him. He didn't know whether to sweep her into his arms and kiss away all of her silly protestations or box her ears. And the worst part was, this ridiculous

96

misunderstanding was all his own fault. Instead of treating his vain, selfish cousin Melanie like the unattainable lady in a medieval romance, he should have encouraged her father to turn her over his knee and spank some sense into her.

"No, you only *think* you have recovered," said Kate maddeningly. "Someday you will look back on this conversation and shudder at your narrow escape."

"Never," he said, appalled to hear such fustian rubbish on his beloved's lips.

"Oh, yes, you will. I promise you. I know you are anxious to find some respectable female and make a home for Serena—"

This was close enough to the truth that Mark immediately began to protest. "Kate, this is ridiculous. I am not offering for you because I want to provide Serena with a home. I am sincerely attached to you."

"No, you only—"

"—*think* so," he snapped, finishing her sentence for her. "I thank you, Cousin. I am older than seven, you know. I apologize for having inflicted my obviously unwelcome attentions upon you. Naturally a young woman of your family would not want to ally herself with a man who possesses neither riches nor a title."

This was so grossly unfair that Kate's usually gentle eyes were on fire, much improving her looks. He felt a masochistic thrill of pleasure at the fury he had aroused in her. He had at least made her stop addressing him in that insultingly kind tone of voice.

"I thank *you*, Cousin," she said angrily. "Because my sister has dashed your hopes, you think all women would reject a worthy man for a rich, though silly, one. I forgive you because I know that your reason has been affected. Surely you don't think I am foolish enough to marry a man who would make me pay for the rest of my life for my sister's perfidy."

He gave her a small, cold bow, which under the circumstances made him feel so ridiculous that he wanted to throw the bowl of water Kate had used to sponge his wound against the wall in his temper. Critically observing the ugly, faded wallpaper, he reflected that this violence could only improve it.

"I will leave you now," said Kate in a chill tone. "You don't want the water to get too cold. The ceremony is at St. James."

"I thank you, Cousin," he said curtly, then bit his lip when she looked at him furiously and scanned his face for signs that he had made the remark in levity. He felt as if she were about to haul him off by the ear, and he didn't find the thought as amusing as he might have under other circumstances.

He had made a ridiculous mull of it, simply because he hadn't waited for the proper time to make his declaration, he scolded himself. It just showed how stupid a man could be when he hadn't had enough sleep. He had had no intention of proposing to Kate so soon after his supposed jilting by her sister, let alone kissing her when he presented a far from dignified figure in his dirty service uniform, with his face unshaven and with blood dripping all over the place from a paltry wound. The words had simply leapt out of his mouth.

He had been overcome by her beauty and her tender ministrations. She was the first person in months who had spared the least thought for his physical comfort except for his batman. For all that his aunt, his cousin Melanie—How he would *love* to wring her graceful white neck at this moment!—and even his own sister cared, he could have bled his life's blood out on the front step.

On this thought he caught himself up. Really, Mark, old man, you are getting morbid, he told himself. He looked regretfully at the freshly made bed, even though long experience had taught him that it was vastly uncomfortable.

Then he began sponging the dirt of travel off his body and donned his second-best uniform for the wedding of his supposed lost love to a young man he was profoundly beginning to pity, for the hapless Lord Windom was about to marry into a family of madwomen.

As he finished his last ablutions, Arabella was inspecting the young ladies of the house with all the keen attention a commanding officer reserves for troops going into battle.

"Melanie, my love, you are exquisite! Perfect! Lord Windom won't be able to take his eyes from you, nor will anyone else," gushed Arabella. "Now, do you go stand in the small salon with your maid. *Stand*, mind you. I don't want you to crush your gown any more than is necessary. We must hope the ride to the church in the carriage won't do too much damage."

The bride dismissed, Arabella turned her attention to Serena. If the flushed look of triumph faded from her face, she looked pleased nonetheless. The girl was impossibly lovely in the sea green, and the pink rosebuds looked charming entwined in her dusky curls.

"You look very well, Serena," said Arabella, gesturing for Serena to turn so she could inspect her completely. "Very well, indeed. Do make sure your behavior is as elegant as your appearance today, my dear."

"Yes, Aunt," said Serena, her eyes shining with

excitement.

"You are to ride in the carriage with Kate and Jeremy," Arabella continued, "and your brother, if he can make himself ready in time."

"He would have been on time if he hadn't had to look for Jeremy," said Serena, resenting the note of censure in Arabella's voice. She couldn't bear to hear Mark criticized.

"Of course, my dear. We must all be very grateful to him," said Arabella, who was so pleased now that Jeremy had been found that she could be charitable, for once, toward the captain. "Now, where is Kate? She was here a moment ago."

"She said something about fetching her fan," said Serena.

"That's all right, then," said Arabella in relief, "although she should have sent a servant. Kate! There you are, my child. Let me look at you."

Kate obediently pirouetted, hoping her reddened eyes weren't noticeable. Apparently cold water hastily applied on her stinging eyelids had improved their appearance, because Arabella found nothing amiss.

"Very lovely, my dear," said Arabella, pleased. "But do try to smile more."

"Have you forgotten something, Mother?" said Kate, catching Arabella's eye with a significant look toward Serena.

"Oh, to be sure! How silly of me! Serena, my dear, come with me," said Arabella. Surprised, Serena glanced at Kate, who nodded. Serena followed Arabella to a low table upon which was set an elaborate casket.

"Your uncle and I want you to have this little gift, child," said Arabella, withdrawing a small box. "It is to wear with your first grown-up gown."

"Oh, thank you, Aunt Arabella," said Serena, giving an unladylike squeal of pleasure when she opened the box. "Oh, Aunt Arabella! How beautiful!"

"Yes, dear, they are," said Arabella, signaling Serena to turn so she could clasp the ornament around her neck. "Pearls are so suitable for a young girl. There, now. Both of you go down and prepare to get in the carriage. Jeremy should be waiting for you."

"Yes, Mother," said Kate, touching Serena's arm. Serena was lost in contemplation of her reflection in the cheval mirror, and she thought she had never seen anything so beautiful as the softly gleaming pearls around her slender throat.

"Come, love," Kate said to Serena, leading her away. Kate forgot her own sadness for a moment in her cousin's pleasure. It had been Kate who reminded her father that Serena had no jewelry of her own, and it had been he who ordered the necklace from the jeweler's, although, as usual, Arabella graciously accepted all of her niece's nearly inarticulate thanks as if the gift had been her idea. Kate was only happy that Arabella was in a pleasant mood.

When the girls were seated in the open carriage, Serena's eyes kept straying to the door.

"I am sure he will join us at the church later, Serena," said Kate kindly, reading her cousin's thoughts. She felt annoyed with herself for being so, but she was relieved that Mark would not be joining them in the carriage. Her emotions were too fragile just then. It took all of her strength not to burst into sobs of sheer reaction. She longed for nothing so much as to be in her own room so she could think through this remarkable thing that had happened.

Mark had actually asked her to marry him, and she had turned him down, although it had taken every ounce of strength at her command not to throw herself into his arms. She could still feel the warm touch of his lips on hers and the shudder of pleasure that had gone through her. Rejecting him had been the hardest thing she had ever done in her life, but how infamous it would have been to accept a man who was in love with her sister. It would have been totally unprincipled of her to take advantage of him, she told herself firmly.

She both feared and hoped to see Mark come out the door and join them. Instead, she saw her sister Melanie, smiling radiantly, descend the steps of the house, attended by most of the female servants of the household, who were charged with the mission of seeing the bride into the carriage without the slightest risk of damage to her gown. Kate had the feeling that if a yawning puddle of mud had opened in her sister's path, a score of black-clad women dutifully would have thrown themselves into it so that Melanie could tread on their backs to safety.

Now that the bride herself had appeared, there was no hope that Mark would be in time to join them. Kate felt the carriage set in motion under her, and out of the corner of her eye she saw her parents join Melanie, who occupied the seat of honor alone so that her skirts could be spread out in the family's best open carriage.

Kate was aroused from her reverie by Jeremy's indignant voice.

"Stop looking at me like that," he said, his eyes shifting guiltily.

"I can't help it," said Serena. "It's all your fault Mark isn't here with us. I wanted him to be there to see me in the wedding procession, and now he'll miss it."

"You'd think *you* were the bride," said Jeremy,

whose conscience bothered him tremendously. He had the vaguest recollection of hitting Mark and hoped he had not injured him. He had always liked Mark, although he could be dashed stiff-necked at times. But, despite his guilt, Jeremy wasn't about to take any sauce from a scrubby schoolgirl, and he told her so.

Serena pointedly ignored him to wave at the crowd of people who had gathered along the street to pay tribute to the bride's beauty. Behind them, the occupants of the first carriage heard smatterings of applause and cheers, evidence that the bride herself had been sighted.

Once at the church, Jeremy, who was to be a groomsman, joined Lord Windom's male supporters inside as a servant helped Kate and Serena out of the carriage.

"I am so nervous," said Serena excitedly.

"You'll be fine," said Kate, watching the carriage containing her sister draw up in front of the church. She felt tears well up in her eyes because the wicked thought came into her head that if she hadn't refused Mark she could have been a bride in a few months, too.

She quickly suppressed her emotion and looked around her in time to see a good-looking man with brown hair and intelligent hazel eyes looking her way with rapt attention. She inclined her head toward him frostily to discourage his impertinence. He gave her a small, grave bow, but his eyes were laughing. Then he turned away to talk with some of the other guests who were arriving.

"Was he a friend of yours?" asked Serena innocently. She had returned the stranger's stare with interest. "He seemed very friendly."

"No. I never saw him before in my life," said Kate.

"And I must say, you could have been more civil, Kate," said her mother, who had shaken out her canary yellow damask skirts and had come up to them just in time to see Kate's exchange with the stranger.

"You have always told me that one should never encourage strangers to stare at one, Mother."

"I didn't mean persons such as that gentleman, my dear. He looked quite distinguished, and you gave him such a *cold* look. He must be some connection of the Bentleys. I must find out."

"Enough, madam," said her husband, taking her by the elbow and winking at Kate. "Let us marry off one daughter at a time."

He escorted her inside the church to her place, then returned to the church door to escort the bride.

"Almost time, my dear," he said kindly to Serena, who gave him a scared look.

Serena was to start the procession down the aisle. She had just taken a deep breath and let go of Kate's hand, which she had been gripping convulsively for support, when she felt her brother's big hand close on her shoulder.

"See, love, I made it, after all," he said, kissing her cheek quickly and walking around her to enter the church before he could get caught up in the procession.

He slipped unobtrusively into the last pew, which was already occupied by the gentleman whose mild overture Kate had snubbed.

"Mark Verelst, is it not?" asked the stranger by way of greeting.

"Morgan, good to see you," said the captain, extending his hand. The gentlemen were about the same age and had met frequently in society when they were in their early twenties. Sir John Morgan had withdrawn from the hub of the polite world in order to breed horses in Scotland soon after that, and Mark had gone into the army.

The men turned as the musicians started playing, in order to watch Serena walk slowly up the aisle. Her eyes looked a little frightened, and her nosegay shook a trifle; but she kept her back straight as she had been lectured repeatedly by Arabella, and she remembered to smile. Not for nothing had she tread solemnly up and down the length of the ballroom at Shallcross House over the past few months to rehearse for this moment. She stifled a nervous giggle when she met Mark's eyes and he gave her a vulgar wink.

Kate followed a few paces behind her. She was smiling, too, but when her eyes met Mark's, she colored and looked away.

Then, on her father's arm, Melanie began her regal progress up the aisle, smiling to the left and to the right, inclining her head graciously to acknowledge the gasps of admiration that greeted her on all sides. There was no sign of nervousness about Melanie. She was the queen of the moment, and she was enjoying every heady moment of it. She joined her affianced husband with a pretty show of even white teeth at the altar. It was the kind of calculating smile one would give socially to a prospective business associate from whom one expects to derive much profit.

The ceremony began, and the wedding guests began to fidget slightly. The ritual itself was a bit of an anticlimax after the parade of fashion that preceded it, and a necessary prelude to the orgy of eating, drinking and dancing that would follow it at the bride's home. The bridegroom's relatives, many of whom lived secluded from the metropolis, were anxious to get a look at the inside of Shallcross House so they could determine whether Lord Windom had done well for himself.

Sir John Morgan, who was distantly connected with the bridegroom's family, had only come down from his estates a few days earlier. He leaned over to whisper to the captain.

"Who is the vision in green?" he asked. "I could see she knew you."

"My cousin Kate," he said, stifling an unfamiliar pang of jealousy which he steadfastly refused to acknowledge. "And I'll have you know it is *not* green. I made the same blunder, and I was told in no uncertain terms by my young sister Serena that it is, in fact, *sea* green, a far superior color. Serena, by the way, is the chit with the dark hair standing next to Kate."

Mark didn't notice the surprised expression in John's eye.

"I see," John said thoughtfully. "Since you know the ladies so well, perhaps you will introduce me."

"To Kate? I am very willing to do so. But I warn you that I am not in the lady's best books right now. Claiming acquaintance with me is not likely to do your suit any good."

"I will risk it," said Sir John solemnly.

After the ceremony, the captain and Sir John left the gloom of the church in time to witness a rather awkward scene between the bride and her new consort, who had trodden upon the bride's lace train and made a small rip in the delicate fabric. Melanie's social mask slipped a little as she sharply reprimanded him for not minding his steps, then, recollecting herself, she blushed and said sweetly that it was of no consequence and she hoped he would forgive her. She was just so *excited* to be his wife.

He made a soothing reply and tenderly helped her into the carriage, making a small place for himself at the edge of the seat which was mostly occupied by the bride's elaborate skirts and several yards of veil as the couple bowled away to Shallcross House. Mark thought cynically that it was probably an ill omen for the hapless young man's future.

"May I offer you a place in my curricle, Captain?" asked Sir John.

"No, I thank you," said Mark. "I think I am expected to join my sister and cousins."

"Until later, then," said the knight. "Remember your promise to introduce me to the young ladies."

"I will remember," said the captain, who was not looking forward to introducing Kate to a possible rival.

He joined the small family group that had gathered around the second-best family carriage and rather cynically watched Kate and Jeremy comfort Arabella, who was shedding crocodile tears of reaction after the wedding.

It confounded Mark if he could understand why women wept at weddings. He had rarely seen anything so unromantic or so cold-blooded as the blatantly ostentatious exhibition he had just witnessed. He put a friendly arm around his sister, who was watching the group around Arabella anxiously. Plainly she was eager to get in the carriage and return to Shallcross House for her first grown-up party.

"You looked beautiful, love," he said, kissing his sister on the cheek.

"Did I? Really?" she asked hopefully. "I was so nervous."

"No one noticed, I assure you," he said. He turned to his aunt and uncle.

"Splendid wedding," he murmured politely. He shook hands with Jeremy, who gave him a shamefaced look. "No hard feelings, Jeremy?"

"None, Mark. Good of you—" his sentence broke off into embarrassed incoherence.

"Don't mention it," said Mark, who glanced at Kate and was cheered to see her watching him surreptitiously. She looked down quickly.

"Come, madam," said Lord Shallcross to his wife, gesturing to a servant to open the door of the carriage.

"My baby," wept Arabella, sniffling gracefully into a wisp of lace handkerchief that matched her gown.

Serena stifled a giggle and received a look of sympathy from Mark. Kate didn't smile, but her eyes danced fleetingly. Mark pressed his advantage by taking Kate's hand and helping her into the carriage before the servant could do so.

"Thank you, Cousin," she said softly.

Her lavender scent tantalized him, and he turned rather abruptly to his sister and handed her into the carriage beside Kate. There was room for two more persons in the open carriage, and both of the younger men properly deferred to Lord Shallcross. Then Mark kindly insisted that Jeremy take the remaining spot, feeling he couldn't endure much more of Arabella's sniveling.

He had just decided to catch a hack when he caught sight of Sir John Morgan, who was talking with one of his Bentley relatives.

"Captain," he said, greeting him. "I thought you were joining your cousins?"

"Cut out of a place in the carriage by my young cousin, as it turns out," said Mark cheerfully.

"My offer of a ride still stands," said John.

Since all of the hacks in sight seemed to be occupied with other wedding guests and Mark thought he would never survive the walk back to Shallcross House in his state of exhaustion, he accepted John's offer, despite the fact he was strangely reluctant to be obligated to a man who had shown an interest in Kate.

Mark found the wind in his face blessedly reviving and was optimistic that he would be able to steal away from the festivities for a nap before long.

He was so cheered by this prospect that he managed to convince himself that with Melanie riveted to her matrimonial prize, things might not be so bad between himself and Kate, after all.

Tonight, he promised himself, he would be rested and more in command of himself. He would tell her the truth—that he never was in love with her tiresome chit of a sister. And he would put to rest her ridiculous conviction that he only wanted a wife so he could establish a home for his sister. That may have been his objective in the beginning, but now he found that he very much wanted to marry his cousin Kate.

Chapter Five

It was cold in the room. Mark struggled to sit up and passed a weary hand over his face. He saw his clothing had been removed and he was wearing a nightshirt.

"Mark?"

He hastily pulled the light blanket up to his neck as Kate entered the room with a tray in her arms. Serena followed with a plate of pastries.

"I have never," he said truthfully, "seen such a beautiful sight in my life."

"Since I know he doesn't mean us, Serena," said Kate archly, "we had better serve the food."

"Wait! I'm not dressed," Mark objected.

"Then put on a dressing gown," said Serena. "Unless you'd rather we left."

"No, not at all. What is the hour?"

"Past eight o'clock, Cousin," said Kate, who politely motioned for Serena to turn her back with her as Mark shrugged into his dressing gown.

"I don't even remember getting into bed," he said.

"Hodge practically carried you up here," said Serena.

"You've missed dinner downstairs, I'm afraid,

110

but if you feel well enough you might attend the ball," said Kate.

She was taking the covers off the serving platters, and an irresistible aroma filled the air. Mark was ravenous. He hadn't eaten anything since the day before on the road, and there had been little enough of that. He fell to with enthusiasm as Kate and Serena looked on indulgently for a few minutes, then left him to it.

When he had finished, he pulled the bell rope, and Hodge came running rather breathlessly into the room.

"Yes, Captain?" inquired the newly obsequious servant.

"Take these things away, if you please, Hodge."

"Yes, Captain," Hodge said, bending to take the trays.

"And Hodge?"

"Yes, Captain?"

"Some water for washing?"

"Right away, sir."

After Hodge left, Mark stretched luxuriously and put his long legs on the floor. He felt like a limp rag, albeit an uncommonly well-fed one. And this was the evening, he reminded himself sardonically, that he was going to convince Kate that she couldn't live without him.

He walked over to the slightly rusted mirror his aunt provided for his convenience and grimaced when he saw the wild man who awaited him there. His hair needed cut, and it bothered him that he had apparently attended Melanie's wedding with his dark mane clinging untidily about his ears.

He looked in his bag, hoping his evening dress uniform, the one with the gold lace that had cost him much of his pay along with a pair of his

111

precious silk stockings, would still be presentable after dangling over his saddle for far too many miles in a satchel. He had forgotten that his bat-man, who would have ordinarily unpacked his gear and made sure his clothing was fit to be seen, had not accompanied him. As it happened, these arti-cles of clothing were missing from his bag.

A search of the wardrobe revealed that they had been neatly pressed and were ready to put on. He knew he had Kate to thank for this consideration. No one else would have thought of it. The thought gave him courage, although he hoped she wasn't beginning to think of him as some sort of bother-some invalid.

Hodge returned with the water.

"Hodge, do you think you could make shift to cut my hair?"

"No, Captain," said Hodge, alarmed. "I have never done so."

"Very well, Hodge. Thank you," said the captain, disappointed.

"Do you know, sir," said Hodge thoughtfully, "I think Mr. Jeremy's valet, Martin, might be of some use to you. I believe he is still in the house. I could find him."

"Do so," said Mark.

After Hodge was gone, Mark donned his best shirt, the one with the fashionably starched collar, his silk stockings and his white pantaloons. His buckled shoes stood by the bed, ready to step into. Hodge returned with Martin, who obviously had been prepared for his task. He carried some compe-tent looking shears and a towel.

"If you would sit here, Captain," he said, mo-tioning Mark to a low stool.

The business was soon done, and the servants

departed, leaving Mark to finish dressing. When he descended the staircase to the drawing room where the guests had gone for conversation after dinner, he flattered himself that he looked very much more the thing, then laughed at himself for his vanity.

He was languidly accosted by Sir John Morgan, who reminded him of his promise to introduce him to Kate and Serena.

"What happened to you, man?" he asked. "I thought you had decided to play truant."

"Too many nights in the saddle," said Mark ruefully.

"I see," said John. "Let me congratulate you on your stamina, in that case."

Mark spied Kate sitting at the pianoforte playing a concerto as Serena turned the pages for her. A smattering of polite applause greeted her competent but uninspired recital. Although she looked poised, Mark knew she disliked playing for company as if she were some sort of performing animal. She smiled at her parents' guests and rose composedly to make way for the next performer. She and Serena were about to join Lord and Lady Shallcross when they caught sight of Mark and walked toward him instead.

"Did you enjoy your dinner, Cousin?" asked Kate with a smile on her lips but a wary look in her eyes.

"I don't know when I have enjoyed a meal more," he said, "except perhaps for the one we stole the night of Melanie's ball."

He realized immediately that mentioning Melanie had been an error. Kate smiled perfunctorily and prepared to glide on.

"Cousin, permit to introduce you to Sir John Morgan, an old friend," he interjected before she could escape. "Sir John, Miss Kate Verelst and my sister, Miss Serena Verelst."

"I am charmed, ladies," said Morgan, shaking hands with each of them. "I hope you will each honor me with a dance."

"I shall be delighted to do so, sir," said Kate, "but my cousin is not yet out. I shall ask my mother—"

"Cannot Mark give permission instead?" asked Serena in a small voice. She wanted so much to dance with this nice stranger with the friendly smile, and she knew her aunt would probably say she must not.

Kate considered this for a moment.

"Surely at a party in her own home it would be permissible for Serena to dance with a gentleman introduced to her by her own brother," said Kate with an understanding twinkle in her eye. "What do you think, Cousin?"

"I see no harm in it," said Mark, who decided he would much rather watch the good-looking knight dance with Serena than with Kate.

"If my mother says it was improper for you to allow it," Kate told him, "we will attribute it to your error of judgment and let her censure fall on your head."

"That would be nothing new," said Mark, laughing.

And so, to Serena's satisfaction, it was decided, although she hoped her aunt would not find out about it until the deed was done.

"And do *you* mean to dance with me, Kate?" asked Mark, quizzing her. "Could you reject a man who has fought in defense of his country—"

"How could I refuse?" she said politely. But the wary note was back in her voice.

Mark realized at that moment that he would have to revise his plans. He had alarmed her with his impetuous proposal, and he had no wish to sabotage his cause by renewing his suit before he had laid to rest her grossly mistaken conviction that he still retained a hopeless passion for her sister.

The bride at that moment was chatting with her in-laws and kept casting languishing looks at Mark, which he steadfastly refused to acknowledge. To his annoyance, he saw that Kate also had noticed the direction of the bride's gaze.

"Whatever happened to Jeremy?" Mark asked. As it happened, this was a happy inspiration, although it was politeness rather than guile that made him ask.

Kate may have been mistaken in thinking that Mark had retrieved Jeremy in time for the wedding in order to gratify Melanie, but she had a highly developed sense of justice and had to acknowledge that it had taken all of his reserve strength to perform this service on behalf of relatives who had not always behaved with consideration toward himself and his sister.

"He's over there. It's hard to see him because of his companion's headdress," said Kate.

This structure was certainly impressive. It consisted of a band of black velvet studded with jewels too large to be diamonds but too bright to be anything else, and several upstanding peacock feathers which provided an immediate peril to the vision of anyone so unwise as to get within range of the young lady's animatedly nodding head.

All of the shades of blue and green and gold in the peacock feathers were represented in a heavy, watered silk gown rather oppressively encrusted with embroidery. A train of priceless lace fell in

115

majestic folds from the lady's white shoulders.

She was certainly an original. Although feathers often adorned the bonnets of fashionable ladies for daytime wear, and the turbans of matrons who wished to make themselves conspicuous by evening, they weren't in the common mode as evening wear for young ladies.

"The heiress?" asked Mark, cocking an intelligent eyebrow.

Serena and Sir John Morgan had drawn a little apart, and John was politely drawing out the suddenly shy young lady. Apparently they were talking about Yorkshire.

Kate glanced their way to make sure Morgan was not paying attention to their conversation and answered Mark's question.

"Yes, indeed. Isn't she remarkable?" she asked, her eyes brimming with laughter.

"Quite extraordinary," he agreed, glad to see the twinkle back in her eye. Perhaps if he did not alarm her again, he could renew his suit at a more propitious time, preferably after Melanie had given birth to a set of lusty twins and had thereby run to fat. He found this thought such a pleasant one after avoiding the bride's simpering attempts to catch his eye that he almost missed what Kate was saying about the heiress.

"She is such a droll little creature," said Kate. "I quite like her."

"Do you think Jeremy means to oblige your mother by offering for her?" he asked. He had heard all about Arabella's plan to marry Jeremy to the heiress from Serena, only he had been given the distinct impression that the heiress was an innocuous little dab of a creature whom her prospective mother-in-law expected to be able to bully.

116

"He certainly is spending enough time in conversation with her," said Kate, "but I think it may be because Mother was so angry with him for defecting that he is determined to do nothing to upset her further."

"How very wise of him," said Mark.

Arabella rose, beginning a general migration toward the ballroom. Kate somehow ended up on Mark's arm, so good manners dictated that Sir John offer his arm to Serena. Serena's cup overflowed. She had expected to sit on the sidelines for a few hours until Arabella made her go to bed like a baby. Instead, she was being escorted into the ballroom on the arm of a gentleman as if she were any other lady of fashion. Her lively, dark sapphire eyes were darting everywhere, enchanted with all they saw. Although these were the rooms she lived in daily, they took on a new magic for her.

Jeremy, also, had given into the dictates of good manners and offered the heiress his arm. He did so with good grace, but his bored look was not missed either by his companion or by her guardians, who had been watching the progress of the couple's stilted conversation closely.

The Honorable Margaret Willoughby, who had pretty brown curls and rather speaking gray eyes, was trying to become accustomed to the sensation of being treated as any other guest in this exclusive company, but she wasn't finding the experience unpleasant. In Yorkshire, where she was reared, she was the queen of that provincial society. She was used to being courted by gentlemen with far more address than seemed to be possessed by Jeremy Verelst, and her evil genius prompted her to utter the veriest commonplaces in order to see how long he would remain at her side to gratify his ambitious mama, who Margaret knew had an eye to her as a daughter-in-law.

A lady of much confidence and some cynicism, she attributed the polite indifference with which she was being regarded at this select London gathering not to any deficiency on her part but to the fact that there were probably many in the room who didn't yet know that her dowry would be in excess of twenty thousand pounds, an incentive quite apart from her lavish income from the extensive lands left to her by her late father.

Although Margaret was accustomed in Yorkshire to a familiar court of attentive gentlemen and fawning ladies who went into raptures and titters of admiration over Margaret's fabled "sparkling wit," the young lady was shrewd enough to guess that the same wit would be deemed to sparkle less if possessed by a person who wasn't blessed with her wealth.

Being an heiress was not always a gratifying experience. Twice she had been kidnapped by impecunious gentlemen bent on compromising her virtue so that she would have to marry them. Only her diligent guardians' intervention had saved her reputation.

On the other hand, her puckish sense of humor appreciated the privileged position in which she found herself. She had once carried a bouquet of weeds to a provincial assembly and gravely accepted fulsome compliments on them the entire evening. She was hugely entertained by the spectacle of several of her female admirers actually going so far as to carry similar bouquets of weeds to the next assembly. But even this kind of flattery fell flat after a time.

Margaret did not come to Shallcross House to

enjoy herself. In fact, she had little expectation of doing so. She had been decked out in this vulgar display of jewels, rich silks and feathers, which were so little to her taste, at her guardians' recommendation in order to impress Lord and Lady Shallcross. Her guardians thought it a wise move in the calculated business of matrimony to let Lady Shallcross's eyes be dazzled by diamonds before she entered into negotiations to sell her son.

Lady Shallcross might have invited Margaret to Shallcross House to judge whether the young lady would be a suitable wife for her Jeremy, but that haughty lady was mistaken if she thought Margaret was by any means anxious to marry a young man who rumor had it was much inclined to strong spirits and whose mother, besides, once had been an actress. A lady with Margaret's assets could afford to shop for a more impressive pedigree in the man upon whom she would bestow her hand and her fortune.

Margaret was indifferent to the fact that she was far too elaborately dressed for a maiden of her tender years. After all, she cared little what the ton thought of her. With all the confidence of one who knew, at eighteen, she could buy and sell most of the people in the room, including the romantically handsome young nobleman forced by his mother into dancing attendance on her, she considered this gathering just one of many parties she expected to attend before she settled down to domesticity, and not a particularly important one at that.

She had, at that time, no intention of committing herself to Jeremy Verelst until she saw what other young men London had to offer. Jeremy's conversation was stiff and polite, imperfectly concealing boredom. Margaret reflected that he probably would be most surprised to learn she was just as bored as he was. He was handsome, yes, but for a lady of her wealth, handsome suitors were hardly a rarity. She decided at the first opportunity to tell him so.

"I beg your pardon," said Jeremy, when he trod accidentally on her train.

"Yes, I think you might do so," said Margaret with a weary sigh, "and not because you were clumsy enough to step on my gown."

Jeremy looked at her in surprise. "What do you mean?" he asked.

"Only that you are obviously bored in my company and haven't the good manners to hide it. Please be assured you are not the only sufferer."

"I am sorry," he said stiffly, "that you do not find my conversation amusing, Miss Willoughby."

"No one could," she said simply.

Affronted, he had an impulse to escort her to the nearest chair and leave her there. After all, he thought with injured pride, it wasn't easy to be scintillating when one's companion will discuss nothing but the London weather and the beauties of St. James Church.

"It's probably not your fault," she said, regretting her rudeness. "It's just that I'm so *weary* of interviewing prospective husbands. They seem so alike after a time."

"I was unaware of having offered for you, ma'am," he said stiffly.

"I suppose you want to put me in my place because I have been rude to you," she said. "I don't blame you. But I imagine you *would* offer for me if my guardians were disposed in your favor."

"You rate your charms very highly," he said dryly, but with a look of far more interest than he had evidenced so far.

"On the contrary," she said quite truthfully. "My looks are passable, and my conversation is, I hope, that of a sensible woman. But I have so much *wealth*, you see, and that is what makes me irresistible to most gentlemen. It would not matter if I were the ugliest beast in nature. I should still have my pick of suitors."

"Please be assured, ma'am, that I am not a fortune hunter, nor am I such a pauper that I am compelled to barter for a rich wife," said Jeremy.

"No," she agreed, "or you would probably exert yourself more to please me. But even if you were as rich as Golden Ball, I doubt you would refuse to offer for me. It is my experience with gentlemen of fortune that they cannot resist the opportunity to add to their wealth by the convenient expedient of marrying an heiress, no matter how little they may need to do so."

"So you are, in fact, a prize of no mean order," he said sardonically.

"More like the proverbial fatted calf, I should think," she said with a sigh. "For, of course, after I am married, I will be like any other wife, subservient to my husband, and dependent upon him because he will hold the purse strings, and not I, even though it *is* my purse."

He sensed real loneliness beneath the bravado.

"I don't think it's true that the only offers you receive will be from men who only want your fortune," he said kindly.

"Possibly not. But I probably won't be able to tell the difference, will I? Not that it matters. Look at your sister."

Jeremy glanced over to where Melanie was laughing up into her husband's face.

"Melanie? What about her?"

"Do you think she consented to marry Lord Windom because she gives two pins for the man?" asked Margaret. "Still, he has a beautiful wife, and she will do him credit despite the fact that even a pompous idiot like Phillip Bentley must know she wouldn't have accepted him if he hadn't been the heir to an earldom. He apparently got what he wanted from the transaction, and that is all that matters in the end. Do you think *you* would do *me* credit Mr. Verelst?"

Jeremy was so taken aback by this speech that he had an unworthy impulse to turn and run. Instead, he waited with the other guests to watch Melanie and Phillip open the ball. Kate was standing next to Sir John Morgan, and Serena was partnered by her brother. When the other guests joined in the dance, Jeremy somehow found himself dancing with the heiress despite his intention of abandoning her.

"I will say you dance very well," she said in tones of approbation.

"Would you like to look at my teeth, ma'am?" he asked silkily.

Kate, meanwhile, was making polite conversation as she danced with Sir John Morgan.

"I don't think I have met you before today, have I, sir?"

"No, Miss Verelst. I don't believe so," he replied. "I have not been in London for some years. I have estates in Scotland, and I breed horses there."

"How interesting," she said. "I have never been to Scotland."

"Perhaps you will go there one day," he said absently. He thought her a pleasant enough young lady, if a bit stiff. But she was one of the prettiest women in the room, and he had no objection to dancing with her.

Serena had been separated by a movement of the dance from Mark and had blundered into another couple by accident. They laughed good-naturedly, and Serena, red-faced, was retrieved by her brother.

"It's hard to mind my steps with so much to look at," she told him apologetically.

"Are you enjoying yourself, Serena?" he asked, amused by the decorous young lady who appeared to have replaced his hoydenish baby sister.

"Oh, yes, ever so much," she said, her eyes dancing. "I had no idea that balls were so *interesting*."

"Well, indulge yourself now, my dear, because this will probably be your last ball until your come-out."

"Will I have a come-out?" she asked in a dismal tone. "I think Aunt Arabella means to keep me locked up in the schoolroom until I'm *twenty*."

There was so much pathos in her voice that she might as well have said *forty*, and been done with it, he thought in some amusement. Twenty must have seemed very old to him, too, at her age, he reminded himself.

"You will not be with your aunt much longer, my dear," he said. "I intend to establish a household for you. It won't be for some months yet, but it will certainly be before you are quite on the shelf."

"Oh, Mark! How long?"

"It will have to wait until I can get a longer leave from the army."

"But Paris has been taken. Bonaparte has been beaten. Why must you go back?"

"If only it were so simple, love," he said regretfully. "I have affairs to put in order. And I must look for a house and find some respectable female to take care of you."

Serena missed a step, and Mark had to catch her to keep her from sprawling headlong.

"Does this mean you are going to marry, Mark?"

"Possibly. Possibly not," he teased her. "Have you met a lady who you think would be a congenial companion for me?"

"If you are going to leave me in order to return to your horrid soldiers, I think it would be more to the purpose to find a congenial companion for *me*," she said.

"Perhaps we can find a lady who would please both of us," he said, laughing. "You can screen the applicants for me and submit a list of prospective brides for my inspection when I return."

"Now you are funning me, Mark," she said reproachfully. "It's probably all a hum, and I'll have to stay with Aunt Arabella until I'm — "

"*Twenty*, I know," he said, laughing at her.

Sir John Morgan had to repeat his last remark twice before his preoccupied companion answered him.

"I beg your pardon, Sir John," Kate said. "What were you saying?"

"It was of no consequence, ma'am," he said politely, but she knew he was annoyed.

Sensing that she had offended him, she searched her mind for some conversational gambit and recalled that he had said something about horses.

"Do you also race the horses you breed?" she asked.

"Not in the common way," he said. "You must ride out with me in my curricle one day so you can judge some of my horses for yourself. I've brought some to London with me. And you must bring your charming young cousin with you, of course."

"How very kind of you!" she said with real

warmth. "We should be delighted."

"Speaking of Miss Serena, I must collect my dance from her."

"Yes, indeed," said Kate. "She will be quite disappointed if you do not. Do you know you probably will be the first gentleman she has ever danced with, except for her brother, of course. It was so kind of you to ask her."

"Not at all," he murmured.

Across the ballroom, Jeremy managed to peek through the heiress's outlandish headgear to see his besotted mother smiling approvingly at him. This sight disgusted him so much that he took the first opportunity of handing Miss Willoughby to a different partner and joining some of the gentlemen around the refreshment table.

"Hard work, eh, Jeremy?" asked Mark good-naturedly. He was balancing two glasses of lemonade destined for Serena and Kate in his hands.

"The devil!" exclaimed Jeremy. "How soon do you think we can shab off?"

"Not until midnight at least. We might plead fatigue. In my case it would be real enough. Do you mean to offer for the heiress?"

"I don't know," said Jeremy thoughtfully. "I had thought not, no matter how much of a dust my mother kicked up, but now I am not too sure."

"Does that mean you like her?"

"The lady has roundly informed me that it is nothing to the point whether I like her," said Jeremy, who was now somewhat amused by the situation. "What matters is whether her guardians approve of me. A lady with such a large fortune can afford to be choosy, you see."

"She never told you so," said Mark, startled.

"Didn't she just? I only wish my mother could

have heard it."

"I, too," said Mark with real regret.

"The lady knows what she wants, at any rate, and finds me wanting."

"Well, no doubt this is very wounding to your vanity, but it's not like you have to hang out for an heiress, after all."

"Miss Willoughby informs me that even if I don't, I will still cast myself at her feet," said Jeremy. "We can't help ourselves, you see, in the face of such an irresistible lure as her father's lands and cows."

"She sounds like a most redoubtable young lady."

"She is," said Jeremy. "Unfortunately, I think I rather like her for it, and I probably have queered my own game."

"Well, buck up, Jeremy, there are many heiresses in the world."

"Indeed, yes," said Jeremy. "I say, do you think there's anything stronger to drink than this appalling lemonade? Except for champagne, that is? I loathe the stuff."

"Not for you, there isn't, my young rascal. Not if you're wise," Mark said frankly. "I don't think it will help your cause with the heiress if you become as bosky as you were at the last ball I attended in this house."

"Don't remind me," said Jeremy, throwing up one hand as if to acknowledge a hit. "I've made a mull of my life so far, haven't I?"

"You're very young," said Mark, unable to disagree.

"The thing is, it's hard to go on the town and play cards and flirt with opera dancers when other men your age are fighting the French. I should be in a cavalry regiment by now, except that I am the heir and my loving mother has decided I'm too precious to be risked in battle."

"Your father must have agreed with her."

"She's finally worn him down," said Jeremy sadly. "What would you expect after twenty-odd years of marriage with a shrew?"

Jeremy regarded Mark's pitying face and managed a crooked smile.

"Eaten up with self-pity, aren't I?" he said. "I'm sure any of those poor devils you fought with in Spain would have been happy to trade places with me, and here I am feeling sorry for myself."

"I think I may have offered you a trade at that," said Mark grimly. The memories were still vivid. "It sounds very romantic to someone who wasn't there, and sometimes it was, but there were more times when I didn't enjoy it much."

Jeremy looked across the room and saw that a sort of court had assembled itself around the heiress. Apparently the news of her fortune had made the rounds of the match-making mamas in search of rich brides for their sons. Margaret caught his eye at that moment and smiled saucily at him. Involuntarily, he smiled back.

At that moment Lord Shallcross joined them.

"Lemonade," said Lord Shallcross in disgust, indicating the glasses in Mark's hands. "You would think that for as much as this barbaric celebration has cost me, my wife could have provided us with something worth drinking besides lemonade and champagne. Let us repair to my library and drink port."

Mark regarded the glasses of lemonade in his hands with a wry grimace. He very much wanted to escape to the library with his uncle and cousin; but both Kate and Serena were dancing, and he would have to wait until they were through to give them their libations.

Jeremy saw his dilemma and solved it neatly by taking the glasses of lemonade from his cousin's hands, walking over to Millicent and Mary Buxted, who were seated on the side of the room trying very hard to pretend they really didn't wish to dance, after all, and bowing graciously, presenting them with the lemonade.

"Compliments of Captain Verelst, ladies," he said gravely.

Both ladies simpered and waved flirtatiously at Mark, who vowed somehow, somewhere to get even with his cousin for this treachery.

The gentlemen then defected to the library, and Jeremy, involuntarily glancing at the heiress from the arched doorway, was gratified to see a look of dismay cross her pert face when she realized he was not going to feed her vanity by watching several obsequious young men make cakes of themselves over her.

"This is more like it," said Lord Shallcross, relaxing in his favorite leather chair. "We're safe, now, from intrusions by the fair sex."

"Don't you wish, sir, that we could escape from all women for a little while longer, say, a month?" asked Jeremy.

"You are both hereby invited to return to the army with me," said Mark. "That would teach you to appreciate your situation."

Jeremy laughed. "My mother would have your scalp at the mere suggestion," he said.

Lord Shallcross seemed gloomily preoccupied for a minute and sat up with an exclamation. "We can, boy," he said.

"I beg your pardon?" asked Jeremy, all at sea.

"Escape. We've done our duty by dancing attendance on her through Melanie's wedding," said Lord Shallcross. "The season will be over in a few months, and my fine new son-in-law can dashed well play host at her evening parties until then."

"What do you propose, sir?" asked Jeremy.

"Do you remember my little hunting box in Hampshire?"

"Of course," he said. "I have not seen it since you took me there after I got out of school."

"Well, how would you like to go there now? Just pack a few rough things and go to Hampshire for some shooting while the weather is still cool."

"That's a *capital* idea, sir," said Jeremy, who longed for fresh air and exercise after being cooped up in drawing rooms. He'd show that smug little Margaret Willoughby that he wasn't going to stand around watching her inspect London's eligible bachelors like so many pounds of beef on the hoof. "When can we start?"

"When do you leave to return to your regiment, Mark?" asked Lord Shallcross.

"Day after tomorrow, sir."

"Then this will be a short leave. I am sorry, my boy, that we cannot take you with us."

"So am I."

"That's settled then," said Lord Shallcross. "We will leave for Hampshire the same day Mark leaves to rejoin his regiment, because it would be too bad to leave him to fend for himself in a house dominated by petticoats, eh?"

The gentlemen enjoyed a long laugh together, smoked some cigars and returned to the ballroom with light hearts. They were like little boys who were about to pull one over on their strict mamas.

Serena, meanwhile, had been intercepted by Sir

John Morgan and reminded of her promise to dance with him. Kate watched their progress to the center of the room with a maternal look on her face, but caught her breath when she saw Arabella striding purposefully toward the couple.

Kate quickly dodged to the left to detain her.

"Mother," she said, taking her mother's arm.

"There you are, Kate," said Arabella, her eyes filled with sparks that boded ill for Serena. "Very careless of you, I must say, not to keep a closer eye on your cousin. The child is not yet out, you know, and there she goes on the arm of a total stranger."

"He is the same stranger," said Kate soothingly, "whom you told me I was wrong to snub at the wedding. He is an old friend of Mark's as it turns out, and Mark has given him permission to dance with the child. He had already asked me to dance while Serena was within earshot, and I think it very civil of him to ask her as well."

"So Mark has given his permission," said Arabella, unappeased. "And where is Mark at this moment, pray? Is he keeping an eye on his sister to make sure the conventions are being observed? No! He has left it up to me to make sure nothing improper happens."

"Good heavens, ma'am," said Kate, nettled. "How improper can one be in the middle of a crowded ballroom?"

Arabella, fuming inwardly, subsided and allowed her daughter to seat her on a sofa, where she could keep an eye on Serena and her cavalier. She didn't seriously think there was any harm in letting Serena dance at her cousin's wedding. It just annoyed her that Serena was dancing with this particular gentleman. An interrogation of her cronies had revealed that he was Sir John Morgan, a wealthy knight who, rumor had it, had come to London in order to find himself a suitable wife.

This fortunate lady would be the chatelaine of no fewer than four desirable residences, one of which was a very pretty property in Herefordshire and another of which was an historic Medieval castle in Scotland. Furthermore, he had just bought a house in London and was renovating it.

However, Arabella was mollified by Kate's explanation that Sir John had asked Serena to dance simply because the child had been standing near when he asked Kate to dance. It quite put her in charity with Mark to learn he had done something so useful as to introduce an eligible bachelor to his cousin.

"You dance very well, Miss Serena," Sir John Morgan was saying politely to Serena.

"Oh, thank you, sir," said Serena, so overcome that she tripped over her partner's foot and would have fallen if John hadn't caught her in his arms. She blushed adorably. "I have not had very much practice, you see, except with my brother and my cousin Kate, only that is not the same thing."

"I am very glad to hear it, Miss Verelst," said John, enchanted.

They finished the dance in companionable silence while Serena carefully minded her steps. Arabella and Kate had been chatting animatedly about household matters when they heard the opening strains of a waltz, and Arabella darted to her feet to prevent Serena from committing the solecism of performing the daring steps at her tender age.

The dance itself was still considered by the old-fashioned to be somewhat indecent, and even the more liberal-minded considered that a young lady not yet out who danced the waltz in public might justifiably earn the fatal reputation of being *fast*.

To Kate's relief, this breech of etiquette was prevented by Sir John Morgan's taking Serena by the hand and leading her toward Arabella and Kate.

"Thank you for the very great pleasure, Miss Verelst," he said politely, handing the child over to Lady Shallcross, who he knew was Serena's aunt, because Serena had pointed Arabella out to him. He plainly expected an introduction.

"Sir John Morgan," said Kate obligingly. "May I present my mother, Lady Shallcross?"

"Your servant, my lady," said John, bowing.

"How do you do, Sir John?"

"Very well, I thank you. Charming party, ma'am."

"How kind of you to say so," said Arabella complacently. "Well, I am sure you don't intend to waste your evening in conversation, my dear sir. I am persuaded you would much rather dance with my daughter."

Kate felt ready to sink with embarrassment; but John seemed willing enough to oblige her mother, so she allowed herself to be swept into the waltz.

Arabella turned to Serena. "I hope you enjoyed yourself at your first grown-up party, child," said Arabella indulgently.

"Oh, yes," breathed Serena, her eyes following Sir John.

"I'm delighted to hear you say so, but it is very late and it is time for you to retire."

"So soon?" asked Serena, crestfallen.

"I am afraid so, my dear," her aunt said firmly. "It is nearly midnight."

Serena cast a last reluctant look at Kate circling the floor merrily in Sir John's arms and obediently turned to go. Mark, who had just returned to the

132

ballroom with his uncle and cousin, joined Arabella and Serena. When Arabella explained that it was time for Serena to go up to bed, Mark tucked Serena's arm in his and offered to escort her. He did not enjoy the spectacle of Kate dancing with Sir John Morgan, and he decided he had had enough of ballrooms for one night.

He thought it grossly unfair that Morgan could flirt with Kate to his heart's content, yet Mark himself was prevented from doing so by his own stupidity. But like every good soldier, he knew when to retreat, and did so.

"There you are, my love," Arabella said in a disapproving tone to her spouse, who was accompanied by Jeremy. "I wondered where you had got to. My son, Margaret Willoughby is about to take her leave. You must go pay your respects."

With an obedient bow, Jeremy walked over to the heiress and kissed her hand in quite the grand manner. Her lively gray eyes twinkled up at him.

"Not angry with me anymore, sir?"

"Certainly not," he said with some reserve in his tone. He spared a contemptuous look for the remains of her small court, which was dispersing now that its lodestar was leaving. "I see that the news about the extent of your fortune has made the rounds of the room at last, ma'am, so the evening wasn't a total loss. I wish you a pleasant good night, and happy hunting."

"Thank you, sir. I have already thanked your mother for her charming hospitality," she said, laughing into his frosty eyes audaciously. "Perhaps we will meet again soon."

"Probably not," he said, pleased by the look of surprise on the lady's face. She obviously expected him to pursue her. He decided he would do nothing of the kind for the present. "I regret that I will be out of the city for some weeks, and I will probably not return until after your return to Yorkshire. Have a pleasant journey, ma'am."

She nodded in some dudgeon and left him, with her guardians in tow.

Jeremy leaned against the wall of the room, his blue eyes alight with wicked amusement. He would show the smug little heiress that Jeremy Verelst was not going to be led about by the nose, no matter how extensive her holdings might be.

He would play her slowly, like a trophy fish, letting her think she was in control until he reeled her in at his leisure. He reflected complacently that he had all the time in the world to capture his prize.

He had no way of knowing that a cruel fate had decreed otherwise.

Chapter Six

"I do believe it is the most barbaric thing I have ever seen," said Serena in awed tones as she walked around the towering red-velvet-draped object.

A winged being, probably an archangel, incongruously dressed in armor, held aloft a torch. Its improbably muscular marble legs melted into a boatlike shape supported by more marble and brass columns encrusted with English lions. A slightly soiled red-velvet miniature pillow was nestled inside the draperies. It was with some difficulty that it had been identified as a cradle.

"I quite agree," said Kate, regarding the cradle, which must have weighed at least two hundred pounds, with equal awe. "In addition, I think it in questionable taste as a bridal gift."

Mark's laugh rang out, echoing eerily through the vaultlike ballroom, now stripped of its finery and lined with all of Melanie's and Phillip's bridal gifts.

"On the contrary, my dear, sweet, prudish cousin," he said, "it is the most appropriate gift for a bridal, at least to the Bentleys. There has rarely been more than one child born in each generation, so filling this cradle amounts to nothing less than a sacred trust on the part of each Bentley bridegroom. Unfortunately, in spite of the fabled prowess in the manly arts which each of the Bentley males claims as his ancestral legacy, the Bentleys appear to find it difficult to fulfill."

Kate gave him a disapproving look, indicating Serena, and he smiled mischievously at her. She had an impulse to inform him frostily that she considered it in poor taste to allude to *that* aspect of the marital relationship in the presence of gentlewomen, particularly one of Serena's tender years. However, since she couldn't think of a way to phrase her reprimand that would not be awkward, she decided to maintain a dignified, disapproving silence instead.

"I should think the baby would be frightened to lie in it," said Serena thoughtfully. To Kate's relief, she had not paid any attention to her brother's suggestive remark.

"I wonder how old it is," said Mark, examining it with interest. Kate retreated a little, feeling very conscious in his presence. He was dressed smartly in his regimentals because he was taking luncheon with his uncle and Jeremy at White's.

"Seventeenth Century, perhaps?" hazarded Kate.

"However old it is," said Serena disapprovingly, "I think it is very shabby to give a new-married couple something that has been lying around as long as that. Moreover, I think it's silly to expect a tiny baby to sleep in it. How would you like to wake up and see that *thing* looming over you?" She gave an eloquent shudder.

The three of them wandered about the room, alternately admiring and criticizing the wedding gifts. According to custom, this bounty would lie in state in the ballroom for several weeks, during which time friends of the happy couples' families were invited to file by it and pay their respects to the couple's consequence. It reminded Mark of quite another sort of social gathering.

"All we need now," Mark teased, "is a corpse."

"Whatever do you mean?" asked Serena innocently.

"Don't ask, my dear," said Kate, giving Mark a stern look that was a dismal failure because her lips were twitching disobediently. He was delighted that she could follow his train of thought so effortlessly.

Jeremy joined them a short time later, coming up abruptly in front of the cradle and giving a loud—and Kate thought extremely vulgar—whistle.

"Oh, lord," he said, impressed. "Is there a chastity belt somewhere, too?"

"Jeremy!" exclaimed Kate, scandalized. She indicated Serena with a gesture.

"I beg your pardon, Serena," he said with elaborate courtesy. "You still think babies are brought by angels, don't you?"

Serena, looking up from her dazzled contemplation of a magnificent silver soup tureen, gave him a decidedly sisterly grimace. He laughed all the louder.

This unbecoming levity was put to an end by Arabella, who ushered Miss Willoughby and the young lady's hired companion into the room. Miss Willoughby gave a start of surprise so artless that Jeremy knew at once it had to be rehearsed since the possibility of encountering him might reasonably have occurred to a young lady embarking on a visit to his parents' home.

Jeremy's sleepy eyes lit up. Margaret was looking very pretty in a rose-colored, sprigged muslin morning dress covered with a matching pelisse and a charming poke bonnet. She colored faintly as she returned his greeting.

"Come to admire the loot, Miss Willoughby?" asked Jeremy.

Arabella, at first glad to see Jeremy so attentive to their guest, glanced at him doubtfully. His ironic tone was hardly what one would wish in a respectful young gentleman smelling of April and May, and she resolved to take him to task about it later. She didn't have much experience in such matters, having never been an heiress herself, but she instinctively knew this was no way to address a young lady who had a dowry rumored in excess of twenty thousand pounds.

"Actually," said Margaret primly, "I came to thank your mother for a charming evening." She flushed at his small, incredulous smile. Nettled, she scolded herself for coming. Of course she had only come to get another glimpse of him. She had wondered if he possibly could be as handsome by daylight in his mother's parlor as he was by candlelight in her ballroom. But she considered it excessively ill-bred of him to show so plainly that he saw through her polite fiction.

"And I am so glad you did, my dear," said Arabella cordially. "The gentlemen were just leaving, so we can have a comfortable cose in the parlor after you examine the gifts."

"We are quite obviously *de trop,* Cousin, so we must be off," Jeremy said archly to Mark, enjoying the look of disappointment that crossed Margaret Willoughby's face before she assumed a mask of unconcern.

"Your servant, Miss Willoughby," said Mark politely.

"Ah, you are the cousin, Captain Mark Verelst, are you not?" Margaret asked, although she knew perfectly well who he was. She had noticed him at the ball and had asked someone his identity. Next to Jeremy, in her opinion, the captain had been the most handsome man in the room. "I have heard much about you from some of my military acquaintances."

He was slightly taken aback by the speculative look she gave him, exactly as if he were a piece of merchandise in a store window. Nevertheless, he returned her direct gaze without flinching.

"Window shopping, Miss Willoughby?" whispered Jeremy provocatively.

Her indignant intake of breath caused him to grin more widely, and she knew he was thinking of the confidences she had been so rash as to make to him the night before. I must have been utterly mad, she thought to herself, to so expose myself to this man. Indeed, she had never before spoken so freely to a prospective suitor. Then, as if taking pity on her confusion, Jeremy's tone grew kinder.

"There are a great many superb objects here," he said, indicating the pile of wedding gifts and giving the others the impression that he had been referring to them when he made the remark that caused Miss Willoughby to look at him so indignantly. He thought she resembled nothing so much as an outraged baby bird, and decided he positively would enjoy the unconventional courtship he had begun. He knew instinctively that flowery words and love tokens would never reach her. He bent his mind to

139

the pleasurable task of inventing more original methods of melting her rather flinty little heart.

Meanwhile, he took his leave, taking Mark along with him. He enjoyed the thought that for the next few weeks her bright little eyes would scan every ton gathering in vain for a glimpse of him. He took it for granted that she would stay in the metropolis until his return instead of repairing to Yorkshire. Then, one day he would call on her, unannounced, and she would be ready to fall into his hand like a ripe plum. And would he catch her? No. He would let her dangle uncertainly for a long, long time, and he would enjoy every tantalizing moment of it. Then he would make her his wife, and not entirely because he had designs on her twenty thousand pounds.

Arabella laid an elegantly manicured hand on Margaret's shoulder.

"My dear," she gushed, after the gentlemen had gone. "I don't know when I've seen Jeremy so attentive to a young lady. He's definitely interested."

"Is he, indeed?" asked Miss Willoughby in a studied tone of polite indifference. "How very gratifying. My, what lovely gifts. However will dear Lady Windom use the half of them?"

"I know it seems like that," said Arabella, "but after many years of marriage even the finest things wear out. Did I tell you Melanie and dear Phillip will be the guests of the Comte Zarcone in Italy for several weeks once this dreadful business with Bonaparte is over?"

"I believe you did mention it, ma'am," said Margaret with some amusement.

Arabella, who was intrigued by foreign titles,

140

had, in fact, mentioned the happy couple's belated honeymoon destination to virtually everyone she knew in London. Margaret resigned herself to an extremely tedious half hour of listening to Arabella expertly drop grand titles and names from her honeyed lips, and decided that it had been worth it for a glimpse of the devastating Jeremy Verelst who was, in fact, even more handsome in the all-revealing glare of day than she had remembered.

She didn't take it amiss that he left as soon as she made her appearance, although few of her admirers would have dared to do so for fear of being backward in any small courtesy to so richly endowed a young lady. Margaret rather approved of this modest show of independence, even though she intended to punish him for it before he was much older. Bringing Jeremy Verelst to heel was going to be rather interesting, after all.

About an hour after Miss Willoughby had taken her leave, the gratified Arabella Verelst received another wealthy caller, Sir John Morgan. He was dressed nattily in a coat of blue superfine and biscuit-colored pantaloons for the promenade in the park and had called to invite the ladies to go driving with him in his open carriage.

He was greeted warmly by Arabella and politely by Kate, who tried to counteract with her coolly polite demeanor the embarrassingly cloying civility Arabella was bent on showing this most welcome guest. Her coy looks from John to Kate made her daughter want to sink.

After exchanging decorous commonplaces with Arabella and declining an invitation to admire the newlywed couple's gifts, John reiterated his invitation to Kate to go driving, and asked politely after

Serena.

"I will tell her you are here," said Kate, seeing that Arabella had a disclaimer ready on her lips that would preempt Serena from the excursion. For her part, Kate had no intention of going out alone with Sir John after her mother's rather broad hints. "I am sure Serena will be happy to go with us. The poor child has been rather cooped up since we left the country, and the air will do her good. If you will excuse me, Sir John."

He inclined his head and proceeded to gratify Arabella very much by complimenting her on both of her daughters' beauty and saying he didn't know when he had enjoyed a wedding ball more.

"And have you been married before, Sir John?" asked Arabella slyly.

"No, never, ma'am," said John, who was asked this question often by hopeful mamas. "Isn't that shocking for a man of my advanced years?"

Kate reentered the room with Serena at that moment, cutting short Arabella's protestation that Sir John, as far as males were concerned, was in his first bloom and precisely the perfect age at which to contemplate matrimony.

Kate, to whom her mother's thought processes were only too predictable, hastily intervened before her mother could make a coy remark about Sir John's being at the age when a man should begin setting up his nursery.

"Ah, here are the young ladies," he said, rising and taking Serena's hand in his. She blushed rosily, although she knew that persons who moved in society frequently touched each other's hands and even kissed without it meaning a thing. Still, she found the touch of Sir John's hand rather alarming

142

and tried to control her trembling limbs enough to convey the impression that handsome knights asked her to go driving with them every day of the week.

"Good morning, Sir John," said Serena.

She was dressed in a new lilac sprigged muslin gown which Kate had cajoled her mother into having made for her by her own modiste, with Mark's money, of course. It wasn't as dashing as the white and rose oriental printed cotton gown that Kate was wearing, but she was pleased with the result. Serena wore a white chip hat decorated with silk violets and secured to her glossy curls with yellow ribbons, and she hoped those horrid Buxted girls, who had made such catty remarks about her old brown dress, would see her being tooled about Hyde Park in a carriage with a titled gentleman handling the reins while they walked along at a sedate pace with their poky, sour-faced old governess.

"It is so kind of you to let me come," said Serena, remembering her manners in time.

"I am delighted to have you, Miss Verelst," he said politely. "I'll have your young ladies home before the hour of three, ma'am," he added to Arabella, who made a show of fussing over her daughter as if she were loathe to let her out of her sight, and then embarrassed Serena very much by telling her to *be good,* with a significant look that practically said out loud that she didn't place much dependence upon such a skittish young female's behaving with propriety.

"Oh, what a beautiful carriage, and what truly splendid horses!" exclaimed Serena when she saw the fine equipage and aristocratic matched grays Sir John's groom was walking up and down the street. She couldn't have said anything that would endear

143

herself more to Sir John Morgan. He was a connoisseur of horseflesh and thought he had found a soul mate in his young guest until she asked him naively if his horses were Arabians.

Upon being told they were not, she said kindly, "Well, I am sure they are very beautiful, just the same."

He was so entertained by this artless remark that Kate had cause later to praise Sir John warmly to Captain Verelst for setting out so good-naturedly to set the self-conscious sixteen-year-old at her ease. Indeed, the captain would have been much gratified by Sir John's graciousness if recounting it hadn't brought such a look of glowing admiration to Kate's face.

Serena was inclined at first to regret not being invited to ride in the curricle, a much more dashing conveyance than a mere carriage, but she was unabashedly pleased to be seen in Sir John's company and couldn't resist the temptation of calling out a greeting to the three Buxted sisters, who, to her satisfaction, were listlessly glumping along with their governess on the promenade. She received their looks of displeased surprise with glee. The Buxted girls later observed to their sympathetic mother that it was positively vulgar the way Serena and Kate had called attention to themselves.

Another green-eyed observer of their party was Captain Verelst, who was cantering through the park with Jeremy after leaving Lord Shallcross with his cronies at the club. They drew up by the side of the carriage just as Kate had thrown back her head in laughter at some scintillating remark of Sir John Morgan's. Serena greeted them with approbation.

"Do ride along the side of the carriage for a little

while," she begged them. Serena was having a wonderful time and thought two more handsome gentlemen, even if they were only her brother and her tiresome cousin Jeremy, could only lend their small party consequence.

They obliged her for one turn about the park with good grace, then Jeremy, who was getting bored, made a fatuous remark about taking his leave because he had no wish to intrude upon Sir John's monopoly of his fair passengers and turned away in search of fresh entertainment. Mark, thwarted in his attempt to converse with Kate, was obliged to go along with him.

"Now, what is wrong with you?" asked Jeremy in surprise, seeing that his cousin looked like a thundercloud.

"Oh, nothing," he said sardonically, "although I am surprised you can be so tolerant of that fellow's attempt to ingratiate himself with our sisters."

"If you don't approve of him," reasoned Jeremy, "then why did you introduce him to Kate and Serena, and to me, for that matter?"

"I had no choice."

"I know what your problem is," Jeremy said as Mark, expecting to be accused of jealousy over Kate, prepared a denial. "You don't like to see him squiring your baby sister around. But remember she's almost as old as Melanie was when she got herself engaged to that silly cawker Phillip Bentley, and after all, Kate is there to keep an eye on her. If I know Kate, there won't be anything havey-cavey going on in her presence. Anyway, he's probably intent on fixing his interest with my sister, not yours."

Naturally, Mark could not tell Jeremy that this

145

was small comfort, so he settled for muttering under his breath.

"M'mother has high hopes in that direction," said Jeremy, compounding Mark's gloom. "She actually had a kind word to say for you this morning because you introduced Morgan to Kate. She's probably smelling orange blossoms already."

"Don't you think that would be a trifle premature, considering the gentleman has only known the lady for one day?"

"Kate's not getting any younger. That's what my mother keeps telling her. She ripped up at me proper at breakfast when she said to Kate—you *know* how she is—'Kate, love, you aren't getting any younger, you know,' when she was telling Kate she was going to invite him to dine one night this week and Kate said it was too early in their acquaintance to issue any such invitation, and I pitched right in with 'Do you know anyone who is, ma'am?' "

"It wasn't the most tactful of remarks, Jeremy," said Mark, amused in spite of himself, "even though I agree wholeheartedly with the sentiment."

"Thing is, I couldn't blame Kate if she wants to get married and cut loose from my mother's apron strings. And, with what my father will probably settle on her, she can afford to look high. I wouldn't be surprised to see Kate a viscount's wife or better before she's much older."

Mark found this thought so appalling that he answered Jeremy's remarks quite at random for the rest of the ride home.

For the first time he entertained the notion that Kate might have refused him because she didn't think him worthy and was using his supposed attachment to Melanie as an excuse. He had, in fact, accused her of rejecting him because of his lack of title and fortune, but he only had said so in anger and hadn't really meant it. Now he seriously considered the idea. Other women of Kate's class wished to marry men with titles and fortunes. Why not his cousin?

They were walking to the house from the stables when the carriage containing Sir John Morgan, Kate and Serena drove up. Mark watched with jealous eyes as John kissed Kate's hand, then Serena's. He handed them down and said something that made them both laugh, then took his leave.

"Can you imagine," said Kate, still laughing when her brother and cousin joined her. "Sir John has offered to give me driving lessons, and Serena, too, of course. I told him I would leave it for more dashing ladies. It was kind of him to offer, although I am persuaded he would have looked nohow if I had taken him up on it."

Serena and Jeremy walked on ahead, Serena regaling her cousin unmercifully with a detailed account of their outing, boring him very much by telling him what certain prominent ladies wore on the promenade, how many persons had stopped to chat with them and what diverting observances Sir John Morgan had made on a variety of fascinating subjects.

Mark and Kate had fallen a little behind, and when Kate would have followed Serena and Jeremy into the house, Mark's voice stopped her.

"Kate," he said compellingly.

She turned and faced him squarely.

"I want to talk with you, if I may," he said.

"Of course," she answered warily.

"I may not return for a long time," he said, relieved to talk at last with a female who didn't assume that when the enemy's capital city fell, a good soldier could simply throw down his arms and pack for the journey home after doing a brisk tidy-up of the battleground like a good housewife. "I wondered if you would do me a service while I'm gone."

"You know I would be delighted," she said, her heart chilled at the thought of his leaving, perhaps never to return.

"You may not be when you learn what a tedious task it will be," he said with a glint of humor. "As you know, I intend to buy a house and establish a home for Serena. I can't support her lavishly on my means, but I will make her comfortable with the exercise of a little judicious economy. I wondered if you could discreetly find out which of our paternal female relatives would be available to undertake the management of a gentleman's home and serve as a duenna for Serena."

"You are taking Serena away?" she asked in a bewildered tone.

"But, of course," he said. "A pretty fellow I should be to leave her in your father's care now that I have the means to provide for her myself. By the way, Kate, I am sure I have you to thank for Serena's new turn-out. She looked quite the young lady of fashion today."

"Oh, pray don't mention it, Mark," she said, flushing slightly. "It takes so little to make her happy."

She looked tearful, and he wondered if it was a good sign.

"Is something wrong, Kate?" he asked.

"It's just that I will miss her so very much," she said, looking so sad that he longed to take her into his arms.

"As I am sure she'll miss you," he said. "Kate—"

"Kate, my love!" called Arabella from the doorway. "Where are you?"

Mark could have sworn in his frustration.

"My love," Arabella was gushing, her slender hands making excited butterfly gestures. "The most delightful scheme! Miss Willoughby is dining with us tonight. It seems a new closed stove is being installed in her kitchen, so of course as a Christian it was my duty to invite her. Only think how cozy!"

"How charming, ma'am," said Kate, genuinely delighted because she had liked Margaret Willoughby very much when she met her at the ball. "Shall I speak with Gaspar about the menu?"

"That isn't necessary, Kate. I hope I am not such a bad housewife that I cannot order a simple dinner in my own home without assistance. I told Gaspar that we would have buttered lobsters removed with a haunch of venison and some squabs in cream, and a basket of strawberries and asparagus, and a raspberry syllabub. And a half-dozen, or so side-dishes. Oh, and I told him we must have duckling, Jeremy's favorite, of course—"

Kate's heart sank as she listened to this recital of elaborate foods which her mother had demanded from the temperamental Gallic genius in the kitchens. She knew Gaspar's sensibilities well enough to be certain he was packing his bags at this very moment.

"I will just look in on him to see how the arrangements are progressing," said Kate, hoping

149

to prevent Gaspar's immediate defection along with, most probably, the second chamber maid with whom Gaspar was enjoying a liaison that according to Higgins was the talk of The Room.

"Very well, my dear, if you think it is necessary," said Arabella, frowning a bit at being interrupted in her recital of what in Mark's opinion sounded like an astonishing array of food.

"I do think that we might do without a few of those dishes, Mother, as delicious as they sound," said Kate soothingly. "It sounds an overwhelming repast to set before one small young lady."

"Oh, but that's the best part of the surprise," said Arabella, in the attitude of someone about to bestow a lovely treat. "I have sent a note around with one of the footmen to Sir John Morgan's lodgings."

"I see," said Kate. "And did you name an hour in your note?"

"I told him about seven o'clock. It's unfashionably early, I know; but your father and Jeremy, and your cousin Mark, of course, intend to begin their journeys early tomorrow, so I thought it was wise to set dinner ahead."

"Did you, indeed," said Kate weakly. She would have her hands full with Gaspar, who was most certainly packing his bags if his mistress not only demanded a banquet but wanted it served in a mere four hours.

Arabella lowered her voice confidingly, but unfortunately not so low that Mark couldn't hear. "Do you know, my love, that Sir John has purchased a charming house and is renovating it?" Her voice dripped with coy significance. Arabella believed that gentlemen were basically slothful creatures and the only thing that would prompt them to endure the inconvenience of making improvements to their homes was the expectation of taking a bride. "Only fancy! Anyway, I thought it would be a charitable gesture to invite him to have pot luck with us as well."

"Well, then I certainly must have a word with Gaspar," said Kate faintly. "If you will both excuse me?"

Mark nodded politely and scolded himself for the unworthy surge of jealousy that rose in him. He knew very well that Arabella did not invite the bachelor out of the kindness of her heart. Arabella was dead to charity.

The captain's old enemy was trying to promote a match between her daughter and Sir John Morgan, and Mark was helpless to prevent it. It frustrated him to no end that tomorrow he would be forced to leave the field to a rival who had the advantages of a handsome face, an engaging address, a title, a large fortune and polished manners to recommend him to a young lady as tender-hearted as his Kate. Mark thought it particularly unscrupulous of Sir John to use kindness toward Mark's own sister to further ingratiate himself with Kate. The captain was not fooled into thinking Sir John was particularly fond of children.

He only hoped that by the time the allied powers had managed to put the Gallic monster on a leash and Mark would have leisure to resume his interrupted courtship, Sir John Morgan would not have captured the heart of the woman Mark was quite sure he could not live without.

Chapter Seven

The usually abstemious Margaret Willoughby was finding her second glass of Lord Shallcross's excellent champagne a heady experience, or perhaps she wouldn't have otherwise been so disastrously frank with Jeremy's sister about the mysterious and altogether disgusting ways of men.

"No doubt you know exactly what I mean, my dear Miss Verelst," said Margaret, whose tone of bravado was fed by pique because Jeremy had treated her with an indifference that offended her sense of what was due a most desirable heiress during dinner.

"I am afraid I have not had much experience with gentlemen bombarding me with proposals of matrimony," said Kate, who was also feeling annoyed with the male sex.

Jeremy had been a perfect boor all evening, and Kate anticipated a stormy scene between her brother and her mother when Miss Willoughby left. Kate could tell that Jeremy was attracted to Margaret, but she also knew that Jeremy disliked having his mother force his hand. When would Arabella learn, Kate wondered in despair, that promoting affairs of the heart required a modicum of delicacy? Arabella's idea of finesse was to seat Jeremy and Miss Willoughby at table together and make coy hints about weddings coming in threes.

"You're thinking of bad news, not weddings," was Jeremy's sour rejoinder.

Kate's lack of enjoyment in the evening was made complete when, because Jeremy paid hardly a scrap of attention to Miss Willoughby, what must Mark do but step into the breech and set Margaret to laughing with humorous anecdotes of his life in the army. Although in her mind Kate knew it was only good manners that prompted Mark as the gentleman on the other side of Miss Willoughby to devote himself to Margaret's entertainment, in her heart she was deeply offended because Mark had heretofore refused to share his wartime experiences with anyone in his family, suggesting they were too painful or, perhaps, too secret.

Yet here he was, thrilling this relative stranger with his first-hand experience in Spain, and later in France with Wellington's army. Miss Willoughby, whom Kate had thought she liked until that moment, hung on every word with bright, animated eyes. If Kate had only known it, most of Miss Willoughby's appreciation of Mark's conversation derived not from any real interest in military strategy but in an unwillingness to let Jeremy Verelst see that his neglect of her was going to spoil her enjoyment of the evening.

It might have been some comfort for Kate to know that she was not the only person who was disappointed in this evening. Sir John Morgan had been dismayed to learn that contrary to his expectation, his little friend Serena would not be one of

153

the dinner party.

Arabella, when asked why Serena was not at dinner, had blandly explained that after all, the young lady was not yet out, and she quite feared she had spoiled the child by letting her mix in adult circles before she was ready. Serena was quite done up by her excursion of the afternoon and was this moment tucked up in her bed, Arabella maintained, a lie so blatant to anyone who knew Serena's tireless constitution that it caused flickers of astonishment and indignation to cross several faces at the table.

Serena had, in fact, cried some secret tears of disappointment when she learned she was to take a tray in the schoolroom instead of joining the company at dinner.

Because Mark was devoting himself to Miss Willoughby's entertainment, Sir John had no choice but to devote himself to Kate. Mark, observing this, gave in to an unworthy impulse and redoubled his efforts to entertain Miss Willoughby. Then Kate became recklessly animated as she discussed the beauties of Yorkshire with Sir John Morgan.

While Arabella was thrilled to see Kate getting on so well with Sir John, she was appalled to see Miss Willoughby practically sitting in Mark's pocket. For that reason, she rose rather early as the signal for the ladies to leave the gentlemen to their port.

Miss Willoughby had never liked the null period of the evening that ladies spent after dinner waiting for the gentlemen to join them. Her experience of Arabella, a manipulative, ambitious woman if ever she had seen one, led Margaret to believe that Kate was as cynical about the male sex as she was herself. Kate's attentions to Sir John Morgan also

154

led Miss Willoughby to make the error of believing Kate was setting her cap at him. Margaret also made the mistake of misinterpreting Captain Verelst's attentions toward herself. Otherwise, Margaret, a good-natured creature beneath her cynicism, would never have uttered words that would be so disastrous in their effect on Miss Verelst's peace of mind.

"Perhaps I'll have your cousin instead," said Margaret pensively.

"I beg your pardon?" asked Kate, not believing her ears.

"Captain Verelst, I mean. Have you another handsome cousin? If so I should be delighted to meet him."

"No," said Kate guardedly. "Captain Verelst is my only cousin, besides Serena, of course, and I'm sure you don't count her."

If she had not had two glasses of wine, Margaret would never have ignored the warning in Kate's tone.

"He's handsome, intelligent, ambitious, and your Captain Verelst would probably make a most amiable husband," said Margaret, hoping Kate would repeat her remarks to Jeremy. "Certainly more comfortable a companion than your brother, and more grateful for the advantages my fortune can bring him."

Kate gave a small start of surprise.

"Don't bother to play the innocent with me, my dear," said Margaret, laughing a trifle too shrilly. "It's perfectly obvious why your mother has honored me with such distinguishing attention. She wants my fortune and my lands for her son. Well, I'm rich enough to choose my own husband, and maybe Jeremy Verelst is not to my taste. Perhaps a military gentleman might suit my purposes better."

"I think you're very cold-blooded about the business of marriage," said Kate.

"It rather *is* a business, you know," said Margaret thoughtfully. "I think your captain knows that. Men have often repaired their fortunes with a judicious marriage. There's no disgrace in that. No, he's no fool, your captain. He has much to recommend him despite his lack of fortune. Good looks. Good birth. Beautiful manners. A distinguished war record. I read about him in the dispatches, you know. Very impressive."

"He's not like that," said Kate, a trifle sharply.

"No? Not handsome and intelligent and the rest?" teased Kate's tormentor. "Or not the type of man who would choose his wife for the material advantages she can bring to him? Don't fool yourself, my dear. *All* men are like that."

Margaret noticed Kate's high color and gave a cruel little laugh. It was contrary to her nature to be vicious; but Jeremy had deliberately hurt her this night, and she needed some outlet for her bitterness.

"He wouldn't have been making up to you, by any chance, would he?" Margaret asked in dulcet tones. She noticed Kate's hesitation and smiled even more brightly. "So, Captain Verelst *has* made some overtures. What better way to repair his fortunes than to marry his cousin? I'm sure with your father's wealth your dowry won't be contemptible. Of course, my dear, there would be no contest if I should enter the lists."

"I am certain you are mistaken," said Kate, her distress all the more painful because Margaret's

156

theory fit so well. Mark did have his own way to make in the world. So, failing to marry Melanie, the woman of his first choice, why not settle for good old Kate and the tidy fortune her father was certain to settle upon her?

Margaret didn't appear to find his lack of fortune a drawback — she was virtually her own mistress because she was an orphan — but most prospective fathers-in-law might be forgiven for considering a military man of good address and little fortune a poor match for well-born, richly dowered daughters who could reasonably aim higher.

It was bad enough to believe the man she loved wanted to marry her because of his disappointment over losing his true love. At least she had been somewhat comforted by the thought that he liked her well enough to consider living with her for the rest of his life. The thought that he might have had his eye on her dowry all the time was devastating.

But it all fit because Mark had been extremely attentive to little Margaret Willoughby at dinner. Of course, it was only good manners to pay some attention to a young lady who was being so callously ignored by the gentleman on her other side. But Margaret's words endowed Mark's courtesy with treacherous significance.

By the time the gentlemen joined them, Kate's head was pounding. Margaret, who had no idea she had caused Kate such distress, compounded her wickedness by looking past Jeremy as if he were invisible and smiling an invitation at Mark, who after a tentative glance at Jeremy, immediately went to her side.

Kate was not to know that he did so only because he thought it shameful of Jeremy to so ignore a young lady expressedly invited to his home to further her acquaintance with him. Mark did not approve of Arabella's manipulative methods, and he certainly understood Jeremy's resentment of them; but he didn't think that excused Jeremy for being rude to Margaret Willoughby, whom Mark rather liked.

Sir John Morgan, entering the room in Lord Shallcross's wake, saw only two places available, one near Lady Shallcross and the other near Kate. Naturally he seated himself near Kate and proceeded to invite her, in Mark's hearing, to try the paces of a charming little filly he had just added to his stables. As an apparent afterthought, he added that he would be delighted to see Serena as well on this excursion.

"Oh, how very kind of you," said Kate, thinking how considerate it was of him to include a schoolgirl in his invitation.

Mark was less impressed by Sir John's courtesy. This episode confirmed his suspicion that Sir John was exploiting his sister in order to recommend himself to Kate, and he resented it.

Lord Shallcross caught his wife's attention.

"I rather miss Serena tonight, my love," he told Arabella with a significant look in his eye. He was among those in the room who didn't like seeing Serena excluded from the family group. She almost always dined with the family, and he thought it a shame that on her brother's last night home she was cooped up in her room. "Perhaps she has recovered enough from her excursion of this afternoon to join us for tea."

"What a capital idea, sir," said Mark with heartfelt gratitude. "I would like it of all things."

"Of course, if she is up to it," said Arabella, who knew when she was forced into a corner. "I'll just step upstairs—"

"Mother, let me go in your place," intervened Kate, who knew her mother was capable of going upstairs for a short while and returning with the announcement that Serena was sound asleep.

"Thank you, my dear," said Arabella, a note of annoyance in her voice. "I'll just ring for tea now, and she can join us as soon as it is convenient for her."

Kate left and returned with Serena a short time later. Under cover of the general greeting to the young lady, Jeremy left his chair by the fireplace and seated himself in the chair Mark had just vacated near Miss Willoughby.

"My dear Margaret," he said, smiling warmly at her. "I do believe you are disguised."

"Don't be ridiculous, Mr. Verelst," said Margaret haughtily. "And I don't believe I gave you leave to address me by my Christian name."

"I'm sorry, Margaret," he said. "I have been beastly to you. And you have given me my own again by flirting with my magnificent cousin."

"I don't have any idea what you're talking about, Mr. Verelst," Margaret said. "Your cousin is a handsome man and an excellent conversationalist. Can you think of any reason why I should need an ulterior motive to flirt with him?"

"None at all," said Jeremy, laughing. "We can't quarrel in my mother's drawing room, my dear. Let us take a walk in the garden by moonlight so we can argue in privacy."

"It's too cold," she said childishly.

"Nonsense. From the look of your charmingly flushed countenance, you could use some fresh air."

He took her arm and raised her to her feet, firmly holding the hand she was attempting unobtrusively to pull from his grasp.

"The room is too hot for Miss Willoughby," Jeremy announced. "We are going to take a turn in the garden."

"How delightful," said Arabella with a huge smile on her surprised face.

"She's almost two years old, she has white stockings and a star-shaped marking on her head," John was telling a fascinated Serena. "Her name is Lady Stockings."

To the surprise of everyone in the room, the butler announced Lord and Lady Windom. To their equal surprise, the newlyweds appeared to be in ill humor.

Since a honeymoon on the continent had been out of the question because of the mess that monster Bonaparte had made of Europe, the couple had repaired to one of Phillip Bentley's estates, which included a medieval castle. Although Lord Windom had been skeptical about this choice of a honeymoon spot, his bride had been adamant. She thought nothing could be so romantic as a honeymoon spent in this setting—except, of course, a month spent shopping in Paris or Vienna—and she felt she was owed her gothic adventure after the disappointment of being denied a wedding trip to the mainland.

Melanie was one of those strong-minded ladies who held the private conviction that if men—and in this classification she grouped her husband, the British forces, and the allied continental powers—

had been more efficient, all traces of Bonaparte's aggression in Europe could have been cleared away in time for her wedding trip. She was not about to be cheated, she told her husband, of her scheme of traipsing about the gothic ruins as well.

The bride had spent only a few hours in this honeymoon retreat before she demanded to be taken back to civilization without delay. The stone walls chilled her through and through, the servants were insolent, and there was no society to admire her lavish trousseau.

Lord Windom had tried to tell her all of these things before they departed for the castle, but by now he knew his bride better than to remind her of this fact. So, in the interest of peace, he bore Melanie to his town house, where she proceeded to be very bored and listless after her long journey. On a whim she thought it might be very pleasant to surprise her parents and dine with them.

Disappointed in her marriage, which in her innocence she thought would be one long cotillion, Melanie perhaps unconsciously sought to return to the scene of her triumph, Shallcross House, the place where she had made her debut, had been pronounced one of the season's most ravishing debutantes, and had stunned society with her brilliant wedding to Lord Windom.

Phillip's old castle might be draughty, his housekeeper might be lacking in respect toward her new mistress, and his new cook might have no idea how to tempt the palate of a lady of sensibility; but Melanie knew that in her mother's home she would still be the pet, the darling, the most cosseted of younger daughters. She looked forward to a meal at Shallcross House, where she could once again enjoy

Gaspar's continental cooking instead of the tasteless messes produced by the incompetent staff installed in Lord Windom's kitchen.

Unfortunately, because Mark, Jeremy and Lord Shallcross intended to rise early to begin their respective journeys, dinner had been moved far forward and Melanie and Phillip arrived, not in time for dinner, but in time for tea.

Nor was Melanie pleased with her reception at her parents' home. Her ethereal beauty had led her to expect immediate attention from male members of any company. In this party, the first she had attended as a married lady, she was to be vastly disappointed.

Mark hardly favored her with a common bow. He was still annoyed with Melanie for sabotaging his courtship of Kate, even though the harm had been done unintentionally. And even if he had been on good terms with Melanie, Mark would hardly flirt with her under the gaze of her husband of only one day.

Jeremy had just returned from the garden with Miss Willoughby, her eyes unnaturally bright and her lips quivering with mischief. Looking smug, Jeremy barely greeted his sister. He didn't even bother to express surprise or pleasure at seeing her.

Sir John Morgan seemed to be sharing his favors between Kate and Serena, and Lord and Lady Shallcross were discussing his lordship's journey into Hampshire and the probability of his return, with Jeremy, before Lady Sefton's ball.

"My darling, I can see you are in high beauty," said Arabella in greeting to her daughter. Lord Shallcross, who thought his daughter looked rather sulky, reflected upon how often Arabella saw only

162

what she wanted to see.

"Good evening, Mother," said Melanie, disappointed. "I see you already have dined."

"Indeed, we have, love," said Arabella distressfully. "If only we had known—"

"It is of no importance," said Melanie, avoiding her husband's eye. Phillip had wanted to send a note to his in-laws to ask them if it would be all right to dine with them since he had given most of his staff time off in the belief that he and his bride would be at the castle for another few weeks. Melanie had overruled him in favor of surprising her parents.

Kate heard her sister's stomach growl.

"It is irregular, I know," Kate said tentatively, "but perhaps a tray—"

"How very kind," said Lord Windom, who was extremely hungry. His bride's stare shot daggers at him, but he didn't care. He didn't see why a married man should have to starve to death for the sake of his wife's crotchets.

Kate slipped from the room and Mark followed.

"May I assist you, Kate?" he asked.

"I don't know what with," she said, remembering Margaret Willoughby's poisoned words and feeling betrayed because Mark had been so attentive to the heiress. "We have footmen to carry trays in this house."

She sounded more abrupt than she had wished to. He looked at her for a long moment and thought he knew the reason for her bad temper. It pained him to think the woman he had thought so different from the rest of her sex was at bottom every bit as ambitious and mercenary as his aunt in her pursuit of Sir John. Kate had treated Mark

163

with reserve since the night of the ball at which Melanie's engagement had been announced, and she had galled him with her patronizing reception of his ill-conceived proposal of marriage. For the first time he felt every bit like the poor relation he truly was.

He was angry enough to have it out with her, then and there.

"Have I done something to offend you, Cousin?" he asked coldly.

"No, of course not," said Kate, turning craven. "Pray don't mention it. It is only the headache, a little."

"Poor Kate," said Mark, his tone softening. "You do seem to be the one who looks after everyone."

"I don't mind," she said.

He returned to the salon, since it was obvious Kate did not want his help. Quite unreasonably, Kate began to feel ill-used. Why was it, she wondered, that she was always the one people turned to for comfort and assistance? For a moment she wondered what it would have been like to be a Toast, like Melanie, or a much-courted heiress like Miss Willoughby.

She could not imagine Melanie, if given the opportunity to entrap the man of her choice into marriage, having qualms about taking advantage of his weakness after he had been repulsed by another. Nor could she imagine Margaret Willoughby putting herself out to brave a temperamental cook who was probably just finishing up for the night in his domain, in order to obtain nourishment for two uninvited guests.

Crossly, Kate fully expected that Melanie would turn up her delightful little upturned nose at whatever Kate managed to procure for her. She was mollified when the genuinely hungry Melanie took the tray borne into the room by a footman and fell to with a little crow of laughter. Phillip seemed equally pleased with his impromptu repast.

"It is good I am in my parents' home and do not have to stand on ceremony. Otherwise I would have starved to death," Melanie said with a warm look up at Kate. "Thank you, my best of sisters."

Kate stole a look at Mark and found him solemnly regarding her, as if trying to find the solution to a puzzle. Serena, who was still hanging on Sir John's every word about Lady Stockings, was firmly dismissed by Arabella to bed on the pretext that it was growing late. After Serena's reluctant departure, Sir John seated himself beside Kate and accepted a cup of the tea she was pouring. He told her he didn't know when he had spent a more charming evening.

Meanwhile, Margaret Willoughby and Jeremy kept exchanging intimate glances, causing everyone to wonder just what had passed between them in Arabella's formal rose gardens.

Margaret eyed Jeremy speculatively. The evening had proven to be quite a success as far as she was concerned, even though it had started out so badly. She was only sorry that Jeremy would be leaving for Hampshire on the morrow.

Growing sleepy, Margaret mused how she rather expected to enjoy the next few weeks of waiting for him to get tired of bucolic peace and tranquility and return to London. It was comforting to reflect that after all, she was young and rich and beautiful or, at least, pretty. Pretty enough, at any rate. Her eyes shone as she anticipated a long, delicious pur-

SOMERSET FAMILY PRACTICE ASSOCIATES
110 REHILL AVENUE
SOMERVILLE, NEW JERSEY 08876
(908) 685-2900

Fu-mai Jam _____ HAS AN APPOINTMENT WITH

DR. _Wu_____

ON _thurs_, _May_ 18 20 05 at _11:00 Am_

PLEASE NOTIFY THE OFFICE AT LEAST 24 HOURS
IN ADVANCE IF YOU CAN NOT KEEP YOUR APPOINTMENT.
THANK YOU.

Chapter Eight

Lord Shallcross and Jeremy had enjoyed a capital day of sport on that lovely April day in Hampshire that was destined to be their last.

They had gone shooting in the morning and bagged several game birds which, following an exhilarating day in the fresh air and sunshine, tasted like ambrosia after being basted with wine and turned on the spit by the female half of the couple from the village who slept elsewhere but came to the hunting box each day to take care of the gentlemen.

"Nothing like this, eh, boy," Lord Shallcross said for the third time as he took another helping of the crispy-skinned fowl and washed it down with a gulp of claret.

"No, sir," said Jeremy, grinning. He wondered what his dainty Margaret would think if she could see him with his elbows on the table like a country gawk and grease dripping down his chin from the roasted bird carcass.

"Now, this is the life for a man," said Charles expansively. "At home with nature. When I am here, I wonder why man ever invented balls and routs and picnics alfresco."

"He didn't," said Jeremy dryly. "Woman invented them. That's why man takes every opportunity he can to escape to hunting boxes."

"If that isn't the truth," said Lord Shallcross, his face clouding. "I suppose we'll be regularly in for it now with that Morgan fellow dangling after Kate."

"Good match for her," said Jeremy.

"Your mother wants you to marry the heiress. Nice gal. I wouldn't mind. Your affair, though. Don't want any of my children forced to live under the cat's paw. Not Kate. Told her so. Not you, either."

"I'm very much obliged to you, sir," said Jeremy, "but damned if I won't oblige Mother and marry the heiress, anyway."

Lord Shallcross laughed aloud. "Well, *I'd* be obliged to you," he said. "I don't mind telling you my life would be a great deal more peaceful if you'd marry the girl and save me your mother's tantrums at not getting her way."

"Father, did you and Mother ever love each other?" asked Jeremy. He had never asked such a question of his parents before. He had always preferred to pretend he didn't notice their discord.

"Oh, yes. You wouldn't think it now," said Lord Shallcross, "but there was a time—but that doesn't bear thinking of. She was a beautiful woman. Still is. Marriage would be well enough if all I had to do is *look* at her. But *living* with her—" He finished his sentence with an eloquent shudder.

"I don't think Miss Willoughby is like Mother," said Jeremy, a bit defensively.

"My boy, *no one* is like your mother," said Lord Shallcross, "thank God."

He wiped his face with a napkin and rose a bit stiffly to his feet. His body had received much unaccustomed exercise that day in the saddle, and he was feeling sore, though satisfied with his day's entertainment.

"I'm for bed," he told Jeremy, stifling a yawn. "Nice thing about being in the country is you don't have to keep town hours. Jeckle and his wife have already left. Are you coming up to bed?"

"No, not yet, sir," said Jeremy, rising as his father got up. "I think I'll go outside, maybe take a ride by moonlight."

"Well, be careful. Mrs. Jeckle thought you were a ghost one night riding that black horse with your cloak flapping in the wind, and I almost was bereft of a housekeeper."

"I'll be good," said Jeremy, smiling in contentment. He lingered over a glass of claret after he watched his father's retreating back stumble slightly on the dark stairs to his room, his candle flickering. Then Jeremy rose, went out to the stables and saddled his horse.

To one who was accustomed to being waited on hand and foot, it was an unaccountable luxury to be in Hampshire and not have servants underfoot every moment.

On that thought he heard a rustling sound from one of the darkened corners of the barn and took his lantern toward the noise to have a look.

"Uh, Mr. Jeremy? Is that you, sir?" asked a hesitant male voice.

Jeremy shone his lantern on the two figures standing against one of the supports of the barn and burst into laughter.

"Good evening, Frank," he said, peering into a

169

face very similar to his own.

Frank Watson and Jeremy Verelst had become acquainted in Yorkshire, where Frank had been born to an unwed chamber maid at Crossley within two years of Jeremy's own birth. This was before the present Lord Shallcross's tenure. If what local gossip said was true, Frank's father was the late Lord Shallcross, Jeremy's grandfather, which would make Frank Jeremy's uncle, in a manner of speaking.

When he was a youth and his resemblance to Jeremy, the Verelst heir, became too often remarked, young Frank had been spirited away to serve an apprenticeship to a craftsman. Since then he had received a fairly good education because the present Lord Shallcross felt somewhat responsible for this tangible result of his father's indiscretion in his dotage, much as he deplored its existence. Frank had been an appealing though not particularly industrious youth, following much in the tradition of legitimate Verelst males.

Frank and Jeremy had met occasionally over the past ten years or so. Frank's apprenticeship in London had been rather a failure, and so was his short tenure as a clerk in a counting house. He had been living off and on without leave at the hunting box in Hampshire, having nowhere else to go. He justified his uninvited visits at the hunting box with the conviction that in a way, he was a Verelst and he wasn't hurting anyone by keeping an eye on things when the viscount wasn't in residence. When Lord Shallcross and Jeremy rather unexpectedly decided to take a jaunt to Hampshire, Frank hurriedly made arrangements to stay with a friend in the village.

His mother still lived in Yorkshire, an invalid of sorts to whom Frank dutifully sent money when he was in a position to earn some. The present Lord Shallcross, who was very nice in his notions of propriety, had made it clear that the illegitimate child of his father's former servant, who so resembled the present heir, was not to be encouraged to linger around Crossley.

Frank was most embarrassed to be surprised by Jeremy in his present occupation. His companion was just fifteen, a buxom, flaxen-haired country lass whose smoky blue eyes held more than a hint of passion.

Since her brother was the friend with whom Frank was staying in the village, the choice of a place for their tryst became a problem. Frank had chosen the stable because he assumed none of the family would be lurking about there. Also, his fair companion was impressed by his connection, be it ever so dubious, with the Verelsts. In a peculiar way, she appeared to think being tumbled in their stable by one of their number, even if he was born on the wrong side of the blanket to be real Quality, would be a novel distinction.

Young Molly had been leaning with her back to the stable support, and Frank had been towering over her, about to make short work of the lacing at her bodice. Both trespassers were considerably disheveled, and Frank's breathing was not quite steady.

"Uh, Mr. Jeremy—" began Frank.

"Don't mind me," said Jeremy, running an expert eye over the young person, who winked at him impudently. He returned the wink. "I didn't know you were still hereabouts, Frank," Jeremy added, eyeing his unofficial relative with curiosity. They were of much the same height, and their hair was the same guinea gold color.

"Not for long," said Frank, making an attempt at a nonchalant tone. "I'm just visiting in the neighborhood before I go to sea."

"To sea?" asked Jeremy, surprised and somewhat envious. He had always thought it would be a grand adventure to go to sea.

"It's all arranged," said Frank. "I leave soon. I have already been to Yorkshire to bid my mother farewell, and there were a few people I wanted to see in Hampshire."

"So I see," said Jeremy with a bark of laughter. "Well, don't let me disturb you. I was just fetching my horse."

Leaving the amorous couple behind, Jeremy rode along the primitive road that served the hunting box, enjoying the feeling of the cold, brisk wind ruffling his short, fair locks and the cadence of his stallion's powerful hooves against the pounded earth.

When he started back toward the stables, he thought he smelled smoke on the air and wondered if some poacher had dared light a campfire.

He returned just before ten o'clock to see the hunting box in flames and a hushed crowd of countrymen roused by Frank. Jeckle and his wife had come up from the village when they smelled the smoke on the wind.

"Father!" Jeremy breathed.

Jeckle materialized from the darkness with Frank close behind him. "Mr. Jeremy. Thank God you wasn't inside," said Jeckle.

"But my father!" Jeremy shouted. "Where is he?"

"Dunno. We hope he got out in time, but there's been no sign of him."

Wordlessly, Jeremy began running for the house, Jeckle and Frank in pursuit.

"Mr. Jeremy! Come back! You can't do him no good!" Jeckle screamed.

"Mr. Jeremy!" Frank shouted at the same time. "This is madness! Perhaps he got out by a window and you will have risked yourself for nothing."

"Father!" shouted Jeremy, breaking into the house by a window. "Where are you?"

"Up here," came a raspy voice, choked with smoke.

"I'm coming," shouted Jeremy, his voice breaking off in a cough.

"No! Save yourself," Charles shouted back. "There are flames between me and the door. Please—"

Jeremy pulled his cloak around himself, hoping it would be some protection from the flames, and tried to make his way to the stairs.

"Mr. Jeremy," came Frank's voice from behind him. "Come back!"

"Father!" rasped Jeremy. "I'm coming!"

He was on the stairway when it collapsed and became engulfed in flames.

Kate looked straight ahead, her face stony, when the messenger of tragic tidings finished.

"He died trying to save his father, miss," said Jeckle kindly. There were tears in the old man's eyes. The sight of them stirred Kate from her shocked stupor.

"I thank you, Jeckle, for coming to tell us yourself. It was very kind of you," Kate said, dimly aware of Serena's sobs behind her. Kate had shed no tears. Her heart was a block of ice. Her whole body was in the grip of a peculiar kind of cold that started inside and radiated out to her extremities. There *were* tears, actually. She could feel them inside of her. They were frozen, too.

Kate turned, painfully dry-eyed, as Serena put her strong young arms around her. She patted Serena's shoulder.

"There, love," Kate said in a brittle voice she did not recognize as her own. "Crying won't bring them back."

Sir John Morgan, who had been with them when Jeckle arrived so unexpectedly, was trying to revive Arabella from a dead faint. Kate, remembering her duty, went to her mother's side and supported Arabella's shoulders as she half sat, half reclined on the sofa.

"Miss Verelst," began Sir John, who honestly had no idea what to do. The grief on Kate's face was so naked that he felt like an intruder for having witnessed it. He started to lay a comforting hand on her shoulder and stopped. She gave him the impression of being made of glass so fragile that she might shatter to bits at a touch.

He turned to Serena, who was gulping convulsively. Her face was stained with red streaks from crying, and her eyes were swollen. She looked so pathetic that he put a comforting arm around her shaking shoulders and started talking to her in low tones.

"My cousin must be informed," said Kate. "He is the heir."

"Never," said Arabella harshly, "will I tolerate

174

Mark Verelst's being set in your father's place."

"I think under the circumstances, Mother, you have no choice in the matter," said Kate firmly, "for Mark is the heir, and he must be informed."

"But, Kate," said Serena, raising her head from John's comforting shoulder. "How does one go about getting a message to someone in the army? We can't just wait until he gets leave again."

"I think I may be of some assistance there," said Sir John, relieved that he could do something for them. "And we should send for Lord Shallcross's solicitors without delay."

"Of course," said Kate, "you are perfectly right."

"What should we do without you?" Serena whispered.

"I wish I could do more," said Sir John. "I'll take my leave, now, if I may, so I can begin trying to reach Captain Verelst."

"Thank you, John," said Kate with a tight smile that was entirely closed off from any answering expression in her eyes. He was to grow too familiar with that smile in the ensuing weeks. He took her hand and pressed it warmly.

"Send for me if I can be of any assistance to you," said John, taking his leave.

It was a sad little cavalcade that set out the next day for Yorkshire and Lord Shallcross's country seat of Crossley, where Charles and Jeremy were to be buried in the family crypt. Arabella, Kate and Serena traveled in the largest carriage with servants and baggage behind them. The weather had turned cold, and their noses were as red as their eyes.

Kate still had not wept. Although her mind had grasped the significance of what had happened, her heart could not accept the fact that she would see

175

neither her father nor her brother again. She knew from Jeckle that their bodies were being sent directly to Crossley, and she braced herself for the ordeal of seeing them.

Jeckle had said the bodies were badly burned, but even so, she had not been prepared for their condition. Her father's was barely recognizable. Her brother's was not. She thought of her handsome brother, his laughter, his wildness, and his sheer deviltry. She scolded herself because she had been angry with him on that last night the family was together. As for her father, when was the last time she had told him she loved him? Probably not since she was a little girl. The Verelsts had not been a demonstrative family. Now they would never have a chance to be.

At last she could cry.

Somehow the three bewildered women got through the funeral and burials. Then, through Sir John Morgan's kind offices, Mark finally arrived.

His reception was not a cordial one. Arriving just at midday, he handed his hat to a footman and was ushered into the dowager Lady Shallcross's parlor by the butler. The widow fixed him with a cold stare.

"You!" she said in accents of loathing.

"Mother!" said Kate, embarrassed, rising to greet her cousin.

Mark took her hand. "I am so sorry, Kate."

"I know," said Kate.

"Sorry!" scoffed the widow. "And why should *you* be sorry, pray? Why couldn't *you* have been taken in their place?"

"Mother!" said Kate, in real distress. "You must not."

"Is Serena here?" asked Mark through narrowed eyes. He had expected to encounter some resentment from Arabella because he was to step into her husband's shoes, so the widow's hostility was hardly a surprise. His expression was unreadable.

"Of course," said Kate. "Forgive me. I'll send for her immediately."

"You don't have to apologize to *him* in your own home, Kate," said Arabella in an overbearing tone. Her eyes were still red with weeping.

Serena, wearing mourning like her aunt and cousin, threw herself into Mark's arms. "I'm so glad you're here," she whispered vehemently. "It has been so horrid!"

"Hush, Serena," he said, caressing her soft hair. "We'll talk later."

He turned to the butler.

"Please tell my uncle's solicitors that I am at their disposal," said Mark, startling the three women with the authority in his voice. Although the commanding tone was a familiar one to the soldiers under him, he had never used it in the presence of his female relatives.

"Very good, my lord," said the butler, his face impassive. Arabella broke into wrenching sobs, and Kate looked shaken at hearing her father's title given to her cousin. The look on Kate's face haunted Mark for a long time.

The solicitors appeared in the doorway, and the ladies excused themselves. Although their fates were being decided in that room, convention dictated that the dear departed's female survivors be spared the reading of the will.

When it was over, and the full significance of her late husband's perfidy dawned on her, Arabella was purple with rage.

Kate clearly remembered that day not so long ago when her father had told her he would protect her from her mother's attempts to force her into marriage against her wishes. She knew now what form that protection would take.

First of all, Arabella was not to have full authority over her husband's personal fortune in trust for her remaining children as she had expected. That honor and responsibility was to go to his heir, in this case, Mark Verelst.

Arabella, who was not perfectly acquainted with entails and other intricacies of English law, naively had assumed she would receive the income from her husband's estate after his death, as he had during his lifetime. But in reality that would go to the heir, who would have no financial responsibility for the dowager. Arabella could depend only on a jointure for her support, and not a particularly generous one at that, in the eyes of a woman who had had unlimited funds at her disposal for many years. It was just large enough for a lady of quality to live in comfort for the rest of her days, provided she lived modestly. Arabella hadn't lived modestly for twenty-three years. She didn't remember how.

Nor was Arabella to be her unmarried daughter's guardian. That responsibility also was to go to the heir. Kate had flushed with embarrassment upon hearing this. Naturally Lord Shallcross had expected Jeremy to survive him.

Because of what she interpreted as her husband's carelessness, Arabella would find it hard to marry Kate off creditably. She had always assumed her elder daughter would have a large dowry, but the terms of her husband's will put this notion to rest.

If she were to marry before the age of five-and-twenty, Kate's dowry would be very small, hardly enough to tempt a man of even modest pretensions to gentility. At the age of five-and-twenty, if still unmarried, Kate was to receive a lump sum to be held in trust by her guardian, a sum which represented a figure far greater than that of the widow's jointure.

If she did marry before the age of five-and-twenty, it would be left to the discretion of her guardian whether she and her husband would ever receive her legacy. If her guardian did not approve of Kate's choice of a husband, he could choose to allow the legacy to revert to the estate.

In the meantime, neither Kate nor Arabella would enjoy even the income from Kate's legacy, although, if Kate chose to live with her mother rather than with her guardian, Arabella would receive a modest sum quarterly to meet the expenses of housing her grown daughter.

To Arabella's resentment, her husband had left generous bequests to both Mark and Serena, apparently in the belief that his son would be the new Lord Shallcross. To his heir he also left the bulk of his personal fortune and property.

In lieu of a settlement, Melanie, whose husband had already received her dowry, was to receive some magnificent emeralds that had belonged to Charles Verelst's mother. Arabella had considered the emeralds her private property since her marriage, and she was determined to fight for possession of them until her dying day, even if she had to fight her own daughter. Melanie was, in fact, closeted with her husband in the west wing of the house at that very moment, prostrated, according to her maid, with grief. Arabella wondered how she could keep her daughter from learning that the emeralds were to be hers.

"My poor Kate!" exclaimed the widow, bending an accusing stare on Mark when all of this had been explained to her. "How are you ever going to be respectably married with things left so awkwardly?"

"Hush, Mother," whispered Kate.

"I will *not* hush," shouted Arabella. Serena backed a pace or two and finally settled on a straight-backed chair near the doorway. She perched on the seat as if ready to take flight.

"Aunt, if you have something to say to me, I would prefer it to be said in private," said Mark, indicating Kate and Serena. "The will is in order. Duly witnessed. There is no putting it aside. If you wish, I will instruct the solicitors to wait upon you to explain it more fully."

Arabella gave a slight, regal inclination of her head, indicating assent. Her nephew's face was implacable, but perhaps she could make some progress with the solicitors, who were most gratifyingly in awe of her.

After an hour of being closeted with these worthy gentlemen, however, Arabella realized she was at her nephew's mercy. Much as this galled her, she was determined to come about by any means necessary. When she joined the rest of her family in the drawing room later that evening, she was much calmer. She had changed her day gown for a most imposing one of black silk trimmed with jet beads and crape. The steely glint in her eye was the same that Mark had seen over many a card table at White's when he went there with his uncle. Cold.

Calculating. Ruthless.

"You will forgive me, I am sure, Mark, for my quite natural agitation upon your arrival," she said with chilly dignity.

"Of course, Aunt," said Mark guardedly. Kate and Serena watched Arabella as if she might explode at any moment. The tension in the room was almost unendurable.

"I think that we must discuss how we are to go on," Arabella continued, as if Mark hadn't spoken. "After careful thought I have arrived at the scheme I think will best serve. May I tell it to you?"

"By all means," said Mark, matching her tone. Serena and Kate unconsciously drew closer together on the sofa, as if for support. They had both lived with Arabella, whereas Mark had not, and they knew the signs that indicated she was up to something dreadful.

"First of all, since you have succeeded to my husband's title, I suppose you should have his room in this house," said Arabella, as if making a most generous concession. "I am sure Kate will see to this. Kate, your father's possessions are to be removed from his room and placed in storage in the attics until one of us has the leisure to go through them."

"Yes, Mother," said Kate, by now accustomed to Arabella's habit of addressing orders to her to be conveyed to Mrs. Bennett the housekeeper, who was suffering under sentence of Arabella's displeasure for the present.

Arabella waited for a denial from Mark that did not come. He was watching her with ominous quiet. She proceeded with a little less of her former assurance, but she still had enough resolution to present a plan to him that left him speechless with astonishment, for a moment, in tribute to her cold-blooded effrontery.

First of all, Arabella required him to place at her disposal a large sum of money for the maintenance of Crossley and Shallcross House because naturally she could not expect to be put to the expense of running both establishments on her slender jointure.

Since she was well aware of his dedication to his military duty (she said) she expected him to return to the army, where she no doubt hoped that he would oblige her by being killed and leaving the title to the next male in line, a doddering gentleman whom Arabella was certain she could manage quite satisfactorily.

Meanwhile, in her nephew's absence, she would use her extensive social connections to present Serena to the ton and, incidentally, to find a husband for Kate, his ward, she reminded him, as well. She would not bore him with the details, she said, but the season would be extremely expensive if the thing were to be done in proper style. She would expect him to disburse additional funds to her for this purpose.

"I see," said Mark in a voice of deadly quiet. "You have neatly arranged the affairs of my wards, ma'am. Serena and Kate are to be married at my expense, and you are, in the meantime, to be housed lavishly in recompense for your services. I am surprised that you have not made plans for my future as well. Or do you place so great a dependence upon my being killed?"

Kate and Serena both flinched at the tone in his voice, and Arabella was taken aback by the ease with which he apparently read her thoughts.

But Arabella, even now, did not realize she had gone too far. Because Mark had always been courteous to her in the teeth of her arrogant behavior toward both himself and Serena, she assumed she would always be able to bully him with impunity. To Arabella, courtesy when there is nothing to be gained by it would always be interpreted as weakness.

"Not at all," she lied graciously, obviously believing that he agreed with her plan. "Perhaps last year I would have done so, but now, with the French beaten, you are most likely to survive." There was just the tiniest tone of regret in her voice.

"You relieve my mind, ma'am," said Mark ironically. Kate and Serena clutched each other more tightly for support. "And how do you plan to dispose, then, of my future?"

"Well, I do believe the best scheme might be for you to marry your cousin," said Arabella, ignoring Kate's sharp intake of breath. "Of course, it would not be necessary if she were to receive an acceptable offer during the season, but, frankly, with things so badly left by her father, I am hardly optimistic. Even the most beautiful girl has difficulty marrying well without a dowry.

"It is all the fault of this cursed war," Arabella added, glaring at Mark as if he, personally, had been responsible for initiating the hostilities between Bonaparte and the rest of Europe. "So many young men have died in it that there are too few eligible men for so many young ladies. Without a dowry, what are her prospects?"

"So, Kate having been 'left over,' so to speak, I am to marry her," said Mark. Kate's cheeks flamed scarlet. She squeezed Serena's hand so tightly that her cousin's fingers were bruised for several days.

"Exactly," said Arabella, pleased with his grasp of the situation. "In fact, being her guardian, it is your duty to do so, provided, of course, no other acceptable gentleman comes forward. That may happen, you know. She is excessively pretty and quite good-natured besides. On the other hand, she *is* more than twenty."

She may well have been talking about a leg of mutton that had been left in the pantry too long. Kate was nearly insensible with embarrassment.

"Mother, pray, stop," Kate said, half rising. "You are not yourself."

Serena pulled Kate back to the sofa, almost as if she were a soldier trying to pull a comrade out of the range of enemy fire.

The combatants ignored them.

"I find your proposal vastly interesting, ma'am," said Mark in that strangely chilling voice of his. "But you are laboring under several misapprehensions."

Arabella's eyes narrowed.

"First of all, ma'am," he said, "it has obviously escaped your notice that I am in civilian dress, nor have I announced any plans for my departure to rejoin my regiment. I sold out upon learning that I am to succeed my uncle."

Arabella looked as if she wanted to interrupt, but he stopped her with a gesture.

"Secondly," he continued, "I am most gratified by your offer to vacate my uncle's room for me. However, one of my purposes in seeking this interview with you was to discover when it would be convenient for you to leave Crossley and remove

184

your personal property from Shallcross House."

"You cannot mean to evict me from my own home!" she exclaimed.

"That is a matter of interpretation, surely, ma'am? I was under the impression that it is my home now."

"My poor husband is hardly cold in his grave, and you cannot wait to throw me into the street," said Arabella awfully. "And my poor child as well, I suppose."

"No, ma'am," he said, glancing at Kate, whose face was bleak. Serena had begun sobbing softly from sheer reaction. "Kate will always be welcome in my home." He raised his voice at the look of triumph that was crossing Arabella's face. "But as my cousin, ma'am," he told her.

"Kate will not stay one night under your roof," said Arabella with bared teeth, "unless it is as your wife."

"When I take a wife," Mark said slowly, "it will be the wife of my own considered choice. I am very fond of Kate, but I'll be damned before I marry her or any other woman on your say-so, Aunt. Serena will be lonely, I know, without Kate. Since Serena is to make her come-out, I am sure Kate would make herself very useful—"

Here Arabella's wrath exploded. "Never! Never will my daughter occupy a menial position in her own home," she shouted. "I would rather see her dead!"

"Aunt Arabella!" exclaimed Serena.

"This conversation does not concern you, miss," said Arabella, lashing out at her niece. "Kindly keep your tongue between your teeth or leave the room."

185

"That will do, Aunt," said Mark. "I hope you do not think that Kate would ever be ill-used under my roof. Kate may stay or leave as she pleases, and"— he glanced at Kate—"I hope she will stay."

"Never," breathed Arabella.

"That is for you and Kate to decide between you," said Mark coldly. "I only wish you to understand that I expect you to leave without delay, Aunt, in, shall we say, two weeks?"

"You wouldn't dare!" she exclaimed. "And where do you expect me to go, if you please?"

"I neither know nor care, ma'am, although, if you wish it, the dower house is certainly at your disposal."

"The dower house! That hovel!"

"If it is a hovel, ma'am, I am sure it can be laid at no one's door but your own since until recently it was part of your late husband's property. May I wish you a cordial good night, Aunt? I am rather tired after my journey."

This was unmistakably dismissal. Arabella rose, gave a huff in her nephew's direction, and imperiously gestured for Kate to accompany her from the room. She did, with an apologetic look in Serena's direction. Mark involuntarily put out a hand to Kate that she either did not, or pretended she did not, see.

"Mark, you cannot let Kate leave, too," Serena said tearfully.

"Kate is a grown woman, Serena," he said, his voice harsh. "I cannot make her stay. In the eyes of the world, indeed, it would present a very odd appearance if Kate did not go with her mother."

"But, Mark—"

"No doubt you think I should have been generous and invited Aunt Arabella to live here as well," he said. "I am not of so magnanimous a nature, my dear. I must insist upon peace in my household, and I will never have it as long as Arabella is under this roof."

"I suppose you are right, Mark," said Serena, digesting the change in her fortunes slowly. Her dearest wish since she had come to live with her aunt and uncle had been to leave their battle-torn household for one of her brother's making, even though she knew the deficiencies of his pay as an officer would have constrained them to live frugally. She realized now that as the sister of the present viscount she suddenly was no humble dependent, but a young lady of consequence. She was both exhilarated and frightened by that knowledge.

"It will be all right, Serena," he told her, as if reading her thoughts.

"I cannot live here with no female to keep me company," she said. "And if Aunt Arabella will not sponsor me in society, I fear we must find some other respectable female to do so. Kate and I never did begin our investigation for a suitable person."

"We cannot go to London until we are out of mourning, my dear, so we have time to find someone. Our parents had a number of widowed relatives, as I recall. Surely one of them is enough up to snuff to present you."

"I wish it could be Kate," said Serena wistfully.

Mark agreed with her, but forbore to say so. The only way Kate could present Serena would be if she would marry Serena's brother. Mark still wanted to marry Kate, but he feared now he had totally bungled the affair by declaring to Arabella that he would not marry Kate at his aunt's command. Now if he offered for Kate, she would believe it was because he felt obligated to do so.

He cursed himself for a fool, although he didn't see how he could have helped himself. He wanted Kate's heart as well as her hand, and he knew he would never capture it if she believed he was marrying her out of duty. That would be even worse, in her eyes, than his marrying her because he was in love with her sister.

The only other way Kate would be able to present Serena would be if she married another eligible gentleman and was willing to take her young cousin under her wing.

Unbidden, a picture of the handsome Sir John Morgan with his lively eyes and gentle smile came into his mind. Mark found this vision so repellent that he ruffled his sister's pretty curls, kissed her on the cheek rather abruptly and took his leave of her.

Kate laid out her oldest, most faded gown before she went to sleep. It was not black, the color prescribed for persons in deep mourning, but that was of no consequence, for no one who mattered was going to see her in it.

It was a long time before she slept. Her mind kept going over the hideous scene in the drawing room. She was haunted by the cold look that had been on her cousin's face when he had outfaced the dowager. This man who had once asked her to be his wife when he was a soldier of modest means now denounced her before her mother and his sister, then made it clear that it was a matter of no interest to him whether she stayed or left his home with her mother.

Was it only a short time ago that Margaret Willoughby had outraged her by suggesting that Mark would marry to his advantage if he could? She had rejected the idea that Mark had offered for her because of her social position and dowry, but the proof seemed to be in what he had said tonight. Now that she was a poor relation as he once had been, he wanted no part of her.

Well, she wasn't about to hang on his sleeve. She had far too much pride for that. Nor was she going to let her mother linger under his roof a moment longer than was necessary.

Tomorrow she was going to ask her cousin for permission to take a few of the servants with her to the dower house, where she intended to wield a broom and a mop with her own hands to make it habitable if necessary. Within a week, she and her mother would be installed there.

And from now on, she promised herself, she was going to be as hard-hearted and cynical as Margaret Willoughby.

Chapter Nine

Although Arabella vowed the day she left Crossley that she and Kate would never speak to Mark and Serena again, the four of them had been obliged to meet each other with at least a show of civility on several occasions.

The landed gentry in their corner of Yorkshire was a sociable lot, and an open breech between the Verelsts would have scandalized most of their neighbors and afforded rather more than a few no mean amount of entertainment, a state of affairs that all parties concerned wanted to avoid.

Because of their mourning, however, these social occasions were few, although Kate did meet Serena quite by accident one morning at the family crypt, each carrying an armful of flowers, and they furtively hugged each other before returning to their respective camps.

"I love you, Kate," said Serena tearfully. "I can't *bear* this."

"Neither can I," said Kate, "but we must for the time being. We are going to London for the little season. Are you?"

"Of course. We leave in September. I am to be

accompanied by my aunt Amelia."

To Kate's surprise, these words were said with a marked lack of enthusiasm. Although Kate knew that a female relative had been installed at Crossley and that some of the neighbors did not take to her, the full evil of Serena's situation did not become known to her until she met Aunt Amelia at Almack's Assembly Rooms several days after she and her mother arrived in London.

Much of the ton was surprised to see Arabella and Kate wearing colors on this occasion. After all, Charles and Jeremy had not been dead a full six months before the 'little season' had begun. But Arabella had confided to everyone who delicately alluded to the situation that one could not be too particular in one's observances to the dead when one had the living to worry about. Then she would give a sad, sentimental smile in Kate's direction.

Arabella didn't know it, but she was fast wearing out her welcome in London's first circles. She had been tolerated as a bride by London's upper crust out of sympathy for her husband, whom no one had wanted to offend. Then Arabella began receiving invitations on her own account because she amused the grand dames who felt their positions secure enough to weather friendship with a former actress.

But Arabella no longer had a claim to society's hospitality. Her husband, whom the prominent had wished to oblige, was dead. She may have survived with her position intact if she had behaved with more dignity, or at least with a show of complaisance toward the new Lord Shallcross and his sister. Instead, Arabella was unwise enough to parade

191

her grievances all over London once she had escaped from the dower house, which she had the bad taste to describe to all who would listen as "that *garret.*" Arabella was no longer amusing; she was, on the contrary, extremely tiresome. She was destined to be dropped from guest lists and, inevitably, her daughter with her.

Kate's intolerable situation soon became food for gossip. It wasn't long before everyone in town knew about her inadequate dowry and the awkward way in which her legacy had been left to her. It would have been most unpleasant for Kate, indeed, if she had cared how society regarded her. Yet she demonstrated how little she cared, in fact, at Almack's on that fateful night.

Kate had appeared in a dress so magnificent that heads turned from every corner of the room when she walked through the doorway. She seemed totally unaware of the sensation she had caused as she accompanied her mother into the room.

Swathed in ruby-red silk, Kate found it hard to walk, let alone dance, on the uncomfortable jeweled slippers that completed a truly remarkable ensemble.

Several pink-dyed ostrich plumes reached for the ceiling from a jeweled band that matched the magnificent rubies dripping in tiers from her throat. The points of her peaked sleeves were parallel with her ears, from which dangled the Spanish silver filigree earrings that Mark had given her so many months ago.

This display of jewels not only positively compelled the interested to look at Kate's low-cut bodice, but also, sniped Arabella's enemies, it was in the worst possible taste for a young lady in Kate's straightened circumstances to wear a king's ransom—even if it did belong to her mother—around her neck like so much bait. She couldn't have more obviously announced she was on the catch for a husband if she had appeared in a wedding veil, in the eyes of her critics.

Further, Arabella's ill-wishers tittered, if the dowager hoped those silly feathers would add height to Kate's diminutive frame, she was sadly mistaken. Rather, more than one person thought Kate's hair ornament would be better suited to an equestrienne at Astley's Amphitheater.

Kate was accosted as soon as her mother left her side by Serena, who looked delightful in light blue muslin heavily embellished with scalloped ecru lace.

"Serena, you look adorable," said Kate, kissing her cousin's cheek with the first animation she had shown since she had entered the room and run the gamut of polite bows of welcome.

"Thank you, Kate," said Serena, tactfully avoiding any mention of Kate's appearance. "Oh, I'm so nervous. This is my first appearance at Almack's. I couldn't believe it when Mark told me Aunt Arabella procured vouchers for us. This must be your doing."

"I'm sure she was happy to do so," said Kate, who had used every tactic short of blackmail to induce her mother to request vouchers for their relatives from the patronesses.

"That's what I thought," said Serena, reading the message on Kate's twitching lips with ease. "Thank you."

"It was my pleasure. My dear, am I to meet this relative who is sponsoring you?" asked Kate with a show of interest.

Serena looked uncomfortable. "I suppose you must, sooner or later," said Serena cryptically, as she led Kate to a rather elderly lady dressed in a dowdy puce gown and an unattractive turban. Aunt Amelia had been delivering a tiresome monologue to another lady who seemed relieved to be able to escape from her.

"Aunt Amelia, may I present my cousin, Miss Kate Verelst?" asked Serena politely.

"How do you do, my dear," said Aunt Amelia. "I am delighted to make your acquaintance. I was just saying to our Serena, it is such a pity we haven't seen anything of your cousins. I have never met your mother, my dear, but I hear she is a most imposing lady. Oh, my dear, isn't it delightful to be at this lovely ball, with all these guests of the first consequence? I declare it does make one mindful of a Kind Providence. To think that I was living in a small house with my widowed sister Esmerelda—she's the one who married the younger son of the nephew of Lord Sherringham's wife's brother—and her five children, when I received a visit from Lord Shallcross that quite changed my life around."

She would have said more, but Mark approached at that moment and took Kate's hand in his.

"Kate, how nice to see you," he said.

"And you, my lord," she said, feeling suddenly conscious of the odd appearance she must present. His gaze dropped to her bosom, then returned an impassive countenance to her face. She could have sworn he was trying not to laugh.

"Blast you, Mark," she whispered, the corners of her mouth quirking upward.

"Will you dance with me, Kate?" he asked.

"Certainly, my lord," she said, placing her hand on his.

"And stop addressing me as 'my lord' every time you open your mouth," he chided her under his breath. "I sat you on your first pony, I'll thank you to remember."

"Certainly, my lord," she said demurely.

"Kate, are you happy? Is your mother treating you well?"

"Of course," she said. "And why, pray, should she do otherwise?"

He knew that he had made another mistake. Kate would not tolerate criticism of her mother in her fall from grace. One of her ostrich feathers tickled his nose and caused him to sneeze.

"Do you like my costume, my lord?" she asked, her voice full of mischief.

"It is a trifle unusual," he said noncommittally. "I suppose it is Aunt Arabella's notion that this eccentric fashion is becoming? If so, she has outdone herself."

"But, of course," said Kate, her eyes dancing. "It is a new experience for me. Although I have worn scores of ball gowns, this is the first time I have ever had the sensation that one of them is wearing me. You must admit there is little probability that I will be overlooked in this rig."

He had to laugh.

"But seriously, Kate, surely you are no longer

forced to do your mother's bidding in the matter of your dress."

"My mother has very little to occupy her mind now," said Kate in an indifferent tone, "and if it affords her gratification to dress me like a Christmas pudding and parade me through Almack's, she may do so with my good grace."

"Kate, I'm sorry—" he began, sensing beneath her gaiety that he had offended her.

"I suppose you think I should assume my most demure demeanor and try my best to oblige you by capturing the affection of a suitor, any suitor?"

"Why would I want you to do any such thing?"

"Certainly you have not forgotten the terms of my late father's will. If I marry, you can withhold my inheritance."

"And you think me capable of such treachery?" he asked, his voice hard.

"Now I've insulted you, and I honestly have no wish to do so," said Kate. "I only meant that I have no reason to be anxious to marry. If I remain single for five years, I will receive a handsome competence. If I do marry, my husband may—depending on your whim, my lord—receive a handsome competence when I become five-and-twenty, which is not, if you will forgive me for saying so, the same as *my* receiving a handsome competence. So, you see, if this ridiculous dress loses me the admiration of gentlemen, it is no great loss, after all. Besides, after living in my parents' home for all these years, I cannot believe marriage is any great thing."

"Your mother does not see it that way."

"No, she does not," said Kate. "She has dreams

of my contracting a brilliant marriage so that she can live with me and my husband. Although one collects she wasn't entirely happy in her own marriage, she insists that matrimony is the only future for a lady of quality. The thing is, nothing will persuade her that her scheme to marry me to a fortune is rather impractical."

He detected a tone of worry in her voice, although she was obviously trying to keep it light.

"What has she been doing, Kate? And don't tell me it isn't any of my business. You *are* my ward."

"And you are going to tear me from my mother's arms by force, if necessary?" asked Kate with a faint smile. "What a figure you should cut!"

"I would if I had to," he said. "Now tell me what she has been doing."

"Only spending rather too much money for my peace of mind," said Kate.

Mark frowned. In accordance with the terms of her father's will, he had been sending the dowager a sum for Kate's support every quarter. Apparently the combination of Kate's allowance and the widow's jointure was not enough to keep them solvent.

"We have *very* expensive lodgings," Kate continued, "because Mother says a good address is crucial for a lady who wants to make the right impression on society. You and Serena must visit us. You will be most impressed. My dress cost her a small fortune, and to very little purpose. But she would hear none of my objections."

"You have taken lodgings?" he said, his brows knit. He had a humorous vision of four rooms packed to the ceilings with fluted columns and hideous little tables on crocodile legs. When he and Serena had opened Shallcross House, they found it practically denuded of its magnificent furnishings, much to the relief of Mark, who lost no time in taking the old furniture out of the attics and setting it once more in its rightful place. "I naturally assumed you would stay with your sister while you were in town."

"And so we would have," said Kate, "if mother had not fallen out with Melanie over the emeralds."

"What emeralds?"

"The emeralds my father left to Melanie. Surely you remember. The ones that had belonged to his mother?"

"Oh, yes. Well, what about them?"

"Mother won't give them up, and Melanie is furious. The whole thing is ridiculous because both of them possess far more jewelry than they could ever wear. But they have quarreled over it, so naturally we cannot drive up to Melanie's door and start unloading our bandboxes. Pretty cool behavior, I should say."

"But surely Melanie would not object to having *you* to stay."

Kate hesitated. After all, there were limits to what one could discuss with impunity about a woman to her former suitor.

"What else?" said Mark, sensing her hesitation.

"No great thing, after all," said Kate. "But Melanie has no wish to sponsor an elder sister into society, and one cannot really blame her."

Mark digested this in silence. He had heard some talk about the dashing young Lady Windom in the short while he had been in London. She had already set up a court of cicisbeos and had one rather public argument with her husband over the amounts she was losing at silver loo. She also had cultivated the friendship of a number of fast young matrons and had scandalized her staid husband by participating in a curricle race with another lady. Lord Windom had retaliated by withholding from her use the little phaeton he had had made for her.

At one party Mark had been astonished to see Melanie disporting herself in a low-cut, one-shouldered diaphanous white gown in the classical style, without so much as a stitch between it and her naked body—or so it seemed to Mark's scandalized eyes—and wearing on her feet a pair of red sandals tied up the leg with red ribbons so they showed through the virtually transparent garment. She may as well have appeared nude, and as if that weren't bad enough, she spent most of the evening at the center of a court composed of the most notorious rakes in town.

It was plain to Lord Shallcross that Melanie was using her falling out with her mother as an excuse to avoid doing her duty by Kate. Melanie apparently had no wish to have an unmarried sister thrust upon her now that she had thrown off the shackles of maidenhood to indulge in more sophisticated entertainments than had been allowed to her under her parents' roof. That enterprising matron would definitely consider demure excursions to the lending library, concerts and rigorously chaperoned balls exceedingly poor sport now that she had been initiated into the mysteries of high stakes racing and faro.

199

"That is enough about me," said Kate, mistaking the grim look on his face for boredom. "Tell me how you are getting on. Do you miss your regiment?"

"To be honest," he said, "I haven't had much time to think about it. I have been very busy, especially now that Serena is to make her debut. I see you have met Aunt Amelia. She has not been of much use, I'm afraid."

"Yes," said Kate. "I suppose I need not ask if she was your only choice."

"No, you do not," he said. "But we get on very well, I promise you. This will amuse you. It seems that I am now a highly eligible bachelor. I have received no less than fifteen visits from matchmaking mamas in three days. Ladies who had nothing to say to me when I was a mere captain cannot show me enough consideration now that I am a viscount. My head would be quite turned if I were susceptible to flattery."

"Now tell me you are not enjoying your new popularity," said Kate.

"But, of course I am," he said, "for Serena's sake, if for no other reason. The house is quite lively now with visitors her own age. Unfortunately, their main purpose for visiting is to captivate me, but I have no objection since it has yielded Serena many invitations to parties."

"On the condition that she bring her excessively desirable brother."

"I know I must sound like an utter coxcomb!"

"Never that," said Kate, laughing.

"I am relieved to hear you say so."

"I suppose," said Kate, sobering suddenly, "that

you expect to marry."

"That depends on a great many things," he said cryptically. "Ah, there is Margaret Willoughby waving at you." The dance was just ending. "I'll take you to her, shall I?"

"Yes, please," said Kate. "I would like it of all things. She came to the funeral, you know."

"I know. She has come to take Serena shopping with her several times, and has dined with us in Grosvenor Square twice," he said. "She was very upset about Jeremy's death."

"I would have welcomed her as a sister-in-law," said Kate. "She would have been exactly the kind of wife who could have stabilized Jeremy's wildness."

By this time, Mark was escorting her to Margaret, who greeted him cordially, then kissed Kate on the cheek.

"I am so happy to see you," said Margaret when Mark had left their side to dance with a young lady whom Lady Sefton was presenting to him. "My dear, what a gown!"

"Isn't it just?" asked Kate, her eyes crinkling in amusement. "Mother is absolutely *desperate* to find me a husband, and she appears to think the solution is to dress me like a ship in full sail."

"You look delightful for all that," said Margaret. "It is a lovely color on you."

Kate thought she heard a hint of censure in Margaret's voice and decided to face the issue head on. That was the only way, she had learned, to deal with Margaret.

"It is too soon, I know," said Kate.

Margaret colored faintly. "That is not what I

meant," she said, in some confusion.

"Yes, it was," Kate returned, "and I agree whole-heartedly. But my mother bought it for me and insisted that I wear it. And you must admit Jeremy would have enjoyed roasting me over it."

"You do it, too," said Margaret, as if making a discovery.

"What is that?"

"Catch yourself wondering what Jeremy would have thought about what has happened, or thinking that you know exactly what he would have said if he'd been with you at that moment."

"Yes. Every day," said Kate. "I wonder the same thing about my father. People say in time I will become accustomed. I hope they are right."

"They are, dear," said Margaret, her eyes bright with unshed tears as she patted Kate's shoulder.

Jeremy's death not only robbed Margaret of the only suitor she had the slightest inclination to marry, but also taught her that her vast wealth could not, for once, buy her what she wanted. For the first time in her life she realized that the security wealth bestowed upon one was only an illusion, and that despite her youth, she was as vulnerable as other mortals to death and tragedy.

Sir John Morgan came up to them at that moment.

"Good evening, ladies," he said. "I wonder if one of you would take pity on a lonely gentleman for the quadrille?"

Margaret said she had been on her way to pay her respects to the dowager Lady Shallcross, so Kate and John were paired for the next dance.

"I am glad to see you," said John as he took

Kate's hand. "I have been worried about you, and about your mother, of course."

"It is so kind of you, sir," said Kate. "As you can see, we are getting on."

In another part of the room, Mark was watching John dance with Kate out of jealous eyes. At that moment he saw Margaret Willoughby leave Arabella's side and asked her for the next country dance.

Kate spotted them as a movement of the dance separated her from John.

"Have you seen much of Lord Shallcross and Serena, Sir John?" she asked when she turned back to him.

"Yes," he said. "In fact, Miss Willoughby had the three of us to dine last Tuesday. She has been very attentive to Miss Verelst, which is fortunate because, if you'll forgive my saying so, her companion doesn't seem to be much company for her. I am sure the young lady is very happy to see you in town."

"I am happy to see her," said Kate. "I have missed her so much, especially now that my sister is married."

"Of course," said John, who had also heard tales of the wild Lady Windom. The dance ended and he escorted Kate to her mother. Later in the evening, Kate happened to see John and Serena dancing as she was procuring tea for her mother and for Aunt Amelia, who had installed herself next to Arabella and was proceeding to bore her very much with an account of her last holiday with her sister Esmerelda at an unfashionable seaside resort.

It occurred to her that Sir John Morgan was a

very considerate gentleman to put himself out to be kind to a nervous debutante, and she was grateful that the women in her family had possessed such a loyal friend during their bereavement.

"Miss Verelst."

Kate turned at the sound of the imperious voice and faced Lady Sefton.

"I just wanted to offer my condolences on your family's terrible loss," said that lady graciously.

"Thank you, my lady," said Kate. "It is very kind of you."

"It is nothing," she said, preparing to move on with a smile and a gracious inclination of the head. "We have seen you here too seldom, child. It is time to forget your sorrow and get on with your life."

"Yes, my lady," said Kate, surprised. Lady Sefton then greeted another couple and Kate understood. This patroness of Almack's had talked loudly enough for several persons to hear her, and her point was made. Kate herself was not to be censured for her gaffe in wearing colors so soon after her bereavement.

As the evening wore on, several more of the patronesses went out of their way to greet Kate, although none seemed inclined to single out her mother for similar attention. It became increasingly clear that although Arabella was out of favor, her daughter was not.

She also noticed that the patronesses frequently presented partners to Mark during the evening, and thought she knew who she could thank for the consideration shown her. It seemed everyone was anxious to earn the new Lord Shallcross's favor.

As she watched him dance for the second time with Margaret Willoughby, it occurred to her that now he had his choice among the most eligible young ladies of the kingdom, and the chance that he would want to marry a mere impecunious cousin seemed even more remote.

It didn't occur to Kate that she was solicited for quite as many dances as Mark was bestowing on eligible maidens, and that he had been watching her out of the corner of his eye, just as she was watching him out of the corner of hers.

Mark, meanwhile, observed with annoyance that Sir John was again asking Kate for a dance, and that she was accepting with every show of pleasure. Mark had, by this time, felt obligated to do his duty by his Aunt Arabella and Aunt Amelia, and stood listening to his Aunt Amelia's monologue with half an ear as he tortured himself by watching Kate laugh at something clever Sir John told her.

When the dancers had finished, Sir John surprised Mark by walking up to him, greeting the ladies, and asking him if he could speak to him about a trifling matter.

Mark excused himself to the ladies and went apart with John, assuming he was about to be invited to dine or something of that nature.

"I wonder, Shallcross, if you are going to be at home tomorrow at two o'clock."

"I should be," said Mark guardedly.

"Then I should like to discuss something with you then, if I may," said Morgan. "It concerns Miss Verelst. You are that lady's guardian, I assume, since you are her only surviving male rela-

Chapter Ten

At two o'clock the next day, Mark and John were in the library at Shallcross House making stilted conversation. Neither was in the best of humor because of his sleepless night.

"And to what do I owe the honor of this visit, Sir John?" asked Mark, wanting to get it over with. He knew that giving this man permission to marry Kate was going to be like tearing the heart from his own body.

"I came to ask for permission to pay my addresses to your ward," said John formally. He was surprised by Mark's coldness, but then, he reflected, perhaps it wasn't easy for a man to give his little sister to another man.

"I see," said Mark, who really thought he did. "I think I should tell you before you proceed any further that the lady's dowry is not as large as you may suppose."

"That is of little interest to me, my lord," said John. "The lady herself is my object. In fact, I would be willing to negotiate settlements with you if you should require it."

"That will hardly be necessary, sir," said Mark

stiffly.

"Does this mean you favor my suit?" asked John, who was also anxious to get the business over with. "You may think, perhaps, the lady could look higher—"

"No," said Mark. "That is not my concern. I am sensible of the fact that it would be a good match for her."

"—or that I might not be kind to her? Let me assure you that I would—"

"I am sure you would," said Mark hastily, not wishing to hear John go into raptures about his devotion to the woman Mark wanted to marry.

Mark swallowed his qualms and made a feeble effort to discourage Morgan from marrying Kate.

"I suppose you realize that you will be expected to house my aunt as well if you marry my ward," Mark said blandly.

He thought his ploy had succeeded when he saw John give a grimace of distaste. If anything could cool a suitor's passion for the delectable Kate, Mark thought hopefully, it would be the prospect of saddling himself with a mother-in-law like Arabella for the rest of her natural life which, judging from the lady's stamina, could be forever. But John manfully pulled himself together.

"I will do so, certainly, if my future wife wishes it," said John, wondering if he could endure meeting the garrulous Aunt Amelia every morning over the breakfast cups. "But I had not thought her so attached to your aunt."

"You were mistaken," said Mark coldly, reflecting that for all of his ardor, this gentleman certainly did not know his Kate. No matter how tiresome Arabella could be, her elder daughter

208

would never abandon her to her fate.

John broke his train of thought.

"If you are thinking she is too young—"

"Too young?" Mark's brows snapped together, and he looked at his guest in astonishment. Kate was almost one-and-twenty. If not precisely on the shelf, she was perilously near it.

"Well, sixteen might be considered rather young," said John, somewhat alarmed by the startled look on Mark's face.

Mark stared at him. He had been a fool. Morgan wanted to marry his sister, not his cousin. Trying to adjust his thoughts to this new idea, Mark reflected that Morgan was, in fact, exactly the sort of man Serena ought to marry. Only she *was* rather young.

"Yes," said Mark, pulling himself together. "That is exactly my own opinion. Still, if she wishes to marry you, I can have no real objection. You have my permission to pay your addresses to my sister, but if she does not like the match, I will not consent to it. After all, the child might be forgiven for wanting to enjoy herself for a season or two before she marries."

John let out a long sigh of relief. "Let us agree then," he said, willing to be generous, "that if your sister wishes it, the engagement can be of long duration. Say, perhaps, six months or a year?"

"I think that an excellent plan," said Mark.

"Thank you, my lord. May I see Serena now?"

"It is customary, I know," he said, "but she left with her cousin for a shopping expedition this morning and has not yet returned. Will you take tea with me, Sir John? I can ask my aunt to pour."

Rather maliciously, he watched John try to control his reluctance to run the gamut of Aunt Amelia's tongue and asked the servant who answered his summons to desire the lady to wait upon them. Mark gave in to an ignoble impulse and didn't exert himself to tell Morgan that he would not be expected to house Aunt Amelia, after all.

Aunt Amelia had poured and returned to her tatting by the time Serena and Kate arrived laden with packages which they surrendered to a footman. The butler ushered them into Mark's library.

Mark greeted them and announced that he had something to show to Kate. Serena, surprised, asked if they were keeping secrets from her. Mark closed the door behind himself and Kate, leaving Serena and John alone.

"What is it, Cousin?" Kate asked warily. Mark had his hand on her elbow and was propelling her through the hall.

"Merely an excuse," he said, ushering her into a small salon. He assumed that Kate had been expecting Sir John to offer for her and was prepared to tell her about the engagement—distasteful though it was to him to be the instrument of her pain—so she wouldn't betray her feelings in front of Serena.

"An excuse?" she asked, puzzled. "Do you realize you just left your sixteen-year-old sister *alone* with a gentleman not related to her—Oh!" Her eyes were wide. "He asked permission to marry her?"

"Yes, Kate," he said, watching her face for signs of impending collapse.

"Well, I am sure I am very happy for them," she said, adjusting her thoughts to this new development. "Of course. I was a fool not to see it. They will suit very well, I think."

It was the truth. She was most apprehensive, however, about the way Arabella would receive the news. Sir John had been most attentive to Kate, visiting her and her mother after the funeral when the rest of the ton had abandoned them in order to enjoy the rest of the season.

Since their arrival in London, Sir John had taken Kate and Serena for drives in the park. He had accompanied her, her mother and Serena to the opera on the very night of their arrival. Although Kate considered the gentleman's interest toward herself to be tepid at best, she knew her mother thought otherwise and had probably made no secret of her expectations to others. Kate was not looking forward to enduring pitying looks from her mother's confidantes when news of the engagement became public. Some of this reluctance showed in her face, and Mark, believing her heart was breaking, despised himself for the surge of elation he had felt when he realized that Sir John had not wanted to marry Kate, after all.

"Please tell Serena I wish her very happy," she said, offering Mark her hand in farewell. He took it automatically. "Now I must go home or my mother will worry."

Then she was gone, her lavender scent lingering behind her.

When the tempest broke, it broke with unmanageable fury. Arabella was absolutely seething with rage when she discovered that Serena, whom she styled That Little Hussy, had stolen Sir John Morgan out from under Kate's very nose.

"It was no such thing, Mother," Kate argued.

"We have nurtured a viper in our bosoms," Arabella declared.

"Mother, how can you possibly call Serena a viper!" exclaimed Kate, appalled. "They will suit very well, and I beg you to accept this very desirable match with at least the show of approval."

It was, unfortunately, expecting rather too much of her mother to expect her to do so.

Arabella told anyone who would listen that Kate had been betrayed by her young cousin, which had the effect of making both Arabella and Kate look ridiculous. There were fewer and fewer invitations being sent to their lodgings these days, and the patronesses had finally turned Arabella away with polite excuses when she desired them to give her vouchers for Almack's.

As if Kate didn't have enough to worry about, she began to see that she and her mother were in serious straits with their creditors. The only solution for Kate was to take rather extreme measures with the household finances, discharging some of her mother's servants, introducing some unpopular economies to the kitchens, and refusing to allow her mother to buy her any more elaborate gowns.

"That will do, Mother," said Kate, adamant in her refusal to allow her mother to buy her a sable-trimmed, sapphire-blue satin creation. "You cannot afford it, and you know very well that I will not receive my inheritance until I am five-and-twenty."

"But if you are to marry, Kate—" Arabella reasoned.

"I will not marry," said Kate. "We have so few invitations these days that I rather doubt I would have an occasion to wear the gown. Anyway, I don't think a mere dress would be enough to convince any gentleman to take me to wife if my dowry is lacking."

The little season was proving a vast disappointment to Arabella. London was becoming thin of company because the fashionable world was already migrating to Vienna to take part in the social swirl that would surround the Congress of Vienna in October. This meant there were even fewer aristocratic gentlemen left in London to admire Kate's charms. Kate firmly vetoed her mother's intention of transporting them both to the continent in pursuit of fresh matrimonial prey.

"That's enough, Mother," said Kate firmly. "We cannot afford it."

To her mother's chagrin, Kate began making her own gowns with the assistance of a rather artistic chambermaid who had managed to keep her position when Kate was ruthlessly slashing the rolls of servants in her mother's household by pointing out that she could sew to perfection.

The result was that Kate began appearing in public in a succession of extremely becoming, though simple, ensembles which had the effect of confirming for the ton that Arabella and Kate were, indeed, living far beyond their slender means and that the man who married Kate would soon be impoverished by his bride's spendthrift ways.

There was so much gossip about the mother and daughter, in fact, that invitations stopped coming into their home altogether.

For that Kate was partially responsible. Many hostesses who thought Kate a nice enough young lady would have been happy to include Kate in excursions with their sons and daughters as long as they would not be expected to entertain the dowager as well. But Kate politely made it known that she would decline all invitations that did not include her mother, pointing out that it would be most disrespectful to her parent for her to do otherwise.

Furthermore, when one or two prominent matrons condescended to sympathize with Kate upon having to endure Lady Arabella's company, Kate told them in no uncertain terms that she considered their pity an impertinence.

Before long, even the dowager's particular cronies began giving her the cut direct in public. That was when Arabella became truly desperate and began inhabiting the demimonde. She was no stranger to this half-world of society that the ton's inferiors inhabited. She had been quite at home in these circles before her marriage.

To Kate, however, this was a most bewildering world in which the vulgar rubbed shoulders with the genteel, and the company was likely to get too rough for a delicately nurtured female. Those on the fringes of polite society embraced Arabella and Kate with open arms, happy to number among their acquaintances a viscount's widow and her daughter.

It was on an excursion to a public masquerade ball frequented by her mother's new friends that they met Mr. Jason Peevers. Mr. Peevers was a London merchant who had made a fortune in trade and wanted to provide an entree into the polite world for his son, William. Mr. Peevers, a well-made, well-spoken man in his mid-fifties, was a downy one when it came to commerce, but he failed abysmally to see that the dowager no longer was on calling terms with the lofty persons he most wished to cultivate.

Mr. Peevers was most impressed by the dowager's elegant gowns, her grand airs and her commanding ways. She was exactly what he expected a fine lady to be. So when she delicately let it drop that she was seeking a husband for her unmarried daughter, he pricked up his ears.

The result of this meeting of the minds was that a tacit understanding grew between Arabella and the merchant that William and Kate would marry. After the father and son had dined quite informally with Kate and Arabella, word reached Mark's ears that Kate was about to contract a shocking misalliance.

Although it was sometimes acceptable for a man to replenish his family's coffers by marrying an heiress of lesser birth or allowing his son to do so, it was simply not done for a gentleman to allow a near female relation to disparage herself by marrying beneath her for the sake of a fortune. A gentleman of quality would be as likely to allow his sister or daughter to hire herself out as a governess or wait tables in a public inn.

When Serena invited her cousin to tea one day, Mark surprised the ladies by joining them and asking Kate if he could see her alone on a private matter when they had finished.

"Yes, my lord?" Kate inquired, seeing from his solemn face that this was to be an unpleasant interview.

"I have been hearing talk about your mother that I cannot like, Kate."

"The gossips have been busy as usual," said Kate flippantly.

"Kate, look at me."

215

She did so, meeting his eyes squarely. What she saw there caused her to unconsciously grasp his fingers when he took her hand.

"Mark, what is it?" she asked, alarmed by the grave look on his face.

"I know it is too soon to ask you this, Kate. I only ask you to consider it. Will you do me the honor of marrying me?"

"Whatever for?" asked Kate, her heart giving a strange little lurch.

"Because I fear your natural disappointment over Sir John Morgan's betrothal to my sister may cause you to do something foolish."

"You are much too busy on my behalf, my lord," said Kate with asperity. She was affronted that he could think her so paltry a creature as to be undone by Serena's good fortune.

"Let me remind you that I am your guardian," he said, tightening his grasp on her hand when she would have withdrawn it.

"So you must marry me to save my face because I have been jilted? Let me assure you there was no understanding of any kind between Sir John and myself, sir. Nor have I any intention of marrying anyone."

"I would not expect—that is, I would not force my attentions on you, Kate, because I know it would be too soon."

"Too soon," Kate repeated, surprised.

"I honor you for accepting the match between Sir John and Serena with good grace; but I fear your mother has made it plain that it was a sad disappointment to you, and she isn't particular about whom she tells."

Kate averted her eyes from his face in embarrassment. This encouraged Mark to continue.

"Believe me, I understand how you feel. I am not without experience in losing someone I love," he said. He was referring to his parents, her father and Jeremy; but Kate thought he meant Melanie, and this was fatal to his cause. As a matter of fact, he had forgotten all about Melanie.

"If you married me," he continued, "the talk would die down after a time. Frankly, I do not trust my aunt, and I fear for your reputation. My sister will soon be leaving my home to marry Sir John, so I cannot provide for you under my roof unless I marry you. The gossip is, and I hope it is mistaken, that my aunt is cultivating a class of persons—"

"That is quite enough, my lord," said Kate, drawing away from him. "I do not intend to stand here in my former home and listen to you abuse my mother. Good day, sir."

"Kate—"

But she was gone.

Kate had considered it imperative to leave because she was so tempted to accept him. She still loved him, and she was just as horrified by her mother's excursions into the demimonde as he was. Furthermore, she was touched that he would offer her marriage to assuage her supposed disappointment. She could acquit him at last of Margaret Willoughby's accusation that Mark was hanging out for a rich wife, and she was glad she had not been deceived in his character.

But she knew she only would be letting herself in for heartbreak if she married a man who was still in love with another. She resolved to remain unmarried, and hoped that her mother would not

217

run through her jointure before Kate could receive her inheritance and support her mother and herself.

A few days later, much to her surprise, she saw Mark at a masked ball. Even though it was the last place she had expected to see him, the company being rather fast, she knew without a doubt the tall masked man by the door was he. She also recognized the smaller figure of his sister wrapped in a domino and assumed he had given in to her pleadings to escort her there.

Kate herself had not wanted to attend, but her mother, who had been invited by Mr. Peevers, was adamant. William Peevers, naturally, was also one of the party and had been drinking rather too heavily for Kate's peace of mind.

In the general way, this young man, who was about Kate's own age, was tongue-tied and nervous in her presence. Tonight, however, he was filled with false courage and had made some rather broad overtures to Kate. To her surprise, her mother accepted this in good part, and Mr. Peevers himself looked on complacently.

"It is nice to see young people enjoy themselves" was Mr. Peevers' verdict on the rather wild activity going on around him. At one point Kate thought she could tolerate no more of this ball that was fast deteriorating into a brawl and attempted to get out of the box. She rather thought she saw her sister Melanie nearby and intended to get some relief from William's heavy-handed ardor by speaking with her.

Unfortunately, William saw her intention and followed her. About that time, Kate realized the blonde in the red domino was not her sister and prepared to retreat to the merchant's box. Instead, she felt hot breath on her neck and moist hands close on her upper arms from behind her.

"Now, where are you off to, my pretty?" asked William, his breath strong with spirits.

"I was returning to my mother, sir," she said, with what dignity she could muster.

"I have a better idea," he said, dragging her toward the gardens. She struggled, but he was stronger than she was. He was attempting to pull her mask off and kiss her when a heavy hand closed on his arm and a fist crashed into his jaw, sending him to sleep in an undignified jumble of black domino on the ground.

Mark put his hands on Kate's shoulders and forced her to look up at him.

"Did he hurt you, Kate?" he asked anxiously.

"No. Mark, if you hadn't come—"

"Who was the fellow? Did you know him?"

"Only too well. This, if you please, is the gentleman my mother wishes me to marry," said Kate, a trifle bitterly.

"Good God. The man looks like a veritable Cit!" exclaimed Mark, appalled.

"He is. His father is with my mother, and she favors his suit. His father is very rich, you see."

Mark's face got such a deadly look on it that Kate cowered.

"Come with me, Kate," he said, pulling her along with him.

"What are you going to do?" she asked in alarm.

"I am going to take you back to your mother. And I am going to put an end to the intolerable pretensions of that Cit."

"Mark, please—"

At that point she was quite out of breath because he was towing her by the hand and had not slowed his long strides out of consideration for her smaller limbs. On the way, he collected Serena, whom he had left in the care of Sir John Morgan and some of his friends.

The three of them converged on the merchant's box, and Kate braced herself for an ugly scene.

"Good evening, Aunt," said Mark.

"Good evening, Mark," said Arabella regally. "My nephew, Lord Shallcross, and his sister, Miss Serena Verelst," she added for Mr. Peevers' benefit. "My lord, this is Mr. Jason Peevers."

"How do you do, sir?" replied Mark coldly. "Aunt Arabella, I would like to call on you tomorrow, if I may. I have just brought Kate to you because she has been accosted by a drunken lout and she is somewhat shaken, so I suggest you take her home immediately."

Serena hadn't said a word, but her widened eyes traveled to Kate. Kate made her a small sign to say nothing and cast her eyes down.

"I hope you know, your lordship, that I wouldn't have had this happen for the world," said Mr. Peevers, truly distressed that his guest had been annoyed while in his care. "We will leave immediately. Miss Verelst, have you seen William anywhere?" he asked innocently.

About that time, William came walking dispiritedly toward the box. He came face to face with Mark. Mark scowled at him. William sat meekly in his place.

"William, we must go at once," said his father. "Miss Verelst has received a shock."

William looked from Kate to Mark and cowered a little. But when he saw that he apparently was going to escape more punishment from this very angry and very powerful gentleman, he meekly rose and offered Kate his arm.

Kate recoiled. Then she realized that it was safe in his father's presence to accept William's escort, and did so.

"I will see you tomorrow, Aunt Arabella," Mark said grimly.

The next day a very polite and very cold young man waited on the dowager Lady Shallcross.

"Good of you to see me, Aunt Arabella," he said.

"I seem to have had no choice in the matter," she said haughtily.

"I'll get right to the point, for I am sure you have other matters to attend to today."

"You are quite right, Mark. I will thank you to state your business and be gone," Arabella snapped.

"Mother!" exclaimed Kate, flushing to the roots of her hair.

"Be silent, miss," said Arabella. "And what is it you wish to say, Nephew?"

"Only that I was appalled to see Kate mixing in the company I saw her with last night. I would not have thought you would countenance your daughter's attending a public ball in such a place."

"And why should she not?" asked Arabella. "Did I not see your sister at the same ball?"

"With her brother and her affianced husband, ma'am. Not with a group of persons from a certain class—"

"I collect you mean Mr. Peevers and his son."

"Precisely, ma'am."

"I'll have you know, Nephew, that Kate is going to marry William Peevers. And if you don't like it, you have only yourself to blame for not marrying Kate yourself."

A sharp intake of breath from Kate's direction steadied Mark, who was about to burst into unwise speech from sheer frustration.

"You forget, ma'am, that I am Kate's guardian. I can, and I will, prevent her marriage to such a person."

"You will be sorry if you do, Nephew, since it is the only eligible offer she is likely to receive, thanks to you."

"Please—" began Kate, who was horribly embarrassed by this bitter exchange.

Arabella pulled the bell rope. When a servant appeared, she pointed to Mark.

"This gentleman," she said haughtily, "was just leaving."

"I have said what I came to say, ma'am," said Mark with a cold bow. "Good afternoon."

A few days later, Arabella fired what she thought was her final volley in this war with her top-lofty nephew. They had just finished their tea when Arabella turned to Kate, her face hardened with resolution.

"You may as well know, Kate, that I have given William Peevers permission to pay his addresses to you," Arabella said. "I may not be your guardian, but I am your mother, and you will obey me in this matter. You *will* marry William Peevers."

Kate rose to her full height. "I most certainly will not," she said. "We would not suit. I intend to remain unmarried until I am five-and-twenty and collect my inheritance."

"And who do you think is going to support you until then, you ungrateful child?" railed Arabella, conveniently forgetting the sum Mark sent her each quarter for Kate's support. "If you won't marry William Peevers, I'll wash my hands of you. You can beg your bread from your cousin, for all I care."

Kate bit her lip.

"Now I suggest you thank Providence for this grand opportunity to recoup our fortunes, Daughter."

"I won't marry him," said Kate quietly. "And you can't force me to."

"No. But I can refuse to house you any longer and, I promise you, I will," said Arabella.

Of course, Arabella meant no such thing. She was angry with Kate for crossing her, but she was, at bottom, fond of her daughter. Kate knew these threats were empty ones, designed only to cow her into submission. She decided, however, that she had done with being a hostage to her mother's ambition.

When her mother went to her room to recruit her strength for an evening party, Kate quietly wrote a note to Mark and sent it around to Shallcross House, instructing Hodge to wait for a reply. She knew he would help her if she asked, and she had no qualms about accepting his assistance. If he renewed his offer to marry her, however, she resolved to be strong. He thought now that it did not matter whom he married because he could not have Melanie, Kate assumed, but she was just masochistic enough to believe that someday he would meet a lady whom he could love and then would regret having married Kate.

Before she could let self-pity overcome her on this last, most unwelcome reflection, she sat down to compose a more difficult letter, this one to her mother:

Dear Mother, I think each of us will be better for some time spent away from the other. Therefore I am leaving without delay for the dower house at Crossley. Once there, I intend to answer some advertisements for employment as a governess or housekeeper. Perhaps you will wish to tell those who inquire about me that I have gone into the country to recover from a trifling illness. Please respect my wish for privacy. I promise I will write often to keep you apprised of my situation. Please believe that I will never marry William Peevers. I will be in the care of my cousin, so I beg you not to worry about me. Your affectionate daughter, Kate.

She propped the letter on the table where she was sure her mother would see it. When Hodge returned with the news that Lord Shallcross was gone into the country for a few weeks, Kate was so dismayed that she didn't realize she had knocked the note off the table and onto the floor. Nor was she to know that the maid would accidentally kick the white paper under one of her mother's oriental rugs pilfered from Shallcross House and that the note would not be found for some months because the maid was very careless in her cleaning.

A moment's reflection convinced Kate that

Mark's absence was not as unfortunate a development as she had at first supposed. He was already at Crossley. She had only to follow him there and explain the situation to him. She was confident he would have no objection to sheltering her at the dower house while she sought a situation. She was not pleased with the prospect of becoming a governess or housekeeper, but she knew she would only have to tolerate a position as a menial until she was five-and-twenty, when she would receive her legacy. Mark, she knew, would help her because he would naturally approve her resolution to do everything in her power to avoid a misalliance with William Peevers.

She stole to her room, packed a bag and sought out the only other gentleman she could be reasonably sure would be willing to help her procure passage to Crossley. After all, Sir John Morgan would soon be related to her, in a fashion, by marriage, and he had always been very courteous to her. She also paid the gentleman the compliment of believing he was discreet enough to honor her desire for secrecy in this most delicate matter.

Sir John was surprised when his butler announced that a young lady had called upon him. A smile came to his lips as he anticipated seeing his young fiancée. He was charmed that she had been so impatient to see him that she would surprise him with an impromptu visit, but he intended to impress upon her that she was not to wait upon bachelor gentlemen at their lodgings, even if the gentleman in question was himself.

He was astonished, then, to see Kate awaiting him without so much as a maid in attendance to lend her consequence.

"Miss Verelst," he said, eyeing the little bag with feelings of foreboding. "How may I serve you?"

She had to laugh at his expression despite the desperation of her situation.

"John, don't look at me that way, I beg," she said, seeing through his scandalized eyes the most disreputable picture she must present in her old blue cloak with her battered little bag, "although I am afraid I do deserve it. I am in a shocking scrape, and my guardian has left London. This is a dreadful request to make of a friend, but we are practically related by marriage, are we not?"

"Of course," he said guardedly, wondering if this woman whom he had heretofore credited with great common sense was about to have hysterics in his lodgings before the interested eyes of his butler. John hurriedly dismissed the man and bade Kate to continue.

"I shouldn't ask it of you, I know, sir," she admitted, "but would you be so obliging as to arrange passage for me to Crossley? I cannot very well take my mother's carriage, you see, and I dare not attempt to hire one for myself without giving rise to the most dreadful scandal—"

"But, Miss Verelst," objected John, "why on earth should you want to go to the country now? The little season is just starting."

"I must. Please don't ask why."

Against his better judgment, he resolved to help her. He knew that Serena was much attached to her cousin. From what his beloved had let slip, he received the impression that Arabella was a veritable dragon, and that Kate's life must be an unenviable one. He did not fear that he was lending his aid to a romantic adventure. He credited Kate with

226

too much common sense to indulge in such foolishness. Nor would he believe any female could be so dead to vanity as to wear such an unbecoming garment to an assignation with her lover.

Sir John proceeded to hire a coach for Kate. He insisted on sending his own man with her to handle the charges at the posting houses along the road and pay her shot at the inn. He also arranged for a young woman who cleaned his lodgings to accompany Kate in the guise of a maid, hoping the servant would return with his man to London before the dust and clutter became intolerable.

All would have been well if Kate's mother had not raised a storm that had her remaining relatives shuddering at the mere mention of it many years hence.

Part of the mischief was done when Kate's note of explanation was lost. Arabella knew only what her servants told her, that her daughter had left the house with some belongings packed in a bag and dressed, to the dowager's outrage, in a shabby old cloak which Arabella had commanded Kate to give to one of the servants months before.

But, even if she had found the note explaining her daughter's intentions, Arabella would still have acted as she did.

Kate, who had endured her mother's acrimony for many years, grossly underestimated that lady's affection for her. She had thought that her mother would consider herself well rid of a daughter who would not conform to her wishes. Although she hadn't believed for an instant that Arabella would bodily throw her into the street, she did think her mother would be gratified to be spared the expense of supporting her. She assumed her mother would be so angry with her for rejecting William that she would not mind her seeking employment as a governess.

In this she was greatly mistaken.

Arabella had emerged from her nap so refreshed that she immediately summoned her daughter so she could renew her arguments in favor of Mr. Peevers' proposal. She had been alarmed to find Kate gone and began questioning the servants with impunity.

Into this scene of confusion walked Lady Buxted with her daughters. Now, the dowager had not received a visit from any of her old cronies for many weeks, and she was much inclined to send Letitia about her business. Unfortunately, because Arabella was questioning the servants, there was no one at the door to deny her to visitors. So Letitia, who had no sense of propriety while on the scent of gossip, merely followed the sound of Arabella's shrieking voice to the parlor.

Arabella stopped abruptly in her inquisition and turned on the visitors.

"Good day, Letitia. As you see I am very busy," she said.

"This will only take a moment, my dear," said Letitia, her eyes alight with curiosity. "I just thought it my duty as your friend to report to you what my Millicent just told me. I brought her along so you could hear it from her own lips.

"And please believe," added Letitia silkily, "that as a mother I feel for you most sincerely."

Arabella gave Letitia a sour look, but saw she was not going to be dislodged until she had heard what her silly chit of a daughter had to say.

"Well, Millicent," said Arabella, turning a fiery

eye on the young lady. Until then Millicent had quite enjoyed anticipating her part in a domestic drama. Now she quaked at Arabella's tone.

"Go ahead, Millicent," her mother coaxed her, giving Arabella a look of cold dislike.

Encouraged, Millicent poured out her tale to Arabella. It wasn't much, but it was enough to send Arabella shouting for her servants to prepare her carriage immediately.

It seemed that Millicent had spotted Kate in a blue cloak and carrying a little bag on the street. She seemed most dismayed at having seen Millicent, and tried to hide her face in her hood as she walked by. She was heading toward Hans Crescent on foot. Arabella knew that Sir John Morgan had lodgings in Hans Crescent.

"Thank you, child, for telling me this. Of course, Kate was on an errand for me," said Arabella desperately, loathing the look of glee in Letitia's eye. "Now, if you'll excuse me, I must go. I have an engagement."

With little ceremony, she ushered her unwelcome guests out and shouted for her maid to bring her pelisse.

Soon she was bowling along toward Hans Crescent in her carriage to the imminent peril of pedestrians and other conveyances.

John had just returned to his lodgings after seeing Kate off in the hired carriage when the dowager Lady Shallcross was announced. He turned a bland face toward that lady, which enraged her so much that she treated him to a display of the temper she had always striven to keep hidden in the presence of gentlemen.

"What have you done with my daughter?" she

demanded shrilly.

"Whatever do you mean?" he asked, his heart hardened by the brave desperation on Kate's face when he had handed her into the hired carriage. When Arabella poured out her accusations of treachery and rapine into his scandalized ears, he was in a fair way to deciding it was very sensible of Kate to leave this woman's influence, inconvenient though he found her method of doing so.

"By God, if you've dishonored my daughter, you'll marry her," snarled Arabella after she had finished her diatribe. "I'll blacken your name from here to Ireland if you do not."

John politely showed her the door.

Getting no satisfaction from him, Arabella next visited Serena, who had just returned from a shopping expedition with her Aunt Amelia.

"We have both been deceived in that villain you call your fiancé," snarled Arabella without preamble as soon as her niece had invited her to sit down.

"I beg your pardon, Aunt?" said Serena stiffly.

"I mean that Sir John Morgan has abducted my innocent child," said Arabella, bursting into tears, "and he will not tell me what he has done with her."

"I don't believe it," said Serena hotly. She jumped up from the sofa and sent a footman back up the stairs for the pelisse she had just taken off.

"Where are you going?" asked Arabella, insulted by her niece's defection before she could finish her tale of betrayal.

"To see my fiancé," said Serena. "And if I find you have maligned him, Aunt, which I fully expect, mind, I shall never speak to you again!"

Arabella had no choice but to return home or fall alive into the garrulous Aunt Amelia's hands. Once there, she sent for Mr. Peevers, who expressed himself much shocked by Kate's disappearance and declared himself ready to render the dowager any assistance necessary to recover her daughter.

Serena, meanwhile, had arrived at John's lodgings, delighting his butler to no end at receiving not one but two unchaperoned ladies to the bachelor household in one day.

"John, it isn't true, is it?" she asked him tearfully.

"What are you talking about?" he asked guardedly.

"My cousin Kate has disappeared. My aunt said you had something to do with it. It isn't true, is it? Is it?" Her voice raised on a hysterical note which made him itch, for the first time in his acquaintance with his beloved, to take her by her slim shoulders and shake her.

"Am I to understand you have so little faith in me that you would believe that woman's hysterical accusations?" he asked coldly.

"You know where she is, don't you?" said Serena, watching his face in disbelief.

"And if I do?"

Serena backed away from him, her eyes haunted. "It's true," she said slowly. "I can see it in your eyes. If you loved my cousin, why did you offer for me?"

"I do not love your cousin," said John desperately, trying to put his arms around her. "Listen to me—"

"Then tell me where she is."

"I cannot," said John. "I promised her I would not."

"You are hiding her," said Serena. "Why could you not have told me instead of acting behind my back?"

"You wrong me, Serena," he said.

"Then tell me where she is."

"I cannot betray the confidence of a lady," he said coldly. "Now I think you should go home before someone sees you. It is not the thing to visit a gentleman's lodgings, you know."

"Particularly if that gentleman is a stranger," said Serena, matching his chill tone. She turned on her heel and fled to the street, several pairs of curious eyes following her.

When she got home she wrote a letter to her brother, dispatched a servant on horseback to Crossley and retired to her room to indulge in a hearty bout of tears.

Kate, meanwhile, blessedly oblivious of the chaos her departure had caused, reached Crossley and the dower house after a leisurely journey of two and a half days. She was disappointed to find her cousin had already left for town.

She did not inquire too carefully into the circumstances of his leaving, feeling it was improper to question another person's servants. Otherwise she would have learned that an urgent summons from his sister conveyed by a servant who had ridden through the night had so alarmed her cousin that he left within an hour of receiving it.

In fact, as she lay sleeping in the best chamber at an inn the last night of her journey, Mark passed by on his way back to London, determined to rescue her from her supposed folly in putting herself under the protection of Sir John Morgan.

An appalling scene awaited Mark at his town house.

"Mark! Oh, Mark!" screeched Serena, whose eyes were red from tears and lack of sleep. "I am so dreadfully unhappy."

He quickly took her into the salon, away from the interested gaze of the butler, and settled her into the crook of his arm, patting her curls as if she were an agitated lap dog.

"Now, Serena. What is this ridiculous tale of Kate's eloping with your fiancé? I don't believe a word of it," he said.

"That's what I thought, too," she said with a gulp. "Aunt Arabella was making nasty accusations, so I went around to his lodgings and asked him to his face if it were true."

"Serena," exclaimed Mark, appalled, "please don't tell me you went to Sir John's lodgings and accused him of eloping with Kate."

"Of course not," said Serena angrily. "I simply asked him if it were true that he knew where she was. And, Mark, I could tell from his face that he d-did!"

"I think I will call on Sir John to see what he knows," said Mark quietly.

Serena sat up with a bounce. "You won't hurt him, will you?" she asked, horrified by the look on his face.

"That depends on what the gentleman has to say for himself," said Mark grimly. He picked up his hat and rode to Hans Crescent.

He soon returned to Shallcross House, frustrated at being cheated of his prey, for John had, his butler told the angry Lord Shallcross, flinching a little at the naked fury in the gentleman's dark eyes, gone into the country for an indefinite period of time. Mark knew that if he could discover John's direction, he would discover Kate's.

He resolved to question every traveler on every road leading out of London if he had to in order to find Kate.

As he was preparing for yet another journey, he was most annoyed to receive a visit from his aunt and Mr. Peevers, who had determined to accompany the dowager on her quest for her daughter.

"There you are," shouted Arabella accusingly when she spotted him. "And you call yourself a guardian! Racketing about the country while my poor girl—"

Here the lady broke off to wipe her tears with a wisp of lace handkerchief as Mr. Peevers rather ineffectually patted her shoulder.

"There, there, your ladyship," the merchant intoned.

"Aunt Arabella, what is the meaning of this shocking news I am hearing," demanded Mark.

"She has eloped with that dreadful Sir John Morgan. Never has a mother been so deceived! I thought he was most truly the gentleman while all the time he was seducing my innocent child. And she, trusting him, has flown to his protection—"

"Yes, Aunt Arabella," said Mark in a tone of intense interest. "Now we get to the part of this most improbable tale that I am anxious to hear. What would cause a sensible woman like Kate to flee her own home and precipitate a scandal?"

Arabella's face turned red. "As to that," she said, "it might have been a silly misunderstanding between Kate and myself—"

"What was it, ma'am? You were attempting to marry her to that silly cawker at the masked ball, were you not? I *told* you I would not tolerate Kate's being forced into a marriage she—"

"And look what's come of it, my fine lord," sneered Arabella, "my poor girl ruined—"

"Aunt Arabella, I will not listen to such calumny against Kate. You are not yourself. I beg you to go home. I will find Kate. You can depend on me. And when I do, I am sure there will be a reasonable explanation for what she has done."

This last sentence was said with so much menace in his voice that both Arabella and Mr. Peevers took their leave without delay. Satisfied, Mark resumed his preparations for his journey, only to be interrupted by tidings of yet another uninvited visitor. Sighing, he repaired to his book room, where the butler had shown the lady.

She was standing with her back to him, staring out the window, in an enveloping cloak with a small portmanteau by her side. Mark gave a long sigh of relief, seeing that the prodigal had returned. He was so happy to see her that he rushed across the room and took her into his arms.

The lady returned his embrace with fervor, and when the hood of her cloak fell down and revealed guinea gold ringlets, Mark released her so quickly she almost fell.

"Oh, Mark," gushed Melanie, preparing to throw herself back into his arms. He held her off with both hands.

"Melanie, what the *deuce* do you think you're doing here?" he said angrily.

"Running away to you, of course," she said. "My marriage was a mistake. I have decided to

235

divorce Phillip."

"You may do so with my blessing, Cousin," said Mark coldly, "but if you think I have any further interest in the matter, you are quite mistaken."

"But, Mark," she argued. "How can you say so after what we have meant to one another?"

"We have meant absolutely *nothing* to one another, Melanie, and so I told you when you tried to convince me to meet you secretly last week."

Melanie flushed delicately. "But it's different now," Melanie said. "Phillip has become intolerable. He is so jealous and spiteful that he says he will take me to the country just because of an odious story that has been circulating about Lady Sefton's party—"

"Melanie, look at me," he said, tilting her chin up. "I do not love you. I have never loved you. I will never love you."

"No, I don't believe it," exclaimed Melanie, bursting into tears. "You said—"

"I know what I said," Mark told her in a bitter tone, "and I have regretted it from the bottom of my heart."

"You do love me. You *must* love me," insisted Melanie, clutching his hands.

To Mark's discomfiture, into this appalling scene came Serena, anxious to discover what he had found out from Sir John Morgan.

"Very pretty, I *must* say, Brother," she said, putting her hands on her hips in outrage. "How can you stand there fondling Melanie in that perfectly disgusting manner—"

"I am *not* fondling Melanie," shouted Mark, appalled at the very thought.

"I want to know what John told you."

"He is not at home," said Mark.

"That means he's with *her!*" Serena seethed. "Who would have thought Kate could be such a designing—"

"That will do," said Mark firmly.

"What *are* you raving about Serena? What is this about Kate? What has she done?" asked Melanie, diverted.

"She's only eloped with my fiancé," said Serena bitterly.

"She has done nothing of the kind, Serena," said Mark, goaded beyond endurance.

"I must say," said Melanie, her eyes brightening, "I never thought Kate would show such spirit. I daresay it's all a hum, though."

Serena looked so fierce at this artless speech that Mark hastily offered to escort Melanie to her mother's lodgings before he set off in pursuit of the truant.

He deposited Melanie in her mother's hall, preparing to take himself off before Arabella could discover him and start screeching at him again. His aunt's butler greeted him and said Lady Arabella had left a note for him in case he happened to call.

Upon learning that Arabella had gone into the country with her Mr. Peevers, Mark hastily tore open the note held out to him and read with horrified eyes that Mr. Peevers had made inquiries and discovered that a single female answering Kate's description down to the shabby blue cloak and the little bag had been seen in a hired coach several days ago heading for Yorkshire. She had been accompanied by a man on horseback and a female presumed to be a servant.

"Crossley," said Mark out loud. "That is where she has gone."

This, coupled with the intelligence that Sir John Morgan had gone into the country also, relieved some of Mark's apprehension. Although Yorkshire seemed like an odd place for an elopement, Mark was convinced that John was joining Kate there. If so, it was probably not so sordid a situation as he had feared. Still, he was anxious to accost the couple.

"Melanie, I must leave you here. I will send word if I discover them," said Mark.

"Who?" she asked, all at sea.

"Kate. Sir John Morgan. Your mother. Anyone at all," he said in exasperation as he stamped out the door.

Upon returning home, Serena surprised him in the act of telling his butler that he would be out of town for a few days.

"Are you going after them, Mark?" she asked. "I'm going with you."

"That you are not, my child," he said. "You must stay here in case they come back, understand?"

She nodded her head grudgingly.

"Good girl," he said. "Try not to worry. I'll send word as soon as I can."

On that note, he turned his efforts toward making his weary body gather strength for yet another long journey within twenty-four hours, unaware that within minutes of his departure Serena would go to her aunt's lodgings and let her enterprising cousin Melanie talk her into following Mark to Yorkshire.

As he pursued the woman he loved and her

238

alleged lover, the only thing that sustained Lord Shallcross in his extreme exhaustion was the thought of wringing Kate's lovely neck when he caught up with her.

Chapter Eleven

Blissfully unaware that no less than four different sets of persons had set out in pursuit of her with various intentions ranging from rescue to murder, Kate had just finished reading the advertisements for positions in the London papers when her first visitor was announced by the unkempt maid Mrs. Bennett had grudgingly spared Kate from Crossley for the duration of her visit.

"Kate!" exclaimed Sir John Morgan, taking Kate's outstretched hand in his. "Thank God you are here!"

"Where else would I be?" asked Kate, startled by his look of desperation. His usually immaculate clothes were spattered with mud from riding horseback through rough country, and his eyes looked a trifle crazed. "Is something wrong?" she asked, alarmed. "My mother? Serena?"

"No, nothing like that," he said hastily. He glanced at the newspapers and writing paper spread all over the desk. "I seem to have disturbed you at something," he added.

"I am answering advertisements for governesses and housekeepers," she said, "and I must say it is most discouraging."

"Kate, you cannot do it," he said, horrified. "If I had thought that was your intention in coming here—Look, dear girl, you must come back with me to London immediately and tell Serena that I haven't abducted you or eloped with you or murdered you or whatever she thinks I've done with you."

"You cannot be serious," said Kate, much diverted. "She actually thinks you've eloped with me?"

"I must say I don't think it is very funny," he said, affronted by her laughter. "I promised you I wouldn't tell anyone where you are; but somehow your mother got wind of the fact that you had been to my lodgings, and I've been accused of all sorts of ramshackle behavior. I'm surprised they haven't searched my lodgings for your dead body. Perhaps by now they have."

"It can't be as bad as all that," said Kate, taken aback.

"Serena has broken our engagement."

"No! She cannot do such a thing!"

"She thinks I was in love with you all the time and now I cannot bring myself to the sticking point, so I have spirited you away and—"

"Please, don't," she said, nearly overset with laughter.

"Kate," he said, eyeing her with disfavor, "you must give up this absurd governessing idea and come back to London with me. You must tell Serena that I am innocent of all these foul crimes your mother has laid at my door. My future happiness depends upon it!"

"I can see something must be done at once," said Kate. "What an absurd tangle. But I don't understand why my mother came to visit you. I left her a letter saying I would be coming to the dower house."

"Then I'll be dashed if I know what her game is this time."

"Nor I," said Kate. "We must leave without delay. I will be ready in a trice. Only let me send Becky back to Mrs. Bennett with a note and—"

"Kate, you are a woman in a million," said John, clasping both of her hands in his. "And don't worry about finding a position. If you can convince Serena I'm innocent so she'll marry me, you can live under my roof for the rest of your life."

Unfortunately, at that moment Lord Shallcross had bullied his way past the maid and entered the room just in time to hear the last part of John's effusion. Although he was generally the last man on earth to resort to violence without just cause, it was no wonder he acted as he did.

He had had a most trying week. He had come to Crossley in order to straighten out some discord among the tenant farmers his bailiff insisted would not wait, and he had just gotten embroiled in estate business when he received an urgent summons from Serena saying Kate had disappeared and her mother was spreading the most shocking stories all over town.

He had ridden through the night to London in order to find out that not only was Kate indeed missing, but also that her name was linked with John's in some havey-cavey gossip doing the

242

rounds of better drawing rooms throughout the metropolis. Not only that, but what must Kate's beautiful ninnyhammer of a sister do but show up in his parlor spouting some fustian rubbish about divorcing her husband to marry him. Then his own ninnyhammer of a sister accuses her fiancé of seducing Kate. Mark, still looking for Kate, calls on John at his lodgings to find that not only has his quarry escaped, but he is reputedly riding post haste to Yorkshire to consummate his fell purpose with Kate.

Mark began his journey wanting nothing so much as to wring Kate's neck, but ended it wanting, instead, to draw John's claret.

It was just too much to find John at dower house holding Kate's hands in his and offering her his home.

So Mark walked up to his rival, grasped his shoulder, turned him around and hit him full on the jaw. Fortunately, Mark's strength was much depleted by his lack of sleep and long hours on horseback, so instead of half killing John as he probably would have done if he had been enjoying his customary vigor, he merely stunned him.

John retaliated by throwing a fist at Mark. Unfortunately, Kate, who could not stand the sight of violence, thrust herself between them at the fatal moment.

"No, Kate!" both men cried at once.

Kate sustained John's blow to her head and tumbled into Mark's arms. Both gentlemen were bending over her in concern when her mother and Mr. Peevers burst into the room.

"Well, I never!" exclaimed the dowager, shocked

to find not one but *two* gentlemen disporting themselves with her prodigal child. Kate was, indeed, a disreputable sight with her disheveled hair streaming part way down her back and her once crisply starched muslin gown hopelessly crushed. "Kate, my love, speak to me!" she screamed, pushing both gentlemen away and enfolding her daughter in a suffocating maternal embrace.

Fortunately for Kate, the full force of John's powerful fist did not come down on her because, although he couldn't stop the blow entirely, he managed to deflect it so it would be little more than a tap. She was not injured, but she was so stunned that she couldn't say so for some moments.

Kate was surprised by her mother's alarm. Years of listening to Arabella's demands and recriminations had led Kate to suppose, quite erroneously, that her mother was not over-fond of her. But all of Arabella's maternal fervor had been aroused by the sight of her abused child. She paused only long enough to ascertain that Kate had not sustained so much as a lump on her head from the dastardly assault of a gentleman at least twice her size before she rounded, like a tigress defending her cub, on the culprit.

"And what is the meaning of this disgraceful carousal?" demanded the dowager of Sir John. "If you've compromised my daughter, I will force you to marry her."

"That I will not, madam," said John, galled beyond endurance. "No offense, Kate," he added apologetically to that lady.

Kate inclined her head gravely, but her eyes were

glinting with amusement. Her mother's next words quite wiped the smile from her lips.

"Then I will have satisfaction," said Arabella. "Mr. Peevers, it is your duty as Kate's prospective father-in-law to call this gentleman out."

Now, Mr. Peevers was, he always told acquaintances, a peace-loving man. And after this day's work he was quite sure his son would be better off married to almost any other lady in London but Kate Verelst, despite the desirability of the lady's pedigree.

Flighty maidens who disappeared without warning to flee to a shabby-looking place like dower house for no apparent reason did not conform to his idea of a proper sort of wife. But he perceived he dared not cross Arabella when she was worked up into this state. Moreover, he was reluctant to show himself a coward in front of two noblemen.

"Very well, my lady," he said manfully. He turned a frightened gaze on John, only faltering toward the end of his challenge. "Sir, I ask you to name your friends."

John looked at him blankly. "See here, my good man, what are you about?" John asked, eyeing the merchant with distaste. "I only *tapped* her, for heaven's sake, and that was an accident." He felt his rapidly swelling jaw gingerly. "Ask her ladyship's precious nephew how this happened to me. How am I going to explain *this* to Serena?" he demanded of the merchant, who seemed, despite the fact that he had just called him out, quite the most sympathetic person in the room.

"That is enough, Mother," said Kate, trying to put her arms around Arabella. "I am quite all

245

right, I promise you. Sir John barely *touched* me."

Arabella caressed her daughter's cheek and crooned, "My love, you are always so kind and gentle, but don't waste your forgiveness on this, this—" she broke off, apparently unsuccessful in finding a word capable of describing the depravity of the gentleman without sullying her daughter's innocent ears.

Arabella extricated herself from Kate's clutching fingers and began circling Sir John and Mr. Peevers menacingly, demanding that Mr. Peevers make an assignation to put a bullet through Sir John without delay and stop allowing the younger man to distract him from the purpose with his disjointed excuses.

Kate was about to intervene when she felt her waist encircled by Mark's strong arms. She turned and was about to entreat her cousin to *do* something about Mr. Peevers and Sir John before someone got hurt when he put his finger on her lips and pulled her close to him.

"My love, I see that you shall have to marry me after all," he told her with a mischievous twinkle in his eye.

She opened her mouth to protest, and he stilled her objection with a quick kiss full on her parted lips.

She stared at him.

"Surely you must see that after this shocking melee you *must* marry someone," he reasoned. "That rather unkempt girl who opened the door to me has been watching us make fools of ourselves for quite five minutes. It will be all over the village by tomorrow, and from there it will spread to the

246

neighboring gentry since it's far too boring in the country for the fine ladies confined here to refrain from gossiping with their servants. And I miss my guess if your mother hasn't told everyone in London who would listen that she has flown to Yorkshire to prevent a rape."

"Oh, no," she objected, flushing. "Surely not."

"Yes," he said solemnly. "I feel certain that not even the worthy William would want to marry you now. Your reputation is quite in shreds."

"I shall try, somehow to endure it," she said, a twinkle in her eye.

"You relieve my mind. But there is no avoiding the fact that clearly *someone* must marry you, and I, as your guardian, am the one to whom this responsibility belongs. Unless you would rather have Sir John, after all?"

"You may accuse me of cowardice if you wish," she said, "but I would be most reluctant to marry a gentleman who has just tried to, er, pop my cork?"

"Certainly not," he said, scandalized. "The most improper expression you are thinking of is to *draw* one's cork, and the fact that you would produce it at such a moment just proves how out of hand you are become."

"I suppose," she said, basking in the loverlike expression in his eyes, "I am quite *ruined* as far as being a governess is concerned?"

Her beloved winced. "My dear, I beg you will not use that most unfortunate expression in your fond mother's hearing," Mark whispered. "Will she have to live with us, by the way?"

"I am afraid so," said Kate, looking up at him

anxiously.

"Well, one cannot have everything after all," he said with a sigh, his arm still encircling her. Suddenly remembering the others, he watched the combatants playing out their farce dispassionately.

"I suppose we ought to try to stop them," he said in a conversational tone, "for Serena's sake, if nothing else. I don't want to be the one to tell her either that I allowed her fiancé to be shot by a Cit or that I stood by while your mother tore him apart with her bare hands, which she seems, at this moment, more than capable of doing."

"No, indeed," she said. "Have you thought of a way to get their attention?"

"No," he said with the air of a man prepared to enjoy a spectacle while it lasted. He settled her into the crook of his arm and whispered, "To them, mother-in-law!" as Kate playfully batted him on the shoulder.

At just this moment Serena and Melanie burst into the room, their tempers much spoilt by having spent the entire drive from London in quarreling while cooped up together in the dowager Lady Shallcross's carriage, which Melanie had had no qualms about appropriating.

"Kate! How *dare* you!" screeched Melanie, outraged by the sight of her sister in the embrace of Lord Shallcross. "He is *mine!*"

"What are you saying?" demanded Arabella, a little hoarse from shouting at Sir John and Mr. Peevers. The dowager took Melanie's arm and turned her to face her. "What are you doing here and *who* is yours?"

"Mark is! He loves *me*," insisted Melanie. "You

and Kate will ruin *everything*. I am going to divorce Phillip. It is all arranged."

"What have you been doing, you wicked, ungrateful girl?" cried Arabella.

"Why do you always assume whatever has happened is my fault?" asked Melanie crossly. "Phillip says he cannot endure being married to a woman who thrives on scandal. Can you imagine one's own husband being so ill-bred? Just because I went to a masquerade with one of Jeremy's old friends and some of the old tabbies heard about it. Ever since I ran that curricle race in the park—"

"Now, you listen to me, Daughter," said Arabella, rounding on her youngest child. "You are going to go to your husband's home without delay and throw yourself on your *knees* in front of Lord Windom and beg him to take you back. You are going to promise him that you will never again do anything to embarrass him in public. To think a daughter of mine would be so abandoned as to throw over a husband like Lord Windom for—"

"I *won't*," insisted Melanie. "And I don't see how you can call *me* abandoned when Kate is standing there allowing herself to be mauled by Mark in that perfectly shameless fashion."

Arabella at once turned to her elder daughter and saw, although Kate and Mark drew a bit self-consciously apart, that Melanie's words were true.

"You!" said Arabella, abandoning Sir John for worthier prey. Her odious nephew was, after all, a viscount and so outranked a mere knight. "If you, sir, have trifled with my daughter, by God, I'll see you married to her!"

"Mother, please—" whispered Kate, mortified.

"With the greatest pleasure on earth," said Lord Shallcross, rising superbly to the occasion. "It will be only a small ceremony, but you, of course, will certainly be invited, Aunt."

"No!" shouted Melanie, drumming her heels on the worn carpet. "No! I won't let her have him!"

Arabella turned with murder in her eye. She took Melanie by the shoulders and shook her, effectively ending the fit of hysterics her pampered daughter was obviously about to inflict upon them.

"Oh, Aunt Arabella—" said Serena, truly shocked by the sight of two females struggling.

John put his arm around Serena and led her to the corner of the room. "My dear, it is best to stay out of these trifling family disputes, it is always said," he informed her.

"But John, if Kate loves Mark, why did she come to you?" asked Serena, genuinely confused.

"My love, there are some things in this world that are impossible to explain. This is one of them. Will you honor me by believing that I have never loved anyone save yourself in my whole life and never will?"

"Well—"

"Serena, I really will not be accountable for my actions if you will not marry me. I can think of few fates worse than to marry your cousin Kate and saddle myself with such a mother-in-law. I wish your brother joy of that connection."

Serena looked up at him with adoration in her eyes. "Yes," she said, "I'll marry you. But I hope you don't want me merely because I am an orphan."

"It is only one of many reasons, my love," he said.

"I won't go back to him," Melanie was screaming at her mother. "I cannot. He wouldn't have me."

"Melanie, I beg you to calm yourself," said Arabella regally. "There is nothing more unbecoming in a lady of quality than strong emotion."

"But if Mark won't marry me, where will I go?" asked Melanie plaintively.

"Indeed, there is no help for it," said Arabella, sighing. "You will have to live with your stepfather and me."

"My stepfather?" asked Melanie, looking puzzled. "But who—"

Her eyes fell on Mr. Peevers, who had the grace to avert his eyes.

"No! Mother, you *wouldn't!*" shrieked Melanie, who thought the prospect of her mother's marrying a Cit was every bit as scandalous as running a curricle race in public and attending a masked ball with a notorious rake.

"And what, miss, does it have to do with you if she does?" asked Mr. Peevers belligerently.

Everyone turned to look at him because until now he had been content to let Arabella do his talking for him.

"I never thought it proper to speak ill of the dead," said Mr. Peevers, rounding on a cowering Melanie, "but if I'd been your late father, I'd have taken a stick to your backside a time or two to teach you some manners. As your ma says, you'll have a home with us, but only so long as you mind your manners! For a start, you'll apologize to your mother. You won't show her any disrespect while you're under my roof, I promise you."

"I beg your pardon, Mama," said Melanie meekly, bursting into tears. Arabella stiffly acknowledged her apology with a slight inclination of her head.

"Sir, I can see you are a man after my own heart," said Mark. He offered his hand to Mr. Peevers with real enthusiasm, perceiving that perhaps his overbearing prospective mother-in-law had finally met her match. He also felt he had been granted a reprieve from a prison sentence when he learned that the dowager would not live with him and Kate after all. "Let us discuss this matter since I am the head of your fiancée's family."

He led a suspicious Mr. Peevers away as Serena, putting her arm around Melanie's sagging shoulders, led her from the scene of her ignominious defeat, beckoning to Sir John to follow them to her aunt's coach. Even Serena, who was blessed with little sensibility, could see she and her companions were very much in the way.

"I cannot understand it," said Melanie earnestly to Serena. "He wants to marry *Kate*."

"It is incomprehensible, I know," said Serena with a twinkle in her eye as she patted her bewildered cousin's shoulder.

The dowager Lady Shallcross vented her spleen by bullying the little maid and congratulating Kate on her conquest with so much enthusiasm that Kate's teeth were on edge by the time the gentlemen returned to the room.

"You sly puss," said Arabella in her most oppressively cheerful tone. "And not a word to your own mother. Why didn't you tell me you were going to marry your cousin? And the best part is, I can marry soon after you do. The only reason why I hadn't married my dear Jason sooner is because I didn't want to jeopardize your chances of attracting a suitor. Now that you will marry Mark, I can marry as well."

"Mother," said Kate wonderingly, "do you *love* Mr. Peevers?"

"Of course, dear, but you must stop calling him Mr. Peevers, you know. And you will have to meet his son now and again."

"Yes, Mother," said Kate, stunned.

Mark and Mr. Peevers came back into the room on excellent terms. While talking with his future father-in-law by marriage, Mark also had learned that the dowager's marriage was imminent. The elder lovers were only waiting for Kate to be married before, as Mr. Peevers so succinctly put it, tying the knot. Mark urged the merchant to marry his lady without delay. Mark felt a trifle guilty about this because he could well imagine Kate's feelings on this occasion. But he was so anxious to seal Mr. Peevers's fate so Arabella would not want to live with him and Kate that he cast compunction to the four winds.

"My dear aunt," said Mark, kissing that lady's cheek, "may I wish you great happiness?"

"Thank you, Mark," said Arabella complacently. "I have the most wonderful idea about your wedding—"

"No, Mother," said Kate firmly. "We will talk when we return to London."

"There is more than enough room for all of us

in my traveling coach," said Mr. Peevers.

"Thank you, no," said Mark. "I intend to conclude my business here on the estate with my bailiff while Kate takes a look at Crossley so Mrs. Bennett can receive her orders about any changes she wishes to make." He raised his hand to still Arabella's objection. "The proprieties will be observed, ma'am," he said. "Kate will live at dower house and I will live at Crossley, and when the time comes to return to London I will ride beside my lady's coach like any other besotted cavalier. Does this satisfy you? If not, I shall write a note to Miss Willoughby, who is at her estate in Yorkshire. I'm certain she will be happy to have Kate visit her for a few weeks."

"Whatever you think best, my dearest nephew," said Arabella happily, leaving the room on the arm of her merchant.

"I have always been excessively attached to that boy," she told her affianced husband in self-congratulatory tones as he guided her to the waiting carriage.

"Mark," Kate asked her cousin as soon as everyone left, "do you *really* love me? You aren't going to marry me just because you want to save me from a shocking scandal?"

"No, my love. I most truly love you."

"But what about Melanie?"

"My sweet Kate, I have never loved Melanie, which is a fortunate thing because there has never been room enough in Melanie's rather shallow little heart for anyone except Melanie."

"But, Mark. You cannot be serious! The night of Melanie's ball—"

"The night of Melanie's ball I only acted the part of the rejected lover to save her from embarrassment. I knew she had told everyone about our wholly imaginary love affair."

"But why did you let *me* believe it?" Kate asked, not sure whether to be relieved or angry.

He took her in his arms again. "Because I have never enjoyed anything so much as I enjoyed being comforted by you, my tender-hearted one, and I have paid dearly for it. Will that do?"

"Yes," said Kate, sighing contentedly. "It will do very well, indeed."

REGENCIES BY JANICE BENNETT

TANGLED WEB
(2281, $3.95)

Miss Celia Marcombe's dark eyes flashed with righteous indignation. She was not a commodity to be traded or bartered to a man as insufferably arrogant as Trevor Ryde, despite what her high-handed grandfather decreed! If Lord Ryde thought she would let herself be married for any reason other than true love, he was sadly mistaken. He'd never get his hands on her fortune—let alone her person—no matter how disturbingly handsome he was . . .

MIDNIGHT MASQUE
(2512, $3.95)

It was nothing unusual for Lady Ashton to transport government documents to her father from the Home Office. But on this particular afternoon a gust of wind scattered the papers, and suddenly an important page was lost. A document desperately wanted by more than one determined gentleman—one of whom would murder to get his way . . .

AN INTRIGUING DESIRE
(2579, $3.95)

The British secret agent, Charles Marcombe, had done his bit against that blasted Bonaparte. Now it was time to nurse his wounds and come to terms with the fact that that part of his life was over. He certainly did not need the likes of Mademoiselle Therese de Bourgerre darkening his door, warning of dire emergencies and dread consequences, forcing him to remember things best forgotten. She was a delightful minx, to be sure, but it would take more than a pair of pleading emerald eyes and a woebegone smile to drag him back into the fray!

Available wherever paperbacks are sold, or order direct from the Publisher. Send cover price plus 50¢ per copy for mailing and handling to Zebra Books, Dept. 2903, 475 Park Avenue South, New York, N.Y. 10016. Residents of New York, New Jersey and Pennsylvania must include sales tax. DO NOT SEND CASH.